Nineteen Seventy Seven

David Peace

A complete catalogue record for this book can be obtained from the British Library on request

The right of David Peace to be identified as the author of this work has been asserted by him in accordance with the Copyright, Designs and Patents Act 1988

First published in 2000 by Serpent's Tail

First published in this edition in 2008 by Serpent's Tail,
an imprint of Profile Books Ltd
3A Exmouth House
Pine Street
London EC1R 0JH
website: www.serpentstail.com

ISBN 978 1 84668 706 8

Printed in Great Britain by CPI Bookmarque, Croydon, CR0 4TD

10   9   8   7   6   5   4   3

This book is printed on FSC certified paper

David Peace grew up in Yorkshire in the 1970s and vividly remembers listening to the hoax tape of the Yorkshire Ripper on his way home from school. He was selected as one of Granta's Best of Young British Novelists 2003. In 2007, he was named GQ Writer of the Year. He lives in Japan.

Serpent's Tail publishes the four volumes of his Red Riding Quartet, *Nineteen Seventy Four*, *Nineteen Seventy Seven*, *Nineteen Eighty*, *Nineteen Eighty Three*.

Praise for the Quartet

Nineteen Seventy Four

'Peace's stunning debut has done for the county what Raymond Chandler and James Ellroy did for LA…a brilliant first novel, written with tremendous pace and passion' *Yorkshire Post*

'Peace's pump-action prose propels the book's narrative with a scorching turn-of-speed to an apocalyptic denouement…One hell of a read' *Crime Time*

'This breathless, extravagant, ultra-violent debut thriller reads like it was written by a man with one hand down his pants and the other on a shotgun. Vinnie Jones should buy the film rights fast' *Independent on Sunday*

'*Nineteen Seventy Four* takes the direct approach: straight to the heart of Ellroy-land, turning his native Yorkshire of the early seventies into a pustulant, cancerous core of complete corruption' *Uncut*

Nineteen Seventy Seven

'Simply superb…Peace is a masterful storyteller, and *Nineteen Seventy Seven* is impossible to put down…Peace has single-handedly established the genre of Yorkshire Noir, and mightily satisfying it is. *Nineteen Seventy Seven* is a must-read thriller' *Yorkshire Post*

'Peace's policemen rape prostitutes they are meant to be protecting, torture suspects they know cannot be guilty and reap the profits of organised vice. Peace's powerful novel exposes a side of life which most of us would prefer to ignore' *Daily Mail*

This book is dedicated to the victims of the crimes attributed to the Yorkshire Ripper, and their families.

This book is also dedicated to the men and women who tried to stop those crimes.

However, this book remains a work of fiction.

*When a righteous man
turneth away from his righteousness,
and committeth iniquity, and dieth in them;
for his iniquity that he hath done
shall he die.
Again, when the wicked man
turneth away from his wickedness
that he hath committed, and doeth that
which is lawful and right,
he shall save his soul alive.*

Ezekiel 18, 26–27

Beg Again

Tuesday 24 December 1974:

Down the Strafford stairs and out the door, blue lights on the black sky, sirens on the wind.

Fuck, fuck, fuck, fuck.

Running, fucked forever – the takings of the till, the pickings of their bloody pockets.

Fuck, fuck, fuck.

Should have finished what he started; the coppers still breathing, the barmaid and the old cunt. Should have done it right, should have done the bloody lot.

Fuck, fuck.

The last coach west to Manchester and Preston, last exit, last chance to dance.

Fucked.

Part 1
Bodies

Caller: So we pull up outside her house and then she says she's got no brass. She's skint like. So I says, what the fuck you gonna do about fare? I'm last white taxi driver as it is; I'm not a bleeding charity, am I?

John Shark: You're a dying breed.

Caller: Aye. So what does she do? She spreads 'em right wide, one on each of seats, and gives me a right eyeful of meat pie. Then she says, take it out of here. Couldn't fucking believe it.

John Shark: Steady on, Don. So what did you do?

Caller: What you think I bloody did? I whipped it out and give her one, didn't I? Right there in back of cab. Good one and all. Best she'd had in a while, she reckoned.

John Shark: Women, eh? Can't live with them, can't kill 'em. 'Cept round Chapeltown.

The John Shark Show
Radio Leeds
Sunday 29th May 1977

Chapter 1

Leeds.

Sunday 29 May 1977.

It's happening again:

When the two sevens clash . . .

Burning unmarked rubber through another hot dawn to another ancient park with her secret dead, from Potter's Field to Soldier's Field, parks giving up their ghosts, it's happening all over again.

Sunday morning, windows open, and *it's going to be another scorcher*, red postbox sweating, dogs barking at a rising sun.

Radio on: alive with death.

Stereo: car and walkie-talkie both:

Proceeding to Soldier's Field.

Noble's voice from another car.

Ellis turns to me, a look like we should be going faster.

'She's dead,' I say, but knowing what he should be thinking:

Sunday morning – giving HIM *a day's start, a day on us, another life on us. Nothing but the bloody Jubilee in every paper till tomorrow morning, no-one remembering another Saturday night in Chapeltown.*

Chapeltown – my town for two years; leafy streets filled with grand old houses carved into shabby little flats filled full of single women selling sex to fill their bastard kids, their bastard men, and their bastard habits.

Chapeltown – my deal: MURDER SQUAD.

The deals we make, the lies they buy, the secrets we keep, the silence they get.

I switch on the siren, a sledgehammer through all their Sunday mornings, a clarion call for the dead.

And Ellis says, 'That'll wake the fucking nig-nogs up.'

But a mile up ahead I know she'll not flinch upon her damp dew bed.

And Ellis smiles, like this is what it's all about; like this was what he'd signed up for all along.

But he doesn't know what's lying on the grass at Soldier's Field.

I do.

I know.

I've been here before.

And now, now it's happening again.

'Where the fuck's Maurice?'

I'm walking towards her, across the grass, across Soldier's Field. I say, 'He'll be here.'

Detective Chief Superintendent Peter Noble, George's boy, out from behind his fat new Millgarth desk, between me and her.

I know what he's hiding: *there'll be a raincoat over her, boots or shoes placed on her thighs, a pair of panties left on one leg, a bra pushed up, her stomach and breasts hollowed out with a screwdriver, her skull caved in with a hammer.*

Noble looks at his watch and says, 'Well, anyroad, I'm taking this one.'

There's a bloke in a tracksuit by a tall oak, throwing up. I look at my watch. It's seven and there's a fine steam coming off the grass all across the park.

Eventually I say, 'It him?'

Noble moves out of the way. 'See for yourself.'

'Fuck,' says Ellis.

The man in the tracksuit looks up, spittle all down him, and I think about my son and my stomach knots.

Back on the road, more cars are arriving, people gathering.

Detective Chief Superintendent Noble says, 'The fuck you put that sodding siren on for? World and his wife'll be out here now.'

'Possible witnesses,' I smile and finally look at her:

There's a tan raincoat draped over her, white feet and hands protruding. There are dark stains on the coat.

'Have a bloody look,' Noble says to Ellis.

'Go on,' I add.

Detective Constable Ellis slowly puts on two white plastic gloves and then squats down on the grass beside her.

He lifts up the coat, swallows and looks up at me. 'It's him,' he says.

I just stand there, nodding, looking off at some crocuses or something.

Ellis lowers the coat.

Noble says, 'He found her.'

I look back over at the man in the tracksuit, at the man with the sick on him, grateful. 'Got a statement?'

'If it's not too much trouble,' smiles Noble.

Ellis stands up. 'What a fucking way to go,' he says.

Detective Chief Superintendent Noble lights up and exhales. 'Silly slag,' he hisses.

'I'm Detective Sergeant Fraser and this is Detective Constable Ellis. We'd like to take a statement and then you can get off home.'

'Statement.' He pales again. 'You don't think I had anything . . .'

'No, sir. Just a statement detailing how you came to be here and report this.'

'I see.'

'Let's sit in the car.'

We walk over to the road and get in the back. Ellis sits in the front and switches off the radio.

It's hotter than I thought it would be. I take out my notebook and pen. He reeks. The car was a bad idea.

'Let's start with your name and address.'

'Derek Poole, with an *e*. 4 Strickland Avenue, Shadwell.'

Ellis turns round. 'Off Wetherby Road?'

Mr Poole says, 'Yes.'

'That's quite a jog,' I say.

'No, no. I drove here. I just jog round the park.'

'Every day?'

'No. Just Sundays.'

'What time did you get here?'

He pauses and then says, 'About sixish.'

'Where'd you park?'

'About a hundred yards up there,' he says, nodding up the Roundhay Road.

He's got secrets has Derek Poole and I'm laying odds with myself:

2–1 affair.

3–1 prostitutes.

4–1 puff.

Sex, whatever.

He's a lonely man is Derek Poole, often bored. But this isn't what he had in mind for today.

He's looking at me. Ellis turns round again.

I ask, 'Are you married?'

'Yes, I am,' he replies, like he's lying.

I write down *married*.

He says, 'Why?'

'What do you mean, why?'

He shifts in his tracksuit. 'I mean, why do you ask?'

'Same reason I'm going to ask how old you are.'

'I see. Just routine?'

I don't like Derek Poole, his infidelities and his arrogance, so I say, 'Mr Poole, there's nothing routine about a young woman having her stomach slashed open and her skull smashed in.'

Derek Poole looks at the floor of the car. He's got sick on his trainers and I'm worried he'll puke again and we'll have the stink for a week.

'Let's just get this over with,' I mutter, knowing I've gone too far.

DC Ellis opens the door for Mr Poole and we're all back out in the sun.

There are so many fucking coppers now, and I'm looking at them thinking, *too many chiefs:*

There's my gaffer Detective Inspector Rudkin, Detective Superintendent Prentice, DS Alderman, the old head of Leeds

CID Detective Chief Superintendent Maurice Jobson, the new head Noble and, in the centre of the scrum, the man himself: Assistant Chief Constable George Oldman.

Over by the body Professor Farley, the Head of the Department of Forensic Medicine at Leeds University, and his assistants are preparing to take her away from all this.

Detective Superintendent Alderman has a handbag in his hands, he's taking a WPC and a uniform off with him.

They've got a name, an address.

Prentice is marshalling the uniforms, going door to door, corralling the gawpers.

The cabal turns our way.

Detective Inspector Rudkin, as hungover as fuck, shouts, 'Murder Room, thirty minutes.'

The Murder Room.

Millgarth Street, Leeds.

One hundred men stuffed into the second-floor room. No windows, only smoke, white lights, and the faces of the dead.

In comes George and the rest of his boys, back from the park. There are pats on the back, handshakes here, winks there, *like some fucking reunion.*

I stare across the desks and the phones, the sweating shirt backs and the stains, at the walls behind the Assistant Chief Constable, at the two faces I've seen so many, many times, every day, every night, when I wake, when I dream, when I fuck my wife, when I kiss my son:

Theresa Campbell.

Joan Richards.

Familiarity breeds contempt.

Noble speaks:

'Gentlemen, he's back.'

The dramatic pause, the knowing smiles.

'The following memorandum has been sent to all Divisions and surrounding areas:

'At 0650 this morning, the body of Mrs Marie Watts born 7.2.45, of 3 Francis Street, Leeds 7, was found on Soldier's Field,

Roundhay, near West Avenue, Leeds 8. The body was found to have extensive head injuries, a cut throat, and stab wounds to the abdomen.

'This woman had been living in the Leeds area since October 1976, when she came up from London. It is believed she worked in hotels in London. She was reported missing by her husband from Blackpool in November 1975.

'Enquiries are requested of all persons coming into police custody for bloodstains on their clothing and also enquiries at dry cleaners for any clothing with blood on it. Any replies to Murder Room, Millgarth Street Police Station.

'Message ends.'

Detective Chief Superintendent Noble stands there with his piece of paper, waiting.

'Add to that,' he continues. 'Boyfriend, one Stephen Barton, 28, black, also of 3 Francis Street. Some form for burglary, GBH. Probably pimped the late Mrs Watts. Works the door at the International over in Bradford, sometimes Cosmos. Didn't show up at either place yesterday and hasn't been seen since about six o'clock last night when he left the Corals on Skinner Lane, where he'd just chucked away best part of fifty quid.'

The room's impressed. We've got a name, a history, and it's not yet two hours.

A chance at last.

Noble lowers his eyes, his tongue on the edge of his lips. Quietly he says, 'You lot, find him.'

The blood of one hundred men pumping hard and fast, hounds the lot of us, the stink of the hunt like bloody marks upon our brows.

Oldman stands up:

'It's going to break down like this:

'As you all know, this is number 3 at best. Then there's the other possible attacks. You've all worked one or more of them so, as of today, you're all now officially Prostitute Murder Squad, out of this Station, under Detective Chief Superintendent Noble here.'

PROSTITUTE MURDER SQUAD.

The room is humming, buzzing, singing: everyone getting what they wanted.

Me too –

Off post office robberies and *Help the fucking Aged*:

Sub-postmasters at gun-point, six-barrels in their faces, wives tied up with a smack and a punch in their nighties, only Scrooge won't give it up, so it's a cosh from the butt of the shotgun and welcome to heart attack city.

One dead.

'Murder Squad'll break down into four teams, headed up by Detective Superintendents Prentice and Alderman and Detective Inspectors Rudkin and Craven. DI Craven will also co-ordinate Admin. from here at Millgarth. Communications will be DS White, the Divisional Officer will be Detective Inspector Gaskins, and Community Affairs and Press will be DI Evans, all based in Wakefield.'

Oldman pauses. I scan the room for Craven, but he's nowhere.

'Myself and Detective Chief Superintendent Jobson will also be making ourselves available to the investigation.'

I swear there are sighs.

Oldman turns round and says, 'Pete?'

Detective Chief Superintendent Noble steps forward again:

'I want every wog under thirty who's not married leant on. I want names. Some smartarse said our man hates women – hold the fucking front page.'

Laughter.

'All right, so let's have every fucking puff in your book in here too. Same goes for the usuals – slags and their lads. I want names and I want them names in here by five. SPG'll round them up. Ladies can go to Queens, rest here.'

Silence.

'And I want Stephen Barton. Tonight.'

I'm biting my nails. I want out of here.

'So phone home, tell them you'll be out all night. BECAUSE THIS ENDS HERE TONIGHT.'

*

One thought – JANICE.

Through the melee and out the door and down the corridor, Ellis trapped back down the hall, calling my name.

Outside the canteen there's no answer and I slam down the phone just as Ellis catches up.

'Fuck you going off to?'

'Come on, we got to get started,' and I'm off again, down the stairs and out the door.

'I want to drive,' he whines behind.

'Fuck off.'

I've got my foot down, flying through the centre back to Chapel-town, police radio still crackling with the New Fire.

Ellis is rubbing his hands together, saying, 'See he has his good points; big-time overtime.'

'Unless they vote to continue ban,' I mutter, thinking *I've got to lose him.*

'More for them that wants it.'

I say, 'When we get there, we should split up.'

'Get where?'

'Spencer Place,' I say, like he's as dumb as he looks.

'Why?'

I want to throw on the fucking brakes and punch him but, instead, I smile and say, 'Try and nip some of the usual bullshit in the bud. Stop them all yapping.'

I turn right, back on to Roundhay Road.

'You're boss,' he says, like it's only a matter of fucking time.

'Yeah,' I say and keep my foot down.

'You take the right-hand side. Start with Yvonne and Jean in 5.'

We've parked up round the corner on Leopold Street.

'Fuck. I have to?'

'You heard Noble. *Names,* he wants fucking names.'

'What about you?'

'I'll do Janice and Denise in 2.'

'Bet you will.' He's looking at me sideways.

I let it go with a wink.

He reaches for the door. 'Then what?'

'Keep going. Meet you back here when you're done.'

He tuts and scratches his knackers as he gets out the car, his mind made up.

I think my heart's going to fucking burst.

I wait until Ellis is inside number 5, then I open the door and walk up the stairs.

The house is quiet and stinks of smoke and dope.

I tap on her door at the top of the stairs.

She comes to the door looking like a Red Indian, her dark hair and skin covered in a film of sweat, like she's just been fucking and fucking for real.

The nights I've dreamt about her.

'You can't come in. I'm working.'

'There's been another.'

'So?'

'You can't stay round here.'

'So how about your place?'

'Please,' I whisper.

'You going to make an honest woman of me, are you Mr Policeman?'

'I'm serious.'

'So am I. I need money.'

I pull out notes, screwing them up in her face.

'Yeah?'

'Yeah,' I nod.

'What about a ring, Prince Bobby?'

I sigh and start to speak.

'One like you gave your wife.'

I look at the carpet, the stupid flowers and birds woven together under my feet.

I look up and Janice slaps me once.

'Piss off, Bob.'

'Fucking give him up!'

'Piss off!'

Ellis pushes her head back, banging it against the wall.

'Fuck off!'

'Come on, Karen,' I say. 'Just tell us where he is and we're away.'

'I don't fucking know.' She's crying and I believe her.

We've been at this now for over six hours and DC Michael Ellis wouldn't know the fucking truth if it walked up and smacked him in the gob, so he walks up to Karen Burns, white, twenty-three, convicted prostitute, drug addict, mother of two, and smacks her in the gob instead.

'Easy Mike, easy,' I hiss.

She falls away against her wallpaper, sobbing and angry.

Ellis tugs at his balls. He's hot, fucked off, and bored and I know he wants to pull down her pants and give her one.

I say, 'Half-time Mike?'

He sniffs and rolls his eyes and walks back down the hall.

The window's open and the radio on. A hot Sunday in May and all you'd usually hear would be Bob fucking Marley, but not today. Just Jimmy Savile playing twenty-five years of Jubilee hits, as every cunt and his stash hide under their beds, waiting for the sirens to stop, the shit to end.

Karen lights a cig and looks up.

I say, 'You do know Steve Barton?'

'Yeah, unfortunately.'

'But you've no idea where he is?'

'If he's any bloody sense, he'll have legged it.'

'Has he any bloody sense?'

'Some.'

'So where'd he leg it to?'

'London. Bristol. I've no fucking idea.'

Karen's flat stinks and I wonder where the kids are. Probably been taken off her again.

I say, 'You reckon he did it?'

'No.'

'So give me a name and I'm out of here.'

'Or what?'

'Or I'll go and get some fucking lunch and let my mate out

there question you, and then I'll come back and we'll take you down Queens Street.'

She tuts, exhales, and says, 'Who do you want?'

'Anyone who likes a bit of strange. Anything odd.'

'Anything odd?' she laughs.

'Anything.'

She stubs out the cigarette on a plastic tray of chips and curry sauce and gets up and takes an address book out of the knife drawer. The room now stinks of burning plastic.

'Here,' she says, tossing the little book over to me.

I scan the names, the numbers, the licence plates, the lies.

'Give me someone.'

'Under D. Dave. Drives a white Ford Cortina.'

'What about him?'

'No rubber, likes to stick it up your arse.'

'So?'

'He doesn't say please.'

I take out my notebook, copy down the licence plate.

'Heard he don't always pay and all.'

'Anyone else?'

'There's a taxi driver who likes to bite.'

'We've heard.'

'That's your lot then.'

'Thanks,' I say and see myself out.

I drop the coins.

'Joseph?'

'Yeah?'

'Fraser.'

'Bobby the bobby. Just a matter of time I says, and see if it ain't so.'

I am in the phone box two down from the Azad Rank, watching a couple of Paki kids bowling at each other. Ellis is sleeping off his Sunday lunch in the car: two cans of bitter and a fat cheese sandwich. There's Sunday cricket on the radio, more heat forecast, birds singing, lilting bass and sax from a terrace.

It can't last.

The man on the other end is Joseph Rose: Joe Rose, Jo Ro. Another Paki kid joins the game.

I say, 'SPG are coming to take everyone away, and not to Zion.'

'Fuck them.'

'See you try,' I laugh. 'You got some names for me?'

Joseph Rose: part-time prophet, part-time petty thief, full-time Spencer Boy with draw to score and debts to pay, he says:

'This be concerning Mrs Watts?'

'In one.'

'Your pirate won't stay away, no?'

'No. So?'

'So people be spooked anyway.'

'By him?'

'Nah, nah. The two sevens, man.'

Fuck, here we go. 'Joseph, give me some fucking names.'

'All I hear is the ladies say it's Irish. Same as befores.'

The Irish.

'Ken and Keith know anything?'

'Same as I say.'

As I hang up two black SPG transit vans fly down the street and I'm thinking, fuck the Spencer Boys:

HEAVY DUTY DISCIPLINE COMING DOWN.

It's going up to eight and the car is getting smaller, light starting to fade. Across Leeds 7 bonfires are going up, and not fucking Jubilee Beacons. Me and Ellis are still sat off Spencer Place, doing fuck all but sweat and get on each other's tits.

Nervous, like the whole fucking city:

Ellis stinks and we've got the windows down, smelling the wood and Rome burn, cat calls and yells upon the hot black air: the ones we've not pinched building barricades, putting out the milk bottles for later.

Edgy:

I'm thinking about giving Louise a ring, wondering if she'll be back from the hospital, feeling bad about Little Bobby and yesterday, coming back to Janice and getting fucking stiff, *and then it all comes down.*

HARD:

Glass smashing, brakes slamming, a red car careering down the road, zig-zagging, its windscreen gone, hitting one kerb, flipping over at the foot of a lamppost.

'Christ,' shouts Ellis. 'That's Vice.'

We're both out of the car, running across Spencer Place to the upturned motor.

I look up the street:

There's a bonfire on a piece of wasteland at the top of the road illuminating a small gang of West Indians, black shadows dancing and whooping, thinking about finishing off what they've just started, sticking the boot in.

I stare into the black night, the barricades and bonfires, the high flames all loaded with pain:

A proud coon steps forward, all dreadlocks and Mau Mau attitude:

Come and have a go.

But I can already hear the sirens, the SPG, the Specials and Reserves, our sponsored fucking monsters let loose on the wind, and I turn back to the red car.

Ellis is bending down, talking to the two men upside-down inside.

'They're all right,' he shouts to me.

'Call an ambulance,' I say. 'I'll stay with them until cavalry get here.'

'Fucking niggers,' says Ellis, running back to our car.

I get down on all fours and peer into the car.

It's dark and at first I don't recognise the men inside.

I say something like, 'Don't try and move. We'll have you out in a minute.'

They nod and mumble.

I can hear more cars and brakes.

'Fraser,' moans one of the men.

I peer in and over at the man trapped in the passenger seat.

Fucking Craven, *Detective Inspector Craven.*

'Fraser?'

I pretend I can't hear him, saying, 'Hang on, pal. Hang on, mate.'

I look back up the road again and see a transit van spewing out SPG, tearing off after the wogs through the bonfire.

Ellis is back. 'Soon as the ambulance gets here, Rudkin wants us back at the Station. Says it's a right madhouse.'

'Like this isn't? You wait with them,' I say, standing up.

'Where are you going?'

'I'll be back in a bit.'

Ellis is muttering and cursing as I tear off back up towards number 2, back up towards Janice.

'Fuck you want?'

'Let us in. I just want to talk.'

'There's a surprise,' she says but opens the door to let me in.

She's barefoot in a long flower skirt and t-shirt.

I stand in the centre of the room, the window open, the smell of smoke and the start of a riot outside.

I say, 'They threw a brick or something at a Vice car.'

'Yeah?' she says, *like it doesn't happen every other night of the fucking week.*

I shut my mouth and put my arms round her.

'So that's what you want?' she laughs.

'No,' I lie, fucked off and hard.

She squats down, pulling at my zip as I fall back and sink into the bed.

She starts sucking, my mind black sky with stars popping in and out, listening to the sirens and the screams, knowing the shit hasn't even begun.

'Fuck you been?'

'Shut up, Ellis.'

'It was fucking DI Craven in the car, you know?'

'You're joking?'

I get into the car, the street still full of blue lights and SPG.

The bonfires out, the wogs nicked, Craven and his mate in St James, and DC Ellis still not content.

I let him drive.

'So where were you?'

'Leave it,' I say quietly.

'Rudkin's going to fucking murder us,' he moans.

'Is he fuck,' I sigh.

I stare out the open window at Black Leeds, Sunday 29 May 1977.

'You think no-one knows about you and that slag?' says Ellis suddenly. 'Everyone knows. Fucking embarrassing, it is.'

I don't know what to say to him. I don't care if he knows or not, don't care who knows, but I don't want Louise to know and now I can't keep little Bobby's face out of my mind.

I turn and say, 'Tonight's not the night. Save it for later.'

For once he takes my advice and I go back to the window, him to the road, steeling ourselves.

Millgarth Police Station.

Ten o'clock going on the Middle Ages.

Live from my own Dark Ages:

Down the stairs into the dungeons, keys and locks turning, chains and cuffs rattling, dogs and men barking.

Let the Witch Trials begin:

DI Rudkin's in his shirtsleeves and crop at the end of the white heat/white light corridor.

'Good of you to join us,' he smirks.

Ellis, pinched face and itching palms, nods in apology.

'Bob Craven all right, is he?'

'Yeah, cuts and bruises,' gabbles Ellis.

I say, 'Got anything?'

'Full house tonight.'

'Anything concrete?'

'Maybe,' he winks. 'And you?'

'Same as before: the Irish, the taxi driver, and Mr Dave Cortina.'

'Right then,' says Rudkin. 'In here.'

He opens a cell door and it's, *aw fuck.*

'One of yours yeah, Bob?'

'Yeah,' I mouth, stomach gone.

They've got Kenny D, Spencer Boy, in his cheap checked underpants bent back over the table in the Black Christ Hold: head and back pinned down against the wood, arms outstretched, feet splayed, cock'n'balls open to the world.

Rudkin shuts the door.

The whites of Kenny's eyes are on their stalks, straining to see who's come into his upside-down hell.

He sees me and takes it in: five white coppers and him: Rudkin, Ellis, and me, plus the two uniforms holding him down.

'Spot of routine questioning was all it was,' laughs Rudkin. 'Only Sambo here, he's got a bit of a guilty conscience and decides to be the black Roger fucking Bannister.'

Kenny is staring up at me, teeth locked in pain.

The door opens behind me, then closes. I glance round. Noble's got his back against the door, watching.

Rudkin smiles at me and says, 'Been asking for you, Bob.'

My mouth's dry and cracks when I ask, 'Has he said anything else?'

'That's just it, isn't it lads,' Rudkin laughs along with the two uniforms. 'You want to tell DS Fraser here, why it was you wanted to have a word with Sambo in first place?'

One of the uniforms, champing for his leg up, gushes, 'Found some of his gear round number 3 Francis Street.'

He pauses, letting it sink in:

Mrs Marie Watts of 3 Francis Street, Leeds 7.

'And then he denies even knowing the late Mrs Marie Watts,' crows Rudkin.

I'm standing in the cell, walls closing in, the heat and stink rising, thinking, *aw fuck Kenny.*

'I've told him,' says Rudkin, 'I'm going to add some blue to that black skin of his if he doesn't start giving us some answers.'

Down on the table, Kenny closes his eyes.

I bend down, my mouth to his ear. 'Tell them,' I hiss.

He keeps his eyes closed.

'Kenny,' I say, 'these men will fuck you up and no-one will give a shit.'

He opens his eyes, straining to stare into mine.

'Stand him up,' I say.

I go over to the far wall opposite the door; there's a news-paper cutting taped to the grey gloss paint.

'Bring him closer.'

They bring him in, eyeball to the wall.

'Read it, Kenny,' I whisper.

There's blood on his teeth as he reads aloud the headline: 'No action against policemen over detainee's death.'

'You want be the next fucking Liddle Towers?'

He swallows.

'Answer me.'

'NO!' he screams.

'So sit down and start talking,' I yell, pushing him down into the chair.

Noble and Rudkin are smiling, Ellis watching me closely.

I say, 'Now Kenny, we know you knew Marie Watts. All we want to know first is how come your fucking stuff was at her place?'

His face is puffed up, his eyes red, and I hope he's fucking smart enough to know I'm his only friend here tonight.

At last he says, 'I'd lost me key, hadn't I?'

'Come on, Kenny. It's not fucking *Jackanory.*'

'I'm telling you. I'd taken some stuff from my cousins and I lost my key and Marie says it was all right to dump it at hers.'

I look up at Ellis and nod.

DC Ellis brings his fists down hard from behind into Kenny's shoulder blades.

He screams, falling to the floor.

I'm down there with him, eyeball to eyeball.

'Just fucking tell us, you lying piece of black shit.'

I nod again.

The uniforms haul him back up into the chair.

He's got his fat pink mouth hanging open, tongue white, hands to his shoulders.

'Oh, why are we waiting, joyful and triumphant,' I start singing as the others join in.

The door opens and another bloke looks in, laughing, and then goes back out.

'Oh why are we waiting, joyful and triumphant, oh why are we waiting . . .'

I give the sign and it stops.

'You were fucking her, just say it.'

He nods.

'I can't hear you,' I whisper.

He swallows, closes his eyes, and whispers, 'Yeah.'

'Yeah what?'

'I was . . .'

'Louder.'

'Yeah. I was fucking her, right.'

'Fucking who?'

'Marie.'

'Marie who?'

'Marie Watts.'

'What about her, Kenny?'

'I was fucking her, Marie Watts.'

He's crying; big fat fucking tears.

'You dumb fucking monkey.'

I feel Rudkin's hand on my back.

I turn away.

Noble winks.

Ellis stares.

It's over.

For now.

I stand in the white corridor outside the canteen.

I call home.

No answer.

They're still at the hospital or up in bed; either way she'll be fucked off.

I see her father in the bed, her walking up and down the ward, Bobby in her arms, trying to get him to stop crying.

I hang up.
I call Janice.
She answers.
'You again?'
'You alone?'
'For now.'
'What about later?'
'I hope not.'
'I'll try and get over.'
'Bet you will.'
She hangs up.

I look at the bleached floor, at the bootmarks and the dirt, the shadows and the light.

I don't know what to do.
I don't know where to go.

Caller: You see this yesterday [reads]: Screaming Mob Sur-
            rounds the Queen. A royal walkabout in
            Camperdown Park turned into a frightening display
            of hysteria as thousands of people, screaming and
            yelling, broke through flimsy rope barriers and
            swarmed around the Queen and the Duke of Edin-
            burgh. Police tried to fend them off but she was
            jostled by people shrieking, 'I've touched the Queen.'

John Shark: Poor cow.

Caller: And if that isn't enough [reads]: Earlier in the day,
            council workmen were called out to erase anti-roy-
            alist slogans from walls and hoardings along the
            Queen's route.

John Shark: Bloody Jocks, worse than the Micks.

                                        The John Shark Show
                                        Radio Leeds
                                        Monday 30th May 1977

Chapter 2

*Ancient English shitty city? How can this ancient English shitty city
be here! The well-known massive grey chimney of its oldest mill? How
can that be here! There is no spike of rusty iron in the air, between
the eye and it, from any point of the real prospect. What is the spike
that intervenes, and who has set it up? Maybe it is set up by the
Queen's orders for the impaling of a horde of Commonwealth robbers,
one by one. It is so, for the cymbals clash, and the Queen goes by to
her palace in long procession. Ten thousand swords flash in the sunlight, and thrice ten thousand dancing girls strew flowers. Then follow
white elephants caparisoned in red, white and blue, infinite in number
and attendants. Still, the chimney rises in the background, where it
cannot be, and still no writhing figure is on the grim spike. Stay! Is
the chimney so low a thing as the rusty spike on the top of a post of
an old bedstead that has tumbled all awry. Stay! I am twenty-five
years and more, the bells chime in jubilation. Stay.*

The telephone was ringing.

I knew it was Bill. And I knew what he wanted from me.

I stretched across the other brown pillow, the old yellow
novels, the strewn grey ashes, and I said:

'Whitehead residence.'

'There's been another one. I need you here.'

I put down the telephone and lay back in the shallow ditch
I'd dug myself among the sheets and the blankets.

I stared up at the ceiling, the ornate brocade around the light,
the chipped paint and the cracked veins.

And I thought about her and I thought about him as St Anne
pealed the dawn.

The telephone was ringing again, but I'd closed my eyes.

I woke in a rapist sweat from dreams I prayed were not my
own. Outside trees hung in the heat, moping in willow pose,

the river black as a lacquer box, the moon and stars cut from drapes up above, peeping down into my dark heart:

The World's Forgotten Boy.

I hauled my tried bag from Dickens to the chest of drawers, across the threadbare flooring, pausing before the mirror and the lonely bones that filled the shabby suit in which I slept, in which I dreamt, in which I hid my hide.

Love you, love you, love you.

I sat before the chest of drawers upon a stool I made in college and took a sip of Scotland and pondered Dickens and his Edwin, me and mine, and all that's thine:

Eddie, Eddie, Eddie.

I sang and hummed along:

One Day My Prince Will Come, or was it, *If I'd Have Known You Were Coming I'd Have Baked A Cake*?

The lies we speak and the ones we don't:

Carol, Carol, Carol.

Such a wonderful person:

All wanked out on my bathroom floor, on my back, feeling for the toilet paper.

I wiped the come off my belly and squeezed the tissues into a ball, trying to shut them out.

The Temptations of St Jack.

Again the dream.

Again the dead woman.

Again the verdict and the sentence come.

Again, it was happening all over again.

I woke on my floor on my knees by my bed, hands together thanking Jesus Christ My Saviour that I was not the killer of my dreams, that he was alive and he forgave me, that I had not murdered her.

The letterbox rattled.

Children's voices sang through the flap:

Junky Jack, Druggy Jack, Fuck You Jack Shitehead.

I couldn't tell if it was morning or afternoon or whether they were just another gang of truants sent to stake my nerves out in the sun for the ants.

I rolled over and went back to *Edwin Drood* and waited for someone to come and take me a little bit away from all this.

The telephone was ringing again.

Someone to save my soul.

'You OK? You know what time it is?'

Time? I didn't even know what fucking year it was, but I nodded and said, 'Couldn't get out of bed.'

'Right. Well, at least you're here. Small mercies, etc.'

You'd think I'd have missed it, the hustle/bustle/tussle etc of the office, the sounds and the smells, but I hated it, dreaded it. Hated and dreaded it like I'd hated and dreaded the corridors and classrooms of school, their sounds and their smells.

I was shaking.

'Been drinking?'

'About forty years.'

Bill Hadden smiled.

He knew I owed him, knew he was calling in his debts. Looking down at my hands, I couldn't quite think why.

The prices we pay, the debts we incur.

And all on the never-never.

I looked up and said, 'When did they find her?'

'Yesterday morning.'

'I've missed the press conference then?'

Bill smiled again. 'You wish.'

I sighed.

'They issued a statement last night, but they've held the meet over until eleven this morning.'

I looked at my watch.

It had stopped.

'What time is it?'

'Ten,' he grinned.

I took a taxi from the *Yorkshire Post* building over to the Kirkgate

Market and sat in a gutter in the low morning sun with all the other dumb angels, trying to get it together. But the crotch of the trousers of my suit stank and there was dandruff all over my collar and I couldn't get the tune of *The Little Drummer Boy* out of my mind and I was surrounded by pubs, all closed for another hour, and there were tears in my eyes, terrible tears that didn't stop for quarter of an hour.

'Well look what the bloody cat dragged in.'

Sergeant Wilson was still on the desk, taking me back.

'Samuel,' I nodded.

'How long's it been?' he whistled.

'Not long enough.'

He was laughing, 'You here for the press conference?'

'Not for the bloody good of my health, am I?'

'Jack Whitehead? Good health? Never.' He pointed upstairs. 'You know the way.'

'Unfortunately.'

It was not as busy as I thought it would be and I didn't recognise anyone.

I lit a cigarette and sat at the back.

There were a lot of chairs down at the front and a WPC was putting out about ten glasses of water and I wondered if she'd let me have one, but I knew she wouldn't.

The room started to fill with men who looked like footballers and a couple of women and for a moment I thought one of them was Kathryn, but when she turned round she wasn't.

I lit another cigarette.

A door opened down the front and out came the police, damp suits and ties, red necks and faces, no sleep.

The room was suddenly full, the air gone.

It was Monday 30 May 1977.

I was back.

Thanks, Jack.

George Oldman, in the middle of the table, began:

'Thank you. As I'm sure you are aware,' he was smiling, 'the body of a woman was found on Soldier's Field, Roundhay, early yesterday morning. The body has been identified as that of Mrs Marie Watts, formerly Marie Owens, aged thirty-two, of Francis Street, Leeds.

'Mrs Watts was the victim of a particularly brutal attack, the details of which we are unable to reveal at this stage of our inquiry. However, a preliminary post-mortem by Professor Farley of the Department of Forensic Medicine at Leeds University, has determined that Mrs Watts was killed by a substantial blow to the head from a heavy blunt object.'

A substantial blow and I knew I shouldn't be here, letting him take me there:

Soldier's Field: under a cheap raincoat, another rollneck sweater and pink bra pushed up over flat white tits, snakes pouring from her stomach wounds.

Oldman was saying, 'Mrs Watts had been living in the city since October last year, after moving up from the London area where it is believed she worked in a number of hotels. We are particularly interested in talking to anyone who can give us more information about Mrs Watts and her life in London.

'We would also appeal to any member of the public who was in the vicinity of Soldier's Field on Saturday night, Sunday morning, to come forward for purposes of elimination only. We are particularly interested in speaking to the drivers of the following cars:

'A white Ford Capri, a red or maroon Ford Corsair, and a dark-coloured Landrover.

'Again, I would stress that we are trying to trace these vehicles and their drivers for elimination purposes only and that any information received will be treated in the strictest confidence.'

Oldman took a sip of water, before continuing:

'Furthermore, we would like to appeal for a Mr Stephen Barton of Francis Street, Leeds, to come forward. It is believed that Mr Barton was a friend of the deceased and could have valuable information about the last few hours of Mrs Watts' life.'

Oldman paused, then smiled: 'Again, this is for elimination purposes only and we would like to emphasise that Mr Barton is not a suspect.'

There was another pause as Oldman went into a whispered huddle with the two men next to him. I tried to put names to the faces: Noble and Jobson I knew, the other four were familiar.

Oldman said, 'As some of you are no doubt aware, there are some similarities between this murder and those of Theresa Campbell in June 1975 and Joan Richards in February 1976, both of whom were prostitutes working in the Chapeltown area of the city.'

The room erupted and I sat there shocked that Oldman had said this so openly, given all his previous form.

George moved his hands up and down, trying to calm everyone: 'Gentlemen, if you'll let me finish.'

But he couldn't stop it, and neither could I:

It was worse than I thought it would be, more than I thought it would be: *white panties off one leg, sandals placed on the flab of her thighs.*

Oldman had paused, his best Headmaster stare on show until the room went quiet. 'As I say,' he continued, 'there are some similarities that cannot be ignored. At the same time, we cannot categorically say that all three murders are the work of the same individual. However, a possible link is one avenue of inquiry we are pursuing.

'And, to that end, I'm announcing the formation of a task force under Detective Chief Superintendent Noble, here.'

That was it, chaos; the room couldn't contain these men and their questions. All around me, men were on their feet, shouting and screaming at Oldman and his boys.

George Oldman was smiling, staring straight back at the pack. He pointed at one reporter, cupping his ear to the question, then feigning indignation and exasperation that he couldn't hear the man. He put up his hands, as if to say, *no more.*

The noise subsided, people sat back down on the edge of their seats, poised to pounce.

Oldman pointed at the man still standing.

'Yes, Roger?' he said.

'Was this latest victim, Marie Watts, was she a prostitute then?'

Oldman turned to Noble, and Noble leant into Oldman's microphone and said, 'At this point in our investigation, we can neither confirm nor deny such reports. However, we have received information that Mrs Watts was known in the city as something of what we would describe as a good-time girl.'

Good-time girl.

The whole room thinking, *slag.*

Oldman pointed to another man.

The man stood and asked, 'What specific similarities have led you to investigate a possible connection?'

Oldman smiled, 'As I say, there are some details of these crimes that we are unable to make public. However, there are some obvious similarities in the location of the murders, the age and lifestyles of the victims, and the way in which they were killed.'

I was drowning:

Blood, thick, black, sticky blood, matting her hair with pieces of bone and lumps of grey brain, slowly dripping into the grass on Soldier's Field, slowly dripping over me.

At the back, I raised a hand above the water.

Oldman looked over the heads at me, frowned for a moment, and then smiled. 'Jack?' he said.

I nodded.

A couple of people down the front turned round.

'Yes, Jack?' he said again.

I stood up slowly and asked, 'Are these the only three murders under consideration at the moment?'

'At the moment, yes.'

Oldman nodded and pointed at another man.

I sat back in my chair, drained, relieved, the questions and answers still flying around me.

I closed my eyes, just for a bit, and let myself go under.

*

The dream is strong, black and blinding at first, then slowly settling, hovering quietly behind my lids.

Open my eyes and she'll still be there:

A white Marks & Spencer's nightie, soaked black with blood from the holes he's left.

It's January 1975, just a month after Eddie.

The fires behind my eyes, I can feel the fires behind my eyes and I know she's back there, playing with matches behind my eyes, lighting her own beacons.

Full of holes, for all these heads so full of holes. Full of holes, all these people so full of holes. Full of holes, Carol so full of holes.

'Jack?'

There was a hand on my shoulder and I was back.

1977.

It was George, a copper holding the door for him, the room now empty.

'Lost you for a minute back there?'

I stood up, my mouth dirty with old air and spit.

'George,' I said, reaching for his hand.

'Good to see you again,' he smiled. 'How've you been keeping?'

'You know.'

'Aye,' he nodded, because he knew exactly how I'd been keeping. 'Hope you're taking it easy?'

'You know me, George.'

'Well, you tell Bill from me that he better be taking good care of you.'

'I will.'

'Good to see you again,' he said again, walking over to the door.

'Thanks.'

'Give us a call if you need anything,' he shouted over from the door, saying to the younger officer, 'Finest journalist I ever met, that man.'

I sat back down, *the finest journalist Assistant Chief Constable George Oldman ever met*, alone in the empty room.

*

I walked back through the heart of Leeds, a tour of a baked, bone-dry hell.

My watch had stopped again and I strained to hear the Cathedral bells beneath the noise; the deafening music from each shop I passed, the car horns punched in anger, hot angry words on every corner.

I looked for the spire in the sky, but there was only fire up there; the midday sun high and black across my brow.

I put my hand to my eyes just as someone walked straight into me, banging right through me, hard; I turned and watched a black shadow disappear down an alley.

I chased into the alley after it but heard horse's hooves fast upon the cobbles behind me but then, when I turned, there was only a lorryload of beer trying to edge up the narrow street.

I pressed my face into the wall to let it pass and came away with red paint down the front of my suit, all over my hands.

I stepped back and stared at the ancient wall and the word written in red:

Tophet.

I stood in the alley in the shadows of the sun, watching the word dry, knowing I'd been here before, knowing I'd seen that shadow before, somewhere before.

'It's not a right good day to be walking around covered in blood,' laughed Gaz Williams, the Sports Editor.

Stephanie, one of the typists, wasn't laughing; she looked at me sadly and said, 'What happened?'

'Wet bloody paint,' I smiled.

'So you say,' said Gaz.

The banter was light, same as it always was. George Greaves, the only one who'd been here longer than me or Bill, he'd got his head down on his desk, snoring his lunch off. There was local radio on somewhere, typewriters and telephones ringing, and a hundred ghosts waiting for me at my desk.

I sat down and took the cover off the typewriter and got a blank sheet and brought it up ready for business, back at my roots.

I typed:

POLICE HUNT FOR SADISTIC KILLER OF WOMAN

Detectives are hunting a killer who murdered Mrs Marie Watts, aged thirty-two, and dumped her body on playing fields not far from Leeds city centre. The body of Mrs Watts, of Francis Street, Leeds, was discovered by a jogger early yesterday morning.

It was lying on Soldier's Field, Roundhay, near Roundhay High School and the Roundhay Hall Hospital. Detective Chief Superintendent Peter Noble, head of Leeds CID, said she had severe head injuries and other injuries, on which he did not wish to elaborate. The killer was sadistic and possibly a sexual pervert.

Sensationally, Assistant Chief Constable George Oldman confirmed that police are investigating possible links to two other unsolved murders of Leeds women:

June 1975:	*Theresa Campbell, aged twenty-six, a mother of three, of Scott Hall Avenue, found dead on the Prince Philip Playing Fields.*
Feb 1976:	*Joan Richards, aged forty-five, a mother of four, of New Farnley, found dead in a Chapeltown cul de sac.*

It is believed that the latest victim, Mrs Watts, had moved to Leeds from London in October last year. The police would like to speak to anyone who has any information about Marie Watts, who was also known as Marie Owens. The police would also like to speak to Mr Stephen Barton of Francis Street, Leeds, a friend of Mrs Watts. It is believed that Mr Barton could have vital information about the last few hours of Mrs Watts' life. It was stressed, however, that Mr Barton is not a suspect.

Assistant Chief Constable Oldman also appealed for any member of the public who was in the vicinity of Soldier's Field last Saturday night to come forward. The police are particularly interested in the drivers of a white Ford Capri, a dark red Ford Corsair, and a Landrover. Mr Oldman stressed that they were attempting to trace these drivers for elimination purposes only and any information would be treated in the strictest confidence.

Anyone with information should contact their nearest police station or the Murder Room direct on Leeds 461212.

I pulled the paper and read it back.

Just a pile of rusty little words, all linked up to make a chain of horror.

I wanted a drink and a cig and not here.

'You finished already?' said Bill Hadden over my shoulder.

I nodded and handed him the sheet, like it was something I'd found. 'What do you think?'

Out of the window there were clouds coming, turning the afternoon grey, spreading a sudden sort of quiet over the city and the office, and I sat there, waiting for Bill to finish reading, feeling as lonely as I'd ever felt.

'Excellent,' grinned Bill, his wager paying out.

'Thanks,' I said, expecting the orchestra to start up, the credits and the tears to roll.

But then the moment was gone, lost. 'What are you going to do now?'

I leant back in my chair and smiled. 'I quite fancy a drink. And yourself?'

This big man, with his red face and grey beard, sighed and shook his head. 'Bit early for me,' he said.

'It's never too early, only too late.'

'I'll see you tomorrow then?' he said, hopefully.

I got up from my chair, giving him a tired wink and grin. 'Undoubtedly.'

'OK.'

'George,' I shouted.

George Greaves looked up from his desk. 'Jack?' he said, pinching himself.

'Coming down the Press Club?'

'Go on then, just a quick one,' he replied, smiling sheepishly at Bill.

At the lift George gave the office a wave and I bowed, thinking, *there are many ways a man can serve his time.*

The Press Club, as dark as home.

I couldn't remember the last time I'd been in, but George was helping me.

'Fuck, that was funny that was.'

I hadn't a clue what he was talking about.

Behind the bar, Bet gave me a look that was too, too knowing. 'Been a while, Jack?'

'Yeah.'

'How are you, love?'

'OK. Yourself?'

'My legs aren't getting any younger.'

'You don't need them,' laughed George. 'Just get legless with us, eh Jack?'

And we all laughed and I remembered Bet and her legs and a couple of times back when I thought I could live forever, back when I wanted to, back before I knew what a curse it really was.

Bet said, 'Scotch?'

'And keep them coming,' I smiled.

'I always try.'

And we all laughed again, me with an erection and a Scotch.

Outside, I was pissed outside, leaning against a wall which said HATE in running white paint.

No subject, no object, just HATE.

And it blurred and whirled and I was lost between the lines, between the things I should've written and the things I had.

Stories, I'd been telling stories in the bar again:

Yorkshire Gangsters and Yorkshire Coppers and, later, Cannock Chase and the Black Panther.

Stories, just stories. Stopping short of the real stories, of the *true stories*, the ones that put me here, up against this wall that said HATE.

Clare Kemplay and Michael Myshkin, the Strafford Shootings and *The Exorcist* killing.

Every dog had his day, every cat her cream, but every camel had his straw, every Napoleon his Waterloo.

True stories.

Black and white against a wall that spelt HATE.

I ran my fingers over the raised paint.

And there I was, wondering just *where have all the Bootboys gone?*

And then there they were, all around me:

Shaved heads and beer breath.

'Aye-up Grandad,' said one.

'Piss off, puff,' I said.

He stepped back among his mates. 'What you fucking have to say that for, you silly old git?' he said. 'Cos you know I'm going have to fucking have you now, don't you?'

'You can try,' I said, just before he hit me and stopped me remembering, stopped the memories for a bit.

Just for a bit.

I'm holding her there in the street in my arms, blood on my hands, blood on her face, blood on my lips, blood in her mouth, blood in my eyes, blood in her hair, blood in my tears, blood in hers.

But even the old magic can't save us now, and I turn away and try and stand and Carol says, 'Stay!' But it's been twenty-five years or more, and I have to get away, have to leave her here alone in this street, in this river of blood.

And I look up and there's just Laws, just the Reverend Laws, the moon, and him.

Carol gone.

I was standing in my room, the windows open, black and blue as the night.

I'd got a glass of Scotland in my hand, to rinse the blood from my teeth, a Philips Pocket Memo to my lips:

'It's 30th May 1977, Year Zero, Leeds, and I'm back at work . . .'

And I wanted to say more, not much more, but the words wouldn't obey me so I pressed stop and went over to the chest of drawers, opened my bottom drawer and stared at all the little tapes in all their little cases with all their neat little dates and places, like all those books of my youth, all my Jack the Rippers and Dr Crippens, the Seddons and Buck Ruxton, and I took one out at random (or so I told myself), and I lay back, feet up on the dirty sheets, staring at the old, old ceiling as her screams filled the room.

I woke up once, dark heart of the night, thinking, *what if he's not dead?*

Caller: During the past two or three decades criminologists in the US have been making systematic attempts to measure and analyse the dark figures of crime . . .

John Shark: The dark figures of crime?

Caller: Yeah, the dark figures of crime, the proportions of people who have locked away in their past offences quite unknown to the authorities or, if known, passed over. In a systematic study of sexual offences, Dr Raazinowicz doubted whether more than 5 in 100 ever came to light.

John Shark: That's outrageous.

Caller: In 1964, he suggested that crimes fully brought into the open and punished represented no more than fifteen per cent of the great mass actually committed.

John Shark: Fifteen per cent!

Caller: And that was in 1964.

The John Shark Show
Radio Leeds
Tuesday 31st May 1977

Chapter 3

The Murder Room, Millgarth.

Rudkin, Ellis, and me.

Just gone six, the morning of Tuesday 31 May 1977.

Sat around the big table, the phones dead, tapping the top.

In through the double doors, Assistant Chief Constable Oldman and Detective Chief Superintendent Noble, dumping two big manila folders on the table.

Detective Inspector Rudkin squints at the cover of the top one and gives it a, 'Ah for fuck's sake, not again.'

I read *Preston, November 1975*.

Fuck.

I know what this means:

Two steps forward, six steps back –

November 1975: The Strafford Shootings still in everyone's face, internal inquiries coming out our ears, Peter Hunter and his dogs still sniffing round our arses. The West Yorkshire Metropolitan Police with our backs to the wall and our mouths shut, if you knew what was good for you, which side your bread was buttered on etc, Michael Myshkin going down, the judge throwing away the key.

'Clare Strachan,' I murmur.

November 1975: COMING DOWN AGAIN.

Ellis puzzled.

Rudkin about to fill him in, but George shuts him up: 'As you know, Clare Strachan, a convicted prostitute, was found raped and battered to death in Preston almost two years ago now, in November 1975. The Lancashire lads immediately came over to review the Theresa Campbell file, and John here and Bob Craven went over there last year after we got Joan Richards.'

Me thinking, *they're cutting Rudkin out, why?*

I glance across at him, he's nodding, eager to butt in.

But Oldman's keeping him out: 'Now whatever you think, whether you count Clare Strachan in or not, we're going to go back over to Preston and review that bloody file again.'

'Waste of fucking time,' spits Rudkin, at last.

Oldman's going red, Noble's face thunder.

'I'm sorry sir, but me and Bob spent two days – was it? – over there last time and, I'm telling you, it's not the same bloke. Wish it was, but it's not.'

Ellis chiming in, 'What do you mean you wish it was?'

'Because he left so much fucking stuff behind him, it's a wonder they haven't nabbed the daft cunt already.'

Noble snorts, like, *that's Lancashire for you.*

'What makes you so sure it isn't?' asks Ellis.

'Well, he'd raped her for a start and then he stuck it up her arse. Come both times, though I don't know how he fucking did it. State of her.'

'Ugly?'

'Doesn't begin to describe it.'

Ellis half-smiling, telling everyone what they already know: 'Not like our boy. Not like him at all.'

Rudkin nods: 'Just lets it fly in the grass.'

'Anything else?' I say.

'Yeah then, when he'd had his fun, he jumped up and down on her until her fucking chest give in. Size ten wellies.'

I look at Oldman.

Oldman smiles and says, 'Everyone finished?'

'Yeah,' shrugs Rudkin.

'Good, because you don't want to be late, do you?'

'Aw, for fuck's sake.'

'Alf doesn't like to be kept waiting.'

Detective Chief Superintendent Alfred Hill, Head of Lancashire CID.

'Me again?' Rudkin asks, looking round the room.

Noble points at Rudkin, Ellis, and me. 'You three.'

'What about Steve Barton and the Irish?'

'Later, John. Later,' says Oldman, standing up.

In the car park, Rudkin tosses the keys to Ellis. 'You drive.'

Ellis looks like he's going to come in his pants. 'Sure,' he says.

'I'm going to get some kip,' says Rudkin, getting into the back of the Rover.

The sun is shining and I switch on the radio:

Two hundred dead in a Kentucky Nightclub fire, five charged in the Captain Nairac murder, twenty-one coloured youths arrested in connection with a spate of street robberies in South-East London, twenty-three million watch the Royal Windsor Show.

'Daft cunts,' laughs Ellis.

I wind down the window and lean my head into the breeze as we pick up speed and head out on to the M62.

'You know the fucking way?' shouts Detective Inspector Rudkin from the back.

I close my eyes; 10CC and ELO all the way.

Somewhere over the Moors, I wake with a start.

The radio's off.

Silence.

I stare at the cars and lorries on either side of us, the Moors beyond, and it's difficult to think of anything else.

'You should've seen it last February when I drove over with Bob Craven.' Rudkin's stuck his head between the front seats. 'Got caught in a fucking blizzard. Couldn't see owt but two foot in front. Fucking frightening it was. I swear you could hear them. We were shitting bloody bricks.'

Ellis glances from the road to Rudkin.

I say, 'Alf Hill was one of the top men, wasn't he?'

'Aye. He was first to interview her. It was his men found the tapes and all.'

'Fuck,' whistles Ellis.

'Hates her more than Brady.'

We're all staring out across the Moors, at the sunshine shining silver, the dark patches of sudden cloud, the unmarked graves.

'Never ends,' says Rudkin, sitting back. 'Never fucking ends.'

Half-nine and we're pulling into the car park of the Lancashire HQ in Preston.

Detective Inspector Rudkin sighs and puts on his jacket. 'Prepare to be bored shitless.'

Inside, Rudkin does the talking at the desk as we shake hands, mention mutual friends, and walk up the stairs to Alf Hill's office.

The uniformed Sergeant knocks on the door and we enter.

Detective Chief Superintendent Hill is a small man who looks like Old Man Steptoe after a rough night. He's coughing into a dirty handkerchief.

'Sit down,' he spits into the cloth.

No-one shakes hands.

'Back again,' he grins at Rudkin.

'Like a bad bloody penny, aren't I?'

'Wouldn't say that John, wouldn't say that. Always a pleasure, never a chore.'

Rudkin edges forward in his chair. 'Anything new?'

'On Clare Strachan? Not that springs to mind, no.'

He starts coughing again, pulls out the handkerchief, and eventually says, 'You're busy men I know, busy men. So let's get on with it.'

We all stand up and head down the corridor to what I presume is their Murder Room, doors closing on either side of us as we go.

It's a big room with big windows and a view of the hills above them and I'm pretty sure they had some of the Birmingham Pub Bombers here.

Alfred Hill pulls open a cabinet drawer. 'Just where you left her,' he smiles.

Rudkin is nodding.

There are other detectives in the room, sitting in their shirtsleeves smoking, the pictures of their dead watching, turning yellow.

Their lot, they eye us like we'd eye them.

Hill turns to one fat man with a moustache and tells him, 'These lads are over from Leeds, reviewing Clare Strachan. If they need anything, give it to them. Anything at all.'

The man nods and goes back to the end of his cigarette.

'Be sure to look in yeah, look in before you go,' says Alf Hill as he heads off back down the corridor.

'Thanks,' we all say.

When he's gone, Rudkin turns to the fat man and says, 'You heard him Frankie, so go get us some pop or something cold. And leave your fags behind.'

'Fuck off, Rudkin,' laughs Frankie, tossing his JPS over to him.

Rudkin sits down, turns to me and Ellis and says, 'Best get to work, lads.'

Clare Strachan: twenty-six going on sixty-two.

Bloated and fucked before he even got to her.

Married twice, two kids up in Glasgow.

Previous convictions for soliciting:

A complete wreck of a human being, said the judge.

Wound up in St Mary's hostel, Preston, living with fellow prostitutes, drug addicts, and alcoholics.

On Thursday 20 November 1975, Clare had had sex with three different men, only one of whom had ever been traced.

And eliminated.

The morning of Friday 21 November 1975, Clare was dead.

Eliminated.

A boot up her cunt, a coat over her head.

I look up at Rudkin and say, 'I want to go to the hostel, then the garages.'

Ellis has stopped writing.

'What for?' sighs Rudkin.

'Can't picture it.'

'You don't want to,' he says, putting out his cig.

We tell the Sergeant on the desk where we're going and walk back out into the car park.

Frankie comes tearing out after us. 'I'll give you a hand,' he pants.

'You're all right,' says Rudkin.

'Boss says I better. Show some hospitality.'

'Going to spring for lunch are you?'

'Think we could manage something, aye.'

'Magic,' grins Rudkin.

Ellis is nodding along like, *this is the fucking fast lane.*

Me, I feel sick.

St Mary's hostel is one hundred years old or more, up the road from Preston Station.

Blood and Fire, tattooed into the wall above the door.

'Any of the same staff still working here?' I ask Frankie.

'Doubt it.'

'What about residents?'

'You're joking? Couldn't find anyone a week later.'

We walk through a dim stinking corridor and peer into the reception cubicle.

A man with lank greasy hair to his shoulders is writing with a radio on.

He looks up, pushes his black NHS frames back up his nose, and sniffs. 'Help you?'

'Police,' says Frankie.

'Yeah,' he nods, like, *what the fuck they done now?*

'Ask you a few questions?'

'Yeah, sure. What about?'

'Clare Strachan. Where can we talk?'

He stands up. 'Lounge through there,' he points.

Rudkin leads the way into another shitty room, draughty windows and rotting sofas covered in cig burns and dried food.

Frankie keeps going, 'And you are?'

'Colin Minton.'

'You the warden?'

'Deputy. Tony Hollis is the senior warden.'

'Is Tony about?'

'He's on holiday.'

Softly-softly: 'Anywhere nice?'

'Blackpool.'

'Close.'

'Yeah.'

'Sit down,' says Frankie.

'I wasn't here when that happened,' says Colin suddenly, like he's had enough of this already.

Rudkin takes over: 'Who was here?'

'Dave Roberts and Roger Kennedy, and Gillian someone or other I think.'

'They still about?'

'Not here, no.'

'They still work for Council?'

'No idea, sorry.'

'Did you ever work with them?'

'Just Dave.'

'He talk about Clare Strachan and what happened?'

'A bit, yeah.'

'Can you remember anything he said?'

'Like what?'

It's Frankie's town so we don't say anything when he starts up again, saying, 'Anything. About Clare Strachan, the murder, anything at all?'

'Well, said she was mad like.'

'What way?'

'Crazy. Should have been in hospital, what Dave said.'

'Yeah?'

'Used to stare out the window and bark at the trains.'

Ellis says, 'Bark?'

'Aye, bark like a dog.'

'Fuck.'

'Yeah, that's what he said.'

Rudkin catches my eye and I take over with, 'Dave say anything about boyfriends, stuff like that?'

'Well I mean, she was on game like.'

'Right,' I nod.

'And he said she was always pissed and she'd let all the blokes here have it off with her and there'd sometimes be fighting and stuff because of her.'

'How was that?'

'I don't know, you'd have to ask them that were here, but like there was some that'd get jealous.'

'And she wasn't right choosey, yeah?'

'No. Not very.'

'She was fucking the staff and all,' says Rudkin.

'I don't know about that.'

'I do,' he says. 'Afternoon she was murdered she'd had a session with your man Kennedy, Roger Kennedy.'

Colin doesn't say anything.

Rudkin leans forward and smiles, 'Still go on, that kind of thing?'

'No,' says Colin.

'You've gone red,' laughs Rudkin, standing up.

I say, 'Which was her room?'

'I don't know. But I can show you upstairs.'

'Please.'

Just me and Colin go upstairs.

At the top I say, 'None of the same residents still here?'

'No,' he says but then, 'Actually, hang on.'

He goes to the end of the long narrow corridor and bangs on a door, then opens it. He talks to someone inside and then beckons me over.

The room is bare and bright, sunlight across an empty chair and table, across a man lying on a little bed, his face to the wall, his back to me and the door.

Colin gestures at the seat, saying, 'This is Walter. Walter Kendall. He knew Clare Strachan.'

'I'm Detective Sergeant Fraser, Mr Kendall. I'm with Leeds CID and we're looking into a possible link between the murder of Clare Strachan and a recent crime in Leeds.'

Colin Minton is nodding, staring at Walter Kendall's back.

'Colin here, he says you knew Clare Strachan,' I continue. 'I'd be very grateful for anything you can tell me about Miss Strachan or the time of her murder.'

Walter Kendall doesn't move.

I look at Colin Minton and say, 'Mr Kendall?'

Slowly and clearly, his face still to the wall, Walter says, 'I remember the Wednesday night, Thursday morning, I woke to terrible screams coming from Clare's room. Real bellowing cries. I got out of bed and ran down the corridor. She was in the room at the top of the stairs. The door was locked and I banged on it for a good five minutes before it opened. She was alone in the room, drenched in sweat and tears. I asked her what had happened, was she all right. She said it was just a dream. A dream, I said. What kind of dream? She said she'd dreamt there was a tremendous weight upon her chest, forcing the air from her lungs, pushing the very life from her, and all she could think was she'd never see her daughters again. I said it must have been something she'd eaten, nonsense I didn't even mean, but what can you say? Clare just smiled and said she'd had the same dream every night for almost a year.'

Outside a train rattles past, shaking the room.

'She asked me to stay the night with her and I lay on top of the covers, stroking her hair and asking her to marry me like I often had before, but she just laughed and said she'd only bring me trouble. I said, what did I care about trouble, but she didn't want me. Not like that.'

My mouth's dry, the room baking.

'She knew she was going to die, Sergeant Fraser. Knew they'd find her one day. Find her and kill her.'

'Who? What do you mean, kill her?'

'First day I met her, she was drunk and I didn't think much of it. I mean, you hear so many tall stories in a place like this. But she was persistent, insistent: *They're going to find me and when they do, they'll kill me.* And she was right.'

'I'm sorry Mr Kendall, but I'm not clear. She say who exactly was going to kill her or why?'

'The police.'

'The police? She said the police were going to kill her?'

'The Special Police. That's what she said.'

'*The Special Police?* Why?'

'Because of something she'd seen, something she knew, or something they thought she'd seen or knew.'

'Did she elaborate?'

'No. Wouldn't. Said it just meant others would be in the same boat as her.'

'Don't suppose you told this to the investigating officers at the time, did you?'

'As if they'd listen. They didn't take any notice of me anyway, especially after what happened to me.'

I say, 'Why? What happened to you Mr Kendall?'

Walter Kendall rolls over in his bed and smiles: his eyes white, the colour gone, the man blind.

'How did it happen?' I ask.

'Friday 21 November 1975. I woke up and I was blind.'

I look over at Colin Minton, who shrugs his shoulders.

'I could see, but now I'm blind,' laughs Kendall.

I stand up. 'Thank you for your time, Mr Kendall. If you think of anything else, please . . .'

Kendall suddenly reaches out, grabbing the sleeve of my jacket. 'Anything else? I think of nothing else.'

I pull away. 'Call us.'

'Be careful, Sergeant. It can strike anyone, anytime.'

I walk away, down the narrow corridor, pausing by the door to the room at the top of the stairs.

It's cold here, out of the sun.

Colin Minton raises his eyes and starts to say how sorry he is.

'Special Police? What fucking bollocks next?' laughs Detective Inspector Rudkin.

We're walking up Church Street, towards the garages.

'These fucking people. They just never accept that the fucking mess they're in is because they're junkies and alcoholics. Has to be someone else or something else.'

Frankie's laughing along. 'Cunt went blind because he drank industrial-strength paint-stripper.'

'See?' says Rudkin.

'Yeah,' laughs Ellis. 'Unlike Bob's mate.'

'If wit were shit,' says Rudkin, shaking his head.

We turn the corner into Frenchwood Street.

On the left are the lock-ups, the garages.

Preston seems suddenly quiet.

That silence again.

'It was that one,' whispers Frankie, pointing to the one furthest from us, the one closest to the multi-storey car park at the end of the road.

'Locked?' asks Ellis.

'Doubt it.'

We keep walking towards it.

My chest starts to constrict, ache.

Rudkin's saying nowt.

Three Pakistani women in black cross in front of us.

The sun goes behind a cloud and I can feel the night, the endless fucking night I've always felt.

'Take notes,' I tell Ellis.

'Like what?'

'Feelings, man. Impressions.'

'Bollocks. It's been two years,' he whines.

'Do it,' says Rudkin.

I can't stop it:

I'm coming up the hill, swaying, bags in my hand. Plastic bags, carrier bags, Tesco bags.

We get to the garage and Frankie tries the door.

It opens.

I'm freezing.

Frankie lights a cig and stands out in the road.

I step inside.

Black, bloody, bleak.

Full of flies, fat fucking flies.

Ellis and Rudkin follow.

The room has the air of the sea bed, the weight of an evil ocean hanging over our heads.

Rudkin is swallowing hard.

I struggle.

Used to stare out the window and bark at the trains.

I've felt this before, but not often:

Wakefield, December '74.

Theresa Campbell, Joan Richards, and Marie Watts.

Today on the Moors.

Too often.

The sweet smell of perfumed soap, of cider, of Durex.

The headache is intense, blinding.

There's a bench, table, wooden crates, bottles, thousands of bottles, newspapers, scraps of this and that, blankets, odd bits of clothing.

'They did go through this, yeah?' says Ellis.

'Mmm,' mumbles Rudkin.

Trains pass, dogs bark.

I can taste blood.

I've slipped on to my knees and he's come out of me. Now he's angry. I try to turn but he's got me by my hair, punching me casually, once, twice, and I'm telling him there's no need for that, scrambling to give him his money back, and then he's got it up my arse, but I'm thinking at least it'll be over then, and he's back kissing my shoulders, pulling my black bra off, smiling at this fat cow's flabby arms, and taking a big, big bite out of the underside of my left tit, and I can't not scream and I know I shouldn't have because now he's going to have to shut me up and I'm crying because I know it's over, that they've found me, that this is how it ends, that I'll never see my daughters again, not now, not ever.

I look up. Ellis is staring at me.

This is how it ends.

Rudkin has a pair of plastic gloves on, pulling a dirt-caked carrier bag out from under the bench.

Tesco's.

He looks at me.

I squat down beside him.

He opens it up.

Porn mags, old and used.

He closes the bag and slings it back under the bench.

'Enough?' he says.

Not now, not ever.

I nod and we go back out into the light.

Frankie lights another cig and says, 'Lunch?'

*

Staring into dark pints, thinking worse thoughts, fucked if there's anything I can do about it.

Frankie brings over the Ploughmans, all withered and bleached.

'Fuck's that?' says Rudkin, getting up off his stool and going back to the bar.

Ellis raises his glass. 'Cheers.'

Rudkin comes back and tips a whisky into the top of his pint and sits back down. He smiles at Ellis, 'Impressions?'

Ellis grins back, reading Rudkin wrong, 'Do I look like Dick fucking Emery?'

'Yeah, and you're about as much fucking use.' Detective Inspector Rudkin's stopped smiling. He turns to me. 'Teach him something, Bob?'

'I'm with you. Different bloke.'

'Why?'

'She was attacked indoors. Raped. Sodomised. She did receive substantial head injuries from a blunt instrument, however none were fatal or immobilising.'

Frankie's got his head to one side. 'Meaning?'

'The killer or killers of Theresa Campbell and Joan Richards attacked them out in the open with one blow to the back of their heads. They were either dead or comatose before they hit the ground. Early indications are that the same is true of the latest one, Marie Watts.'

'And it couldn't be the same bloke over here using a different m.o.?'

'It doesn't really add up. If anything, the resistance, the struggle, was what kept him going.'

'Turned him on?' asks Ellis.

'Yeah. He'll have raped before, probably since.'

'So why kill her?'

I've only one answer:

'Because he could.'

Rudkin wipes ale from his face. 'What about the placing of the boot and the coat?'

'Similar.'

'Similar how?' repeats Frankie.

Ellis is about to chime up, but Rudkin cuts him off dead, 'Similar.'

Frankie smiles and looks at his watch, 'Best be getting back.'

'No offence, mate,' says Rudkin, patting Frank's back.

'None taken.'

We sup up and pile into the car.

It's almost three and I'm fucking tired, half-pissed.

We're going to drop Frankie back at the station, say our goodbyes, and head home.

I'm thinking of Janice, half dozing.

Ellis is telling Frankie about Kenny D.

'Dumb fucking monkey,' he laughs.

I can see Kenny's splayed legs, his cheap underpants and shrivelled dick, the pleas in his eyes.

Rudkin's going on about how we'll hold him until they bring Barton in.

I picture Kenny in his cell, sweating and shitting it.

They're all laughing as we swing into the car park.

Detective Chief Superintendent Hill is waiting for us as we come through the front door.

'Got a minute?' he says to DI Rudkin.

'What is it?'

'Not here.'

Me and Ellis stand around at the desk as Alf Hill takes Rudkin upstairs.

We wait, Frankie hanging around, talking up Lancs/Yorks rivalry.

'Fraser, up here now,' yells Rudkin from the top of the stairs.

I start up the stairs, stomach hollow.

Ellis starts to follow.

'Wait there,' I snap.

Rudkin and Hill up in the Lancashire Murder Room.

No-one else.

Hill's putting down the phone.

'Get that fucking file,' shouts Rudkin.

I pull it out from the cabinet.

'The Inquest in there?'

'Yeah,' I say.

'What was the blood group they got off her?'

'B,' I say from memory, flicking through for the report.

'Check it.'

I do and nod.

'Read it to me.'

I read: *'Blood grouping from the semen taken from victim's vagina and rectum, blood group B.'*

'Pass it here.'

I do it.

Rudkin stares at it, flat on his palms:

'Fuck.'

Hill too:

'Shit.'

Rudkin holds it up to the light, turns it over, and hands it to Detective Chief Superintendent Hill.

Rudkin picks up the phone and dials.

Hill has sucked his lower lip in, waiting.

'B,' says Rudkin into the phone.

There's a long silence.

Eventually Rudkin repeats, '9 per cent of the population.'

Another silence.

'Right,' says Rudkin and passes the phone to Alf Hill.

Hill listens, says, 'Will do,' and puts down the phone.

I stand there.

They sit there.

No-one speaks for about two whole minutes.

Rudkin looks up at me and shakes his head like, *this can't be fucking happening*.

I say, 'What is it?'

'Farley pulled some semen stains off the back of Marie Watts's coat.'

'And?'

'Blood group B.'

*

9 per cent of the population.

It's somewhere around eight or nine in the evening, the light still with us.

My eyes, my shoulders, my fingers ache from the writing.

The phone from here to Leeds hasn't stopped:

Panic Stations.

Rudkin keeps looking up at me like, *this is fucked,* and I swear sometimes there's bloody blame there.

We keep at it:

Transcribing, copying, checking, re-checking, like a gang of fucking monks hunched over some holy books.

Me, I keep thinking, *didn't Rudkin fucking know this? What the fuck were him and Craven doing over here?*

Ellis is just sat there scribbling away, totally blown away, head spinning like the fucking *Exorcist.*

I sketch the scene, the boot and the coat, and I look up and say, 'I'm going to go back up there.'

'Now?' says Ellis.

'We're missing something.'

'We going to stay night?' asks Rudkin.

We all look at our watches and shrug.

Rudkin picks up the phone.

'I'll sort you out,' says Frankie.

'Somewhere nice, yeah?' calls Rudkin, a hand over the receiver.

Up Church Street, the light almost gone, a train snaking out the station.

Yellow lights, dead faces at the glass.

Searching, looking for the lost, trying to find a Thursday night two years ago:

Thursday 20 November 1975.

It had rained during the day, helping keep Clare in the pub, the one at the bottom of the hill, St Mary's, same name as the hostel.

To the left the multi-storey and Frenchwood Street.

I cross the road.

A car slows behind me, then passes.

A tramp on the corner, asleep on a bed of cans and newspapers.

He reeks.

I light up and stand over him, looking down.

He opens his eyes and jumps:

'Don't eat my fingers please, just my teeth. Take them, they're no use to me now. But I need salt, have you got any salt, any at all?'

I walk past him, down Frenchwood Street.

'SALT!' he screams after me. 'To preserve the meat.'

Shit.

The street is dark now.

Estimates put the time of death between eleven and one. About the time she was thrown out of the pub.

The street would have been darker, after the rain, before the wind got going.

The bricks beside the garage have practically given up, wet even now with damp in May.

And then I feel it again, waiting.

I pull open the door.

It's there, laughing:

You just can't keep away, can you?

I've got a torch in my hand and I switch it on.

She's pulling up her skirt, taking down her tan tights, letting the flab of her thighs fall loose.

I sweep the room, the weight pressing down.

I'm not going to be able do this.

There's music, loud, fast, dense, from a car outside.

She's smiling, trying to make it hard.

The music stops.

I'll make it hard.

Silence.

I turn her round, pull down the black shiny briefs with their white streaks, and I'm getting bigger now, better, and she's backing on to me.

There's rats in here.

*But I don't want that, I want this: her arse, but she reaches round
and moves me towards her huge fucking cunt.*

Big fucking rats at my feet.

*And I'm in her and then I'm out again and she's slipped on to her
knees . . .*

Outside, I puke, fingers in the wall, bleeding.

I look up the street, no-one.

I wipe away the spit and shit, sucking the blood from my
fingers.

'SALT!' comes the scream.

I jump.

Fuck.

'To preserve the meat.'

The tramp's standing there, laughing.

Cunt.

I push him back into the wall and he stumbles, falls over,
staring up at me, into me, through me.

I swing my fist down into the side of his face.

He goes into a ball, whimpering.

I punch him again, a disconnected blow that bounces my fist
off the back of his head and into the wall.

Frustrated I kick him and kick him and kick him again until
there are arms around me, holding me tight, and Rudkin is
whispering, 'Easy Bob, easy.'

In a corner of the Post House, I'm begging, pleading into a
phone:

'I'm sorry, we thought it'd be just a day trip and back but
they want us to . . .'

She's not listening and I can hear Bobby crying and she's
telling me I've woken him up.

'How was your Dad?'

But it's how the fuck do I think he is and apparently I don't
fucking care so I needn't even waste my breath.

She hangs up.

I stand there, the smell of fried food from the restaurant,

listening to everyone in the bar: Rudkin, Ellis, Frankie, and about five other Preston coppers.

I look down at my fingers, my knuckles, the scuffs on my shoes.

I pick up the phone and try Janice again, but there's still no answer.

I look at my watch: gone one.

She's working.

Fucking.

'They're bloody closing up, can you fucking believe it?' says Rudkin on his way to the bogs.

I go back into the bar and drink up.

Everyone's pissed, really pissed.

'You got any fucking decent clubs round here?' says Rudkin coming back, still doing up his fly.

'Think we could manage something,' slurs Frankie.

Everyone tries to stand, talking about taxis, and this place and that, telling stories about this bloke and that lass.

I break away and say, 'I'm going to hit the hay.'

Everyone calls me a fucking puff and an arse bandit and I agree and feign drunkenness as I stumble off down the low-lit corridor.

Suddenly Rudkin's got his arms round me again. 'You all right?' he asks.

'I'll be right,' I say. 'Just knackered.'

'Don't forget, I'm always here.'

'I know.'

He tightens his grip: 'Don't be afraid, Bob.'

'Of what?'

'Of this,' he says, waving at everything and nothing, pointing at me.

'I'm not.'

'Piss off then, you puff,' he laughs, walking off.

'Have a good time,' I say.

'It'll make you blind,' he shouts down the corridor. 'Like Old Walter.'

A door opens and a man peers out at me.

'What you fucking want?'

He closes the door.

I hear the lock turn, him check it.

I knock on his door hard, wait, and then walk off to my room, digging the key into my arm.

Sat on the edge of the hotel bed in the middle of the night, the lamp on, Janice's phone ringing and ringing, the receiver beside me on the sheet.

I go over to Rudkin's bed and pick up the file.

Turn the pages, the copies we're to take back.

I come to the Inquest.

I stare at that single, lonely, bloody letter.

Wrong, the *B* looks wrong.

I hold the paper over the lamp.

It's the original.

Shit –

Rudkin's left them with the copy.

I put the paper back and close the file.

Pick the receiver up from the bed.

Janice's phone's still ringing.

I put it down.

I pick up the paper again.

Put it down again.

I switch off the lamp and lie there in the dark of the Preston Post House, the room unbearably fucking hot, everything heavy.

Scared, afraid.

Missing something, someone.

At last I close my eyes.

Thinking, *don't be afraid.*

Caller: You see this [reads]: *Silver Jubilee appeal reaches £1,000,000?*

John Shark: You're not happy, are you Bob?

Caller: Course I'm bloody not. Same day IMF come to London to meet Healey.

John Shark: Bit strange.

Caller: Strange? Nonsense is what it is, John. Sheer bloody nonsense. Country's lost its mind.

The John Shark Show
Radio Leeds
Wednesday 1st June 1977

Chapter 4

The court is a narrow yard of six houses, whitewashed up to the
first storey, the windowframes showing the remnants of green paint.
Entrance to the court is obtained through an arched, tunnel-like
passage which runs between numbers 26 and 27 Dosset Street, both
of which are owned by a Mr John McCarthy, a 37-year-old naturalised
British subject born in France. Number 27, to the left of the passage,
is McCarthy's chandler's shop, but the building doubles above and
behind as a lodging house. Number 26 is also a lodging house and the
rear ground floor has been partitioned, so that a second room has been
created. This is her room, number 13.

It's small, about twelve feet square, and is entered through a door
at the right-hand side of the passage at the furthest end from the street.
Apart from the bed, there are two tables, another smaller table and
two dining-type chairs, one of which has a broken back. A fierce fire
has been burning in the grate and the ashes disclose the remains of
clothing. Above the fireplace opposite the door hangs a print entitled
The Fisherman's Widow. In a small wall cupboard next to the print
there's some crockery, some empty ginger beer bottles, and a piece of
stale bread. A man's pilot coat doubles as a curtain over the window,
one of two looking out into the courtyard at right angles to the door
of the room.

I woke before the light, the rain clattering against the window,
ladies' heels down a dark alley.

I sat up in the sheets to see them perched upon the furniture,
six white angels, holes in their feet, holes in their hands, holes
in their heads, stroking their hair and wings.

'You're late,' said the tallest one, coming over to my bed.

She lay down beside me and took my hand, pressing it
against the walls of her stomach, hard beneath the white cotton
cloth of her gown.

'You're bleeding,' I said.

'No,' she whispered. 'It's you.'

I put my fingers to my face and they came away bloody.

I pinched my nose in a dirty old handkerchief and asked, 'Carol?'

'You remembered,' she replied.

'Thank you for seeing me at such notice.'

'Not a problem,' said Assistant Chief Constable George Oldman.

We were sat in his brand new Wakefield office, modern to the bone.

It was Wednesday 1 June 1977.

Eleven in the morning, the rain gone.

'Listen to that,' said George Oldman, nodding to the open window and the shouts and stomps of cadets drifting up from the Police College. 'We'll lose almost fifty per cent within five years.'

'That many?'

He looked down at the papers on his desk and sighed, 'Probably more.'

I looked round the room, wondering what he wanted me to say, wondering why I'd asked Hadden to set this up.

'Looks like you been in the wars too, Jack?'

'You know me,' I said, touching the bruise beneath my eye.

'How've you been, seriously now?'

Taken aback by the real concern in his voice, I smiled, 'Fine, really. Thanks.'

'It's been a long time.'

'Not really. Three years.'

He looked down at his desk again. 'Is that all?'

He was right: *100 years*.

I wanted to sigh, to lie face down on his floor, to be taken back to my bed.

George waved his hand across the desk and asked sadly, 'But you've kept up with all this?'

'Yeah,' I lied.

'And Bill wants you on it?'

'Yeah.'

'And you?'

Thinking about choices and promises, debts and guilt, nodding and keeping on lying, saying, 'Yeah.'

'Well, in a way, it's good because we could use all the publicity we can get.'

'Not like you.'

'No. But neither's this and . . .'

'And it can only get worse.'

George handed me a thick white bound dossier and said, 'Yeah.'

I read:

Murders and Assaults Upon Women in the North of England.

I opened up the first page and the bloody contents:

Joyce Jobson, assaulted Halifax, July 1974.

Anita Bird, assaulted Cleckheaton, August 1974.

Theresa Campbell, murdered Leeds, June 1975.

Clare Strachan, murdered Preston, November 1975.

Joan Richards, murdered Leeds, February 1976.

Ka Su Peng, assaulted Bradford, October 1976.

Marie Watts, murdered Leeds, May 1977.

'It's top secret.'

I nodded. 'Of course.'

'We've circulated it to all the other forces across the country.'

'And you think each of these women was attacked by the same man?'

'The three we've publicly linked, definitely. The others we can't discount simply because we've no evidence either way.'

'Fuck.'

'Clare Strachan looks more and more likely and, if she's in with the others, that'll be a big help.'

'Evidence?'

'More than we got over here.'

I flicked through the pages, skimming words:

Philips screwdriver, abdomen, heavy Wellington boots, vagina, ball-pein hammer, skull.

Black and white photos leaping out:

Alleys, terrace backs, wasteland, rubbish tips, garages, playing fields.

'What do you want me to do with it?'

'Read it.'

'I'd like to interview the survivors.'

'Be my guest.'

'Thanks.'

He looked at his watch and stood up. 'Early lunch?'

'That'd be nice,' I lied again, another angel dying.

At the door, George Oldman stopped. 'There's me doing all the bloody talking and it was you who asked for the interview.'

'Just like old times,' I smiled.

'What was on your mind?'

'We covered it. I wondered if you'd connected any other attacks or murders.'

'And?'

We were standing in his doorway, half in and half out, women in blue overalls polishing the floors and the walls.

'And if he'd made contact?'

Oldman looked back at his desk. 'None.'

George brought the pints over.

'Food'll be five minutes.'

The College was quiet, a couple of other coppers drank up when they saw us, everyone else was either a lawyer or a businessman.

George knew them all.

'How's Wakefield?' I asked.

'Good, you know.'

'You miss Leeds?'

'Oh aye, but I'm over there every other bloody day. Especially now.'

'Lillian and the girls, they keeping well?'

'Yes, thanks.'

The wall was still there, as high as ever:

A car crash, four maybe five years ago. His only son dead, one daughter paralysed, all kinds of rumours.

'Here we are,' said George, two big plates of liver in front of us.

We ate in silence, stealing glances, forming questions, abandoning them under the weight of a thousand bad tangents, worse memories, mires and traps. And then for a moment, just one moment, between the liver and the onions, the dartboard and the bar, I felt sorry for the big man before me, sorry like he didn't deserve the things he'd been through, the lessons he'd got coming, like none of us deserved our cruel cities and faithless priests, our barren women and unjust laws. But then I remembered all we'd done, the cuts we'd taken, the lives stolen and lost, and knew I was right when I said it could only get worse, so much more worse, the lessons we'd all got coming.

He dropped his knife and fork on to his empty plate and said, 'Why did you ask if we'd had any contact?'

'Just a hunch, a feeling.'

'Yeah?'

I swallowed the last of my lunch, the first in a long time. 'If it's the same fellow, he'll want you to know.'

'What makes you think that?'

'Wouldn't you?'

I drove back to Leeds, the long way, stopping for a third pint at the Halfway House.

'Not at all. Secrets should stay secret.'

And another.

Radio on:

Princess Anne greeted by noisy protesters as she opens the Kensington and Chelsea Town Hall, police urged not to cooperate on new complaints procedure, Asian man given three years for killing white man.

Three years, that's all it had been.

It was Wednesday 1 June 1977.

The office Derby-crazy.

Gaz was shouting, 'What you got, Jack?'

'Haven't looked.'

'Haven't bloody looked? Come on, Jack. It's the Derby. Jubilee Derby at that.'

'Your common people's race,' echoed George Greaves. 'None of your Royal Ascot here.'

'They reckon there'll be over a quarter of a million there,' said Steph. 'Be great.'

I opened up the paper, hiding the file.

Bill Hadden looked over my shoulder and whistled, 'Minstrel five to one.'

'It'll be Lester's eighth Derby if he does it,' said Gaz.

I wanted to fold up the paper, but I didn't want to see the file again. 'Can't see him not, can you?'

'Go on, Jack. Back Baudelaire,' smiled Bill.

I made an effort. 'What you fancy George?'

'A large one.'

'Slap him Steph,' shouted Gaz. 'Can't let him talk about you, like that.'

'You hit him, Jack,' laughed Steph.

'Royal Plume,' said George.

'Who's on it?'

'Joe Mercer,' said Gaz.

George Greaves was talking to himself. 'Royal Plume in Jubilee year, it's fate.'

'Come on, Jack. I want to get down there before they're in the stalls.'

'Hang on, Gaz. Hang on.'

'Milliondollarman?' laughed Steph.

'Can't fucking rebuild Jack, can they,' said Gaz.

I said, 'Hot Grove.'

'Carson and Hot Grove it is,' said Gaz, out the door.

An hour later, Piggott had won his eighth Derby and we'd all lost.

We were down the Press Club, drowning our sorrows.

George was saying, 'Trouble with racing is it's like sex, great build-up but it's all over in two minutes thirty six point four four seconds.'

'Speak for yourself,' said Gaz.

'Unless you're French,' winked Steph.

'Yeah, they don't even have a great build-up.'

'What would you know George Greaves,' screamed Steph. 'You haven't had it in ten years and bet then you never took your socks off.'

'You told me not to, said they turned you on.'

I picked up the file and left them to it.

'Should've backed it for a place, Jack,' shouted Gaz.

Grey evening sky, still hot with the rain to come, leaves green and stinking, tapping on my window like I LOVE YOU.

The moon down, the file open.

Murders and Assaults Upon Women in the North of England.

Sugar spilt, milk spoilt.

Mind blank, eyes hollow.

Unlucky stars fallen to the earth, they mocked me with their idiot lines, taunted me with their playground rhymes:

Jack Sprat who ate no fat.

Jack be nimble, Jack be quick.

Little Jack Horner, sat in his corner.

Jack and Jill went up the hill.

No Jill, the Jills all gone, just Jacks.

Jack in a box, Jack the lad.

Jack, Jack, Jack.

Yeah, I'm Jack.

Union Jack.

The same room, always the same room:

The ginger beer, the stale bread, the ashes in the grate.

She's in white, turning black right down to her nails, hauling a marble-topped washstand to block the door, falling about, too tired to stand, collapsed in the broken-backed chair, spinning, she makes no sense, the words in her mouth, the pictures in her head, they make no sense, lost in her own room, like she's had a big fall, broken, and no-one can put her together again, messages: no-one receiving, decoding, translating.

'What shall we do for the rent?' she sings.

Just messages from her room, trapped between the living and the dead, the marble-topped washstand before her door.

But not for long, not now.

Just a room and a girl in white turning black right down to her nails and the holes in her head, just a girl, hearing footsteps on the cobbles outside.

Just a girl.

I woke panting, burning, sure they'd be waiting.

They smiled and took my hands and feet.

I closed my eyes and let them rip me right back into that room, the same room, always the same room –

Different times, different places, different towns, different houses, always the same room.

Always that same bloody room.

The body is lying naked in the middle of the bed, the shoulders flat, the axis of the body inclined to the left side of the bed. The left arm is close to the body with the forearm flexed at a right angle, lying across the abdomen. The right arm is slightly abducted from the body and resting on the mattress, the elbow bent and the forearm supine with fingers clenched. The legs are wide apart, the left thigh at right angles to the trunk, the right forming an obtuse angle with the pubes.

The whole of the surface of the abdomen and thighs has been removed and the abdominal cavity emptied of its viscera. The breasts cut off, the arms mutilated by several jagged wounds and the face hacked beyond recognition of the features. The tissues of the neck have been severed all round, down to the bone.

The viscera are in various parts viz: the uterus and kidneys with one breast under the bed, the other breast by the right foot, the liver between the feet, the intestines by the right side, and the spleen by the left side of the body. The flaps removed from the abdomen and thighs are on the table.

The bed clothing at the right side is saturated with blood and on the floor beneath is a pool of blood covering about two feet square. The wall by the right side of the bed and in line with the neck is marked by blood which has struck it in a number of separate splashes.

The face has been gashed in all directions, the nose, the cheeks, eyebrows and ears being partly removed. The lips have been blanched and cut by several incisions running obliquely down to the chin. There are also numerous cuts extending irregularly across all the features.

The neck has been cut through the skin and other tissues right down to the vertebrae, the fifth and sixth being deeply notched. The skin cuts in the front of the neck show distinct eccymosis.

The air passage has been cut at the lower part of the larynx through the cricoid cartilage.

Both breasts have been removed by more or less circular incisions, the muscles down to the ribs being attached to the breasts. The intercostals between the fourth, fifth, and sixth ribs have been cut through and the contents of the thorax are visible through the openings.

The skin and tissues of the abdomen from the costal arch to the pubes have been removed in three large flaps. The right thigh is denuded in front to the bone, the flap of skin, including the external organs of generation and part of the right buttock. The left thigh has been stripped of skin, fascia, and muscles as far as the knee.

The left calf shows a long gash through skin and tissues to the deep muscles, reaching from the knee to five inches above the ankle.

Both arms and forearms have extensive and jagged wounds.

The right thumb shows a small superficial incision about one inch long, with extravasation of blood in the skin and there are several abrasions on the back of the hand showing the same condition.

On opening the thorax it appears that the right lung is minimally adherent by old firm adhesions. The lower part of the lung is broken and torn away.

The left lung is intact: adherent at the apex and there are a few adhesions over the side. In the substance of the lung are several nodules of consolidation.

The pericardium is open below.

In the abdominal cavity is some partly digested food and fish and potatoes and similar food was found in the remains of the stomach attached to the intestines.

Spitalfields, 1888.

The heart is absent and the door locked from the inside.

I woke to find them still perched across the sofa.

I flew from the bed and, casting them aside, I flung open Oldman's dossier:

Murders and Assaults Upon Women in the North of England.

I read and read till my eyes were blood-red and bleeding from all that I'd read.

And then I began to type, type as they chattered among themselves, wheeling around the room in dreadful disharmony, Carol taunting me, scolding me:

'You're late. You're late. You're always so late.'

One bitten finger in my ear, I kept typing, texts rewritten in a matching, fetching, fresh blood-red.

In the darkest part of the night, before the dawn and the light, I'd finished, just one last thing to do:

I picked up the telephone and pulled the numbers round the dial, my stomach turning with each digit.

'It's me, Jack.'

'I thought you'd never call.'

'It's not been easy.'

'It never is.'

'I need to see you.'

'Better late than never.'

With the dawn and more soft rain, I woke again. They were sleeping, wilted across my furniture.

I lay alone, staring up at the cracks in the ceiling, the chips in the paint, thinking about her, thinking about him, waiting for St Anne.

I rose and tiptoed past them to the table.

I pulled the paper from the typewriter.

I held the words in my hand and felt my belly bleeding:

Yorkshire, 1977.

The heart absent, the door still locked from the inside.

She came up behind me, leaning over my shoulder, warm against my ear, staring at the words I'd written:

Yesterday's news, tomorrow's headline:

The Yorkshire Ripper.

Caller: I'd like to ask Dr Rabonwick . . .

John Shark: Raazinowicz.

Caller: Yeah, right. I'd like to ask him like, he's saying
             that all these crimes have been committed and no-
             one knows about them . . .

Dr Raazinowicz: Over eighty-five per cent, yes.

Caller: Right. So my point is then, where are all the
             victims?

Dr Raazinowicz: The victims? The victims are everywhere.

The John Shark Show
Radio Leeds
Thursday 2nd June 1977

Chapter 5

Spade work:

Twenty-four hours' solid digging.

No sleep since we left Preston –

The drive back over Wednesday morning, Rudkin and Ellis as hung-over as fuck, passed out in the back.

Home, Millgarth still chaos and bodies, tips coming in one a bloody minute, no fucker free to follow them through. Me thinking, his name could be right here now in this room, right here now written in ink, right here now waiting for me.

Me, flying through slips, chasing up calls.

3.30 p.m. and I get the last call I want: another post office, another sub-postmaster.

Rudkin giving Noble shit: 'Fuck's it got to do with bloody Bob?'

'We haven't got anyone else.'

'Neither have I.'

OT ban kicking in, Uniforms having voted to continue the ban while we were over the hills in Preston, Rudkin with his, 'Who can fucking blame them?' speech.

'You're getting to be a right whining bastard, John. It's just for a couple of days.'

'This is bollocks. We haven't got a couple of days. He's supposed to be Prostitute Murder Squad.'

But Noble's gone and I'm back on the fucking post office jobs:

Hanging Heaton, Skipton, Doncaster, and now Selby.

Fuck-ups from start to finish.

Would be Robbery Squad and five years maximum if the dumb bastards had kept their fucking fingers off their bloody triggers in Skipton and didn't insist on battering each of the old gits half to death.

Murder: life for a life.

Well done, boys:

Suspects believed to be four, gloved and masked with local accents.

Could be gypsies: surprise, surprise.

Could be black: no surprises.

Level of violence suggested white, late teens/early twenties, previous form and too much *Clockwork Orange*.

I speak to Selby on the phone:

Mr Ronald Prendergast, sixty-eight, closing up his corner shop sub-post office on the New Park Road when he's confronted by three masked intruders, armed.

A struggle ensues, during which Mr Prendergast is clubbed repeatedly by a blunt instrument, rendering him unconscious with severe head injuries.

There by half-five and spend the evening between the crime scene and the hospital, waiting for Grandad Prendergast to come round.

Wife had been doing the flowers at Church, the lucky bitch.

Eight o'clock on, I stalk the hospital corridors, phoning and phoning:

Calling Janice.

Zero –

Knowing she'll be working, me desperate to crawl the streets, desperate to see her, desperate to stop her.

Calling home:

Zero –

Louise and Bobby in one hospital, me in another, the wrong one.

Calling Millgarth:

Less than zero –

Craven picking up, no sign of Noble or Rudkin, all them slips full of tips and no-one to work through them. Craven hanging up, seeing him limping back to Vice, thinking they must have invented it just for him and that fucking sneer.

Nine and it doesn't look like Mr Ronald Prendergast will be saying much, just drooling and looking like warmed-over-death-in-waiting, me praying and praying that he hangs on so it won't turn into a double-murder and knowing now, knowing now how much I want this:

Prostitute Murder Squad.

And knowing now, knowing now why:

Janice.

Two hours later all my prayers pay off, answered:

'Sergeant Fraser, would Sergeant Fraser please come to reception.'

Down the corridor, out of Intensive Care, back into Intensive Hell – Rudkin in Leeds, calling me home: 'We found Barton.'

Foot down into town, the whole of Millgarth humming, buzzing, burning. The Midnight Briefing:

BRING HIM IN.

The radio spits into life: 'Right, now,' cackles Noble's voice across the night: Thursday 2 June 1977.

Ellis is howling, 'Thank fucking Christ for that.'

And we're out the car and walking across Marigold Street, Chapeltown, Leeds.

Rudkin, Ellis, and me:

A shotgun, a sledgehammer, and an axe.

Up the top end of the terrace I can see Craven's boys coming down the street, the rest of them round the back.

We've got the front door.

Ellis raises the sledgehammer.

Rudkin looks at his watch.

We wait.

4 a.m.

Big John gives Ellis the nod.

Tick-tock, no need to knock:

He heaves it up over his head and yells, 'Rise and fucking shine you black bastard,' and brings it crashing down into the green door and there's splinters everywhere, and he pulls it out and does it again and then Rudkin sticks the boot in and in we go, me shitting it in case the fucking shotgun goes off, but half cracking up when we see one of Prentice's lads with his fat arse stuck in the fucking kitchen window, neither in nor out and us with the jump up the stairs where Steve Barton, Mr Sleepyhead himself, is standing in his blackest birthday suit, rubbing his gollylocks and scratching his knackers and shitting them, all in the five seconds it takes him to clock me and my fucking axe as I hit the stairs screaming at the dumb cunt, Rudkin and Ellis and the two barrels of the shotgun right behind me, giving full fucking voice to the four hours we've been sat in that car, sat in that unmarked pitch of hell, no phone, no Janice, no nothing, sat waiting for the bloody word, and I wind Barton straight off so he doubles over and topples down the stairs straight into Rudkin and Ellis who help him on his way with a kick and a punch and then they're back down there after him cos they don't want Prentice or Craven to beat them to it, and I'd be right behind them but Barton's cousin or his aunty or his mother or whatever part of his huge extended fucking tribe's been sheltering him, they go and put their head out the door of one of the bedrooms and I give her a quick squeeze on the tit and grab a feel of her cunt and push her back inside the bedroom where a baby's started crying and the woman's too scared to go to it cos she's too busy thinking about hiding, thinking she's going to get raped, which is what I want her to think so she'll stay in the room and leave us be, but I want her to shut that bloody baby up, to stop it sounding like Bobby and making me hate it and hate her and hate Bobby and hate Louise and hate everyone in this whole fucking world except Janice, but mainly because it's making me hate me.

I slam the door.

Back down the stairs they've got Barton outside, naked in the road, lights going on up and down the street, doors opening and then there's Noble, Detective Chief Superintendent Peter Noble standing there, bold as the fucking brass he is, standing in the middle of the street like he owns the place, hands on his hips like he don't give a fuck who sees this and he walks right up to Barton who's trying to curl up into the tiniest little ball he can, whimpering like the tiny little dog he is, and Noble looks up just to make sure everyone is watching and just to make sure everyone knows he knows everyone is watching and he bends down and whispers something into Barton's ear and then he picks him off the road by his dreadlocks, twisting them tight around his fist, pulling him on to the tips of his toes, the man's cock and balls nothing in the dawn and Noble looks up at the windows and the twitching curtains of Marigold Street and he says calmly, 'What is it with you fucking people? A woman gets to wear her guts for bloody earrings and you don't lift a fucking finger. Didn't we ask you nicely to tell us where this piece of shit was? Yeah? Did we come and turn all your shitty little houses upside down? Did we have you all down the Nick? No we fucking didn't. But all the time you're hiding him under the fucking bed, right under our bloody noses.'

A maria comes down the street and stops.

Uniforms open the back.

Noble spins Barton into the side of the van, bringing him round all bloody and reeling, and then he tips him into the back.

Detective Chief Superintendent Peter Noble turns and looks again at Marigold Street, at the empty windows, the still curtains.

'Go on hide,' he says. 'Next time we don't ask,' and with a spit he jumps inside the van and is gone.

We head for the cars.

By the time we get to Millgarth, they've got Barton down in the Belly – the huge fucking hole of a cell right down in the gut, all strip lights and wash-down floors.

There's about twelve or fifteen blokes standing around.

Steve Barton's on the floor, still stark-bollock naked, shivering, shaking, shitting it.

We stand there, smoking, flicking ash here and there, Craven showing off his cuts and bruises, all black hate, the rest of us looking bored, waiting for the show.

And just as I'm thinking about Kenny D and wondering if I can sit through another nigger beating, Noble shoulders through the crowd and everyone breaks into a circle, leaving Barton and Noble in the centre, the Christian and the Lion.

Noble is holding a white plastic cup, the kind you get from the coffee machine upstairs.

He looks into it, looks at Barton, then tosses it on to the floor in front of him and says, 'Come into that.'

Barton looks up, eyes all wide red streaks.

'You heard,' says Chief Superintendent Peter Noble. 'Put your fucking jungle juice in that.'

Barton is here and there, searching the room for a friendly face, some kind of help, and for a brief second his eyes light on mine but finding nothing there they keep on going till they end up back on the white plastic cup in the centre of the room.

'Fuck,' he whispers, the fucked-up horror of his situation sinking into them dense black bones.

'Get it hard,' hisses Noble.

And then the slow handclap starts up and I'm right there, beating out the rhythm, banging out the time, as Barton slithers around in the smallest circle his body'll let him, this way and that, twisting and turning, this way and that, no escape at all, that way or this, no escape.

Noble nods and the claps stop.

He bends down and cups Barton's head in his hand:

'Let me help you out, boy. Let's imagine that dead woman of yours isn't dead any more and it was all just some ugly dream. Yeah? Let's get her all naked and hot, get her wet, yeah. Bet you could make her wet Steve, yeah? Bet you can get a right big cock on you when you want, can't you Steve? Go on, show us what a big black cock you got. Show us how big you got it for Marie. Come on boy, don't be shy. Among friends here, all lads together. Don't want to have to put you in with some big fat babber-stabber from Armley, now do we? No need for that. Let's just picture dear old Marie, hot and naked and waiting for that big old cock o'yours, stroking that big old bush of hers, getting it all big and pink and hanging out like a little fat juicy cherry, just waiting for you. Ooh. Ooh. What's that? A drop of the good stuff slipping out, sneaking off. Come on Steve, she's not dead, you didn't kill her, she's here and she's hot and she's waiting for you to stick that big old cock of yours inside and give her a good seeing to, a right good time. Come on, get it hard. Come on, she's all wet and waiting, begging for it, flipping on to her belly, her fat little fingers right up her juicy chute, wondering where the fuck you are when she needs you. Where's Stevie, she's thinking, and then the door opens and in comes a big black dick, but it isn't you is it Stevie? It isn't your big black dick, is it? Well, well, if it isn't your old mucker Kenny D and he's looking at her all wet and naked and lying there with her fingers up her cos you're nowhere to be seen and so he whips it out and puts it in and out, in and out, in and out, till she's got it running down her legs and then here you come and you clock him and her, your woman and your mate making the old beast with two backs and you're pissed off aren't you Steve? Pissed off and who wouldn't be? Him with his big black cock up your white woman, your white woman who should be out earning your cash not fucking around with your mate giving it away for nowt. Makes you sick, just fucking sick eh? Your mate and your woman. Hard to take, eh? That's what happened, isn't it Steve? And you had to get her back, pay her back big time didn't you Stevie, didn't you?'

'No, no, no,' he's whimpering.

Noble stands up, Barton sobbing between his legs.

'So you come, then you go.'

Steve Barton reaches for the cup and puts it over his shrivelled dick.

Fifteen white faces stare at the black man on the floor before us, a white plastic cup on his dick, his other hand shaking it, stopping it shrinking anymore.

There's a shove in my back and there's Oldman.

He looks at the scene before him, at the black man on the floor before him, a white plastic cup on his dick, his other hand shaking it.

Oldman looks at Noble.

Noble raises his eyes.

Oldman looks pissed off.

'Get the black cunt some porn and get his fucking spunk down the lab,' he says.

'You heard him,' shouts Noble at the man nearest the door, me.

Craven makes a move, but Noble points at me.

I'm down the corridor, up three flights of stairs and into Vice, Craven's lair.

Dead, half of them back down in the Belly.

I pull open a cabinet: envelopes.

Next drawer the same.

And the next.

Thinking, this is fucking Vice, there ought to be some.

And then it hits me and I look back at the door, the thought right in front of me: JANICE.

Back into the cabinets, eyes every second second at the door, ears bleeding for the slightest footfall.

Ryan, Ryan, Ryan . . .

Nothing.

Nowt.

Nil.

I'm almost out the door before I remember the fucking porn.

I reach across the desks and pull open a drawer: two magazines, cheap and nasty, a fat blonde woman with a sun visor and her cunt wide open.

Spunk.

I grab them and go.

Back down into the Belly, the crowd parting, Barton still lying on the floor in a ball, still fucking crying, a blanket beside him.

I chuck the magazines down on the ground next to him.

He turns his head and pulls the grey blanket slowly across the concrete towards him.

'Had an Aunty Margaret,' Rudkin is saying. 'Went by the name Mags. We all called her Nuddy for short.'

Titters and giggles.

'Should get one of the women to do it for him,' says someone else.

'Do rest of us while she were down here.'

'Long as she does me before Sambo.'

Noble kicks the magazine closer. 'Get on with it.'

Barton lies on his side beneath the blanket, the magazine before him.

Ellis bends down and opens it.

Everyone laughs.

'Go on, Mike,' shouts Rudkin. 'Give him a hand.'

Belly laughs in the Belly.

Barton's started moving beneath the blanket.

More laughter.

'Here, don't forget the fucking cup,' says Oldman. 'Don't want it all over the blanket.'

Steve Barton keeps moving, eyes closed, tears open, teeth clenched, the curses burning into his brain.

The clapping starts and I'm right there again but I'm thinking about Bobby and how Steve Barton must have been someone's little boy not so long ago, with his trains and his cars and his hopes and his dreams and the food he liked and the food he didn't but here he is now, a bouncer, a pimp, and a drug user, wanking into a white plastic cup from a coffee machine in front of fifteen white coppers.

And then, just as he picks up speed, Rudkin reaches down and pulls away the blanket, just as Barton's dick spits up its come, just as Craven snaps a Polaroid and the claps break into a round of applause.

'Detective Constable Ellis,' says Oldman. 'Take Mr Barton's semen up to Professor Farley.'

Everyone's laughing.

'And don't be having a fucking sip,' I add, everyone clapping, Ellis giving me his best hard-as-nails fuck-you-later face.

And Barton, Barton's still in a ball, shaking and shaking, dry heaving big gulping sobs, the party over.

And just as it's breaking up, I reach down, pick up the magazines and hand them to Craven.

'I think these are yours,' I say.

Craven takes them, eyes cold and dark and far away until he glances down at the covers and stops: 'Fuck you get these?'

'Your wife, why?'

The room's all silent smiles, everyone hanging back to see
what comes next.

'Funny man, Fraser. Funny man.' And Craven limps off, back
to Vice.

I'm sat up in the canteen, wiped out.

Rudkin's getting the coffees.

We've been told to wait while Prentice and Alderman question Barton, wait while the tests come back, which is a load of
bollocks when we all know it isn't him, wish it was, but know
it's not.

'Could've taken a fucking blood test,' says Rudkin, pissed
off he's not in on the questioning, staring to get the big fucking
picture, those two words:

SPADE WORK.

'What, going to scrape under your nails?'

'You really are a funny man,' he laughs as we heap sugar
into our coffees, and lots of it.

I want to sleep but, if they let me loose, I've got so many
fucking fences to mend.

'What time is it?' asks Rudkin, too tired to look at his own
watch.

'What am I? The speaking fucking clock?'

'Speaking cock, more like.'

And we keep this up for about two minutes till we fade back
into another one of them fucked-up knackered silences in which
we hide.

'We're letting him go.'

Out of silence and back into the bright, bright lights of the
police canteen, the world of Chief Superintendent Peter Noble.

'Quel surprise,' mutters Rudkin.

'Not a B?' I say.

'O,' says Noble.

I ask, 'Get anything else from him?'

'Not much. He was pimping her. Hadn't seen her since the
afternoon.'

'Should've let us at him,' spits Rudkin.

'Well, now's your chance. He's waiting for you downstairs with DC Ellis.'

'You don't need us. Ellis can take him home.'

Noble takes a wad of fivers from his jacket and leans over and stuffs them inside Rudkin's top pocket. 'The Assistant Chief Constable wants you to take Mr Barton out and get him pissed, give him a good time. No hard feelings etc.'

'Fuck,' says Rudkin. 'We're up to our fucking eyes in work, Pete. We got all the stuff from Preston, then you put Bob on these fucking robberies. Now this. We haven't got the time.'

I'm looking at the table top, the lights reflecting in the Formica.

Noble bends over and pats Rudkin's top pocket. 'Stop whining John and just do it.'

Rudkin waits till Noble's out the door and then gives it, 'Cunt. Fucking cunt.'

We stand up, stiff as a pair of wooden puppets.

Ellis is in the Rover, sat behind the wheel waiting.

Barton's in the back in oversize trousers and a tiny jacket, dreadlocks against the window.

Rudkin gets in next to him. 'Where to?'

I get in the front.

Barton's just staring out the glass.

'Come on, Steve. Where to?'

'Home,' he mumbles.

'Home? You can't go home now. It's only three o'clock. Let's all have a drink.'

Barton knows he's no fucking choice.

Ellis starts the car and asks: 'Where to then?'

'Bradford. Manningham,' says Rudkin.

'Bradford it is,' smiles Ellis as we pull out of Millgarth.

I close my eyes as he sticks the radio on.

I wake up as we get into Manningham, Wings on the radio, Barton silent as some black ghost in the back.

Ellis pulls up outside the New Adelphi.

Rudkin says, 'What do you reckon, Steve?'

Steve says nowt.

'Heard it's all right,' says Ellis and out we get.

There's day-old puke on the steps and inside the New Adelphi is a big old ballroom, high ceilings and flock wallpaper, the crowd mixed, stirred, and well fucking shaken and it's not even four o'clock in the afternoon.

I'm shattered, shoulders down, head killing, the stripper not on again until six and they're playing some reggae bollocks:

'Your mother is wondering where you are . . .'

Rudkin turns to Steve and says, 'See, right up your street.'

Steve just nods and we plonk him down in the corner under the stairs up to the balcony, me on one side, Rudkin on the other, Ellis at the bar.

The three of us sit there, saying nothing, scanning the ballroom, the black faces and the white.

'Know anyone?' asks Rudkin.

Barton shakes his head.

'Good. Don't want folk thinking you're a bloody grass now do we?'

Ellis gets back with a tray of pints and shorts.

He hands Barton a large rum and coke. 'Get that down you.'

'Here Steve,' laughs Rudkin. 'You come here often?'

And we're laughing, but not Steve.

It's going to be a long time before he starts laughing again.

Ellis goes back to the bar and brings over more drinks, more rum and cokes, and we drink them and then back he goes.

And we sit there, the four of us, talking here and there, the endless reggae, the Paki cab drivers coming in and out, the slags falling about on the dancefloor, the old blokes with their dominoes, the rat-faced whites with their v-necked sweaters and no shirts, the fat-faced blacks nodding their heads to the music:

'What do you see at night when you're under the stars . . .'

Rudkin and Ellis have got their heads together, laughing at one of the women at the bar, the one sticking two fingers up at them.

'*Stay at home sister, stay at home . . .*'

And Barton suddenly leans across to me, his hand on my arm, his eyes yellow, breath rank, and he says: 'That shit about Kenny and Marie, that true?'

I look at him, his tight jacket and baggy trousers, seeing him back down in the Belly under that grey blanket, his hands moving, the magazines beside him.

'You got to tell me. I know you're tight with Kenny and Joe Ro. I ain't going to do nothing, but I got to know.'

I take his hand off my arm and push it away, spitting in his face: 'Fuck I care about your shit. You got bad information, boy.'

And he sits back in his chair and Rudkin throws another cigarette at him and Ellis goes back to the bar and brings more drinks, more rum and cokes, and the reggae keeps on going:

'*Baby keep on running but you won't get far . . .*'

And when I next look at my watch it's almost six and I want to be gone, gone like Steve who's pissed now, head down on the table, dreadlocks in the ashtray.

The music stops, the microphone wails across the room, and a spotlight hits the heavy red curtains at the back of the stage.

Dancing Queen starts up, the curtains go back, and there's a flabby brunette in a sequined bikini standing there, eyes glazed, limbs slack.

'Dumb fucking monkey's going to miss the show,' lisps Ellis, nodding at Barton as the woman jerks into some kind of life.

'Mike, you're fucking boring,' hisses Rudkin and gets up and wanders off up the stairs to the balcony.

'Fuck's got into him?'

I say, 'You got to learn to bloody read people.'

Mike starts up again, moaning, whining, injured.

'Keep an eye on Sleeping Beauty,' I say, following Rudkin upstairs.

He's leaning over the balcony, staring down at the bleached stripper.

'Good view,' I say, elbows next to his.

All the blokes downstairs are facing the stage, women lolling about between them, one woman tossing peanuts in the air and catching them between her tits.

Rudkin swirls the whisky about in the bottom of his glass and says, 'You know what it's going to be like from now on, don't you?'

Thinking, *here we fucking go,* saying, 'No. What's it going to be like?'

Rudkin keeps staring into the bottom of his glass. 'He'll keep killing them and we'll keep finding them. Always behind, never in front.'

'We'll catch him,' I say.

'Yeah? How?'

'Hard bloody work, patience, and he'll fuck up. The usual way.'

'The usual way? There's no usual way here.'

'You know what I mean.'

'No, I don't. You seen this kind of thing before?'

I think of little girls and lost years and I say, 'Similar.'

'I don't think you have.'

I can't be arsed: 'We'll catch him.'

'You're a good man, Bob,' he says and I wish he hadn't because it's been said before and it wasn't true then and it's even less true now, just fucking patronising.

So I say, 'What the fuck's that supposed to mean?'

'It means what I say: you're a good bloke, but all the fucking good blokes and all the hard work in the world isn't going to catch this cunt.'

'And what makes you so fucking certain?'

'You read that *Murders and Assaults Upon Women in the North of England* shit?'

'Yeah.'

'And?'

'We'll catch him, John.'

'The fuck we will. We haven't got a clue, not a bloody one. This cunt, he looks back out the mirror at us and he's laughing. He's watching us and he's pissing himself.'

'Fuck off. You got a point to make, make it.'

Rudkin looks up from his glass, shadows heavy across his face, big black tears in pitch black eyes, a man who keeps a cricket bat by his front door, just in case, and this man he takes hold of my arm and he says, 'That shit in Preston, that bollocks is nothing to do with what we got here.'

My heart's beating fast, stomach twisted tight, the man still staring into me, still holding me, still scaring me.

'The blood groups,' I say. 'They're the same.'

'It's bollocks, Bob. Something's going on and I don't know what the fuck it is and I don't want to know what the fuck it is but we're right in the fucking middle of it and I'll tell you this: it's going to fuck up your life if you let it.'

What's to fuck up, I'm thinking but I let him go on.

'You don't know them, Bob,' he's saying. 'I know them. I know the kind of shit they'll try and pull. Specially for their own.'

I stare down at the stage, at the tops of the stripper's flaccid white titties, the men at the bar bored already.

I say, 'One minute you're telling me not to be afraid, the next minute we might as well jack it in. Which is it, John?'

Rudkin looks at me and shakes his head, half smiling, then walks off back down the stairs, leaving me wanting to punch the arrogant twat.

I stare back down at the stripper's tits, look at my watch, and decide to get the fuck out of here.

Downstairs Rudkin's thinking the same, kicking Barton awake, ignoring Ellis and all his apologies.

Barton staggers to his feet and Rudkin takes what's left of the fivers and stuffs them inside Barton's tight little jacket.

I look at the stripper gathering up her bikini from the floor of the stage, her arse fat with spots and I look at the bar and the faces of the dead, wondering if he's here, here with us now, and then I'm back at the table, nowhere left to look.

And Barton's standing there, coming round, still filled full of rum, and he takes the notes out of his jacket and tosses them on to the table.

'Keep them,' he says. 'Keep them for the next one.' And he turns and walks out.

'Thought we were supposed to let him get his dick sucked,' laughs Ellis.

I pick up one of the rums and drain it.

Ellis, suddenly scared his whole evening'll fall about his ears and we'll leave him, sighs, 'Fuck we going to do now?'

'Do what you fucking want,' says Rudkin, going over to the bar, walking into people, looking for a fight to make him feel better.

'Where you going?' shouts Ellis as I head for the door.

'Home,' I say.

'Yeah, right,' he's saying as I push through the double doors and escape.

I'm in the back of a cab, crawling out of Bradford with the windows down, my eyes dropping, heart heavy, brain in flames:

Got to see Janice, got to see Bobby, got to see Louise, and I've got to see her Dad.

Four murdered whores, maybe more.

Shotguns in Hanging Heaton, shotguns in Skipton, shotguns in Doncaster, shotguns up Selby way.

Four murdered whores, maybe more.

My son and my wife, her father's days numbered.

Janice, my lover, tormentor, my own private whore in my own numbered days.

'Here OK?'

'Cheers,' and I pay him.

I walk up the stairs, suddenly thinking, *help me, I'm dying here.*

On her landing thinking, *you don't answer the door, I'm dead.*

I knock once thinking, *help me, I don't want to die here on your stair.*

She comes to the door and smiles, hair damp, her skin browner than before.

The radio's on inside.

'Can I come in?'

Her smile broadens, 'You're a policeman. You can do what you want.'

'I hope so,' I say and we kiss hard; hard kisses to forgive and forget all that went before and is yet to come.

We hit the bed, my hands all over her, trying to get deeper inside her, her nails in my back, getting deeper inside me.

I pull off her jeans, kick off her shoes, death all gone.

And we fuck, then we fuck again, and she kisses me and sucks me until I fuck her one last time and we fall asleep to Rod on the radio.

I wake as she's coming out of the bathroom, just a t-shirt and knickers.

'You going out?' I ask.

'Got to,' she says.

'Don't.'

'Told you, I got to.'

I get out of bed and start to dress.

She starts putting on her make-up in front of the mirror.

I ask her: 'It doesn't worry you at all?'

'What?'

'These fucking murders?'

'What? You mean because I'm a prostitute?'

'Yeah.'

'Like your wife, she's no need to worry?'

'She doesn't walk the streets of bloody Chapeltown at two in the morning, does she?'

'Lucky bitch. Probably got herself a nice husband to keep her off the streets with his big fat salary . . .'

I've got my wallet open. 'You want money, I'll give you fucking money.'

'It's not the money, Bob. It's not the fucking money. How many more times?'

She's standing in the middle of the room, under the paper lampshade, her hairbrush in her hand.

'I'm sorry,' I say.

She goes to the drawer and puts on some kind of black PVC top and a short denim skirt, the kind that buttons up the front.

My eyes are stinging, filling.

She looks so fucking beautiful and I don't know how any of this happened, where we came in.

I say, 'You don't need to do this.'

'Yes, I do.'

'Why?'

'Please. Don't start.'

'Don't start? It never stops.'

'It can stop any time you want.'

'No, it can't.'

'Just don't come around any more.'

'I'll leave her.'

'You'll leave your wife and baby for a Chapeltown scrubber, a whore? I don't think so.'

'You're not a whore.'

'Yes, I am. I'm a dirty little fucking whore, a woman who fucks men for money, who sucks for money on her knees in parks and cars, who'll have at least ten blokes tonight if I'm lucky, so don't pretend I'm not.'

'I'll leave her.'

'Shut up, Bob. Shut up,' and she's gone, the sound of the door ringing through the room.

And I sit down on the edge of the bed and I cry.

I walk the streets down to St James.

Visiting time is almost up, people filing out, their duty done.

I take the lift up to the ward and walk down the corridor, past the overlit rooms of the nearly dead with their shaven heads and sunken faces, their sallow skin and cold, cold hands.

No air, only heat.

No dark, only light.

Another night in Dachau.

And I'm thinking, *never sleep, never sleep.*

Louise is gone and her father almost, eyes closed and alone.

A nurse comes by and smiles and I smile back.

'Just missed them,' she says.

'Thanks,' I nod.

'Hasn't half got your eyes, your lad,' she laughs.

I nod and turn back to her father.

I sit down beside his bed, beside the packets of drugs, the drips and the tubes, and I'm thinking of Janice, there beside the half-dead body of my wife's father, hard at the thought of another woman, of a Chapeltown whore, and while he's on his back dying, she's on her knees sucking, bleeding me.

I look up.

Bill's looking at me, bloodshot and watery, trying to place me, seeking answers and truth.

A hand reaches through the bars on the side of the bed and he opens his mouth, cracked and dry, and I lean closer.

'I don't want to die,' he whispers. 'I don't want to die.'

I pull away, away from his striped pyjamas and terrible breath, away from his coming threats and ramblings.

He tries to sit up but the restraints work and he can only raise his head. 'Robert! Robert! Don't leave me here, take me home!'

I'm on my feet, looking for the nurse.

'I'll tell her! I'll tell her,' he's screaming.

But there's no-one, only me.

I open the door, the house dark.

I pick the evening paper up off the mat.

Bobby's little blue anorak is hanging from a peg.

I switch on the kitchen light and sit down at the table.

I want to go upstairs and see him but I'm afraid she'll be awake, waiting.

So there I sit under the kitchen light, alone, just thinking.

Under the kitchen light, late into the night, pacing cancer wards, cradling Bobby, parked in a car; these are the places where I do my thinking, beside the dirty dishes and my father-in-law, looking at my son's scribbles on the fridge door and the crumbs under the toaster, thinking.

I look at my watch, almost midnight.

I sit there, my head in my hands as they sleep upstairs, a broken Jubilee mug on the draining board, in the middle of my family, thinking about HER.

Thinking, this is where I came in:

I'd heard of her, heard the others talk about her, knew she used to tip some Bradford copper called Hall the odd word for a blind eye, but I'd never seen her, never seen her until 4 November last year.

Mischief Night.

I'd picked her up for soliciting near the Gaiety, drunk and weaving, trying to flag down lorries, dragged her down to Millgarth only to be driving her home five minutes later, the laughter loud and long in my ears, thinking fuck *'em.*

I'd been married five years and I had one son, almost a year then, and wanted another.

But what I got was the fuck of my life in the back of an unmarked police car and my first taste of her, licked off her lips, off her nipples, out of her cunt, out of her arse, off the lids of her eyes, off the tips of her hair.

And that night I went home to Louise and Bobby and watched them sleeping, the cot squeezed in beside our bed.

I'd had a bath to wash her off but ended up drinking down the water just to taste her again.

And later that night I'd woken up screaming that Bobby was dead, rushing to the cot, checking he was still breathing, the sweat stinking the room out, then lying in the bath again, hard, wanking.

And it never stopped:

From that night on I thought about her every second, flying through arrest sheets, asking questions I shouldn't, combing the streets, pulling files, knowing one wrong word and the whole thing'd come tumbling down.

So I learnt to keep secrets, to lead two lives, to kiss my son with the same lips I kissed her with, learnt to cry alone in overlit rooms while all three of them slept, learnt to control myself, to ration, knowing there'd be famine and drought, worse plagues than this, learnt to kiss three sets of lips.

Under the kitchen light, between the fridge and the washer, thinking:

She's twenty-two, I'm thirty-two.

She's a half-caste prostitute and I'm a white Detective Sergeant, married to the daughter of one of the finest Yorkshire coppers there ever was.

I have an eighteen-month-old baby boy called Bobby.

After me.

And then, when I can think no more I go upstairs.

She's lying on her side, wishing I was dead.

Bobby's in the cot, and later he'll wish I were dead too.

She swears in her sleep and rolls over.

Bobby opens his eyes and looks up at me.

I stroke his hair and bend down into the cot to kiss him.

He goes back to sleep and, later, I go back downstairs.

I walk through the dark house, remembering the day we moved in, the first Christmas, the day Bobby was born, the day he came home, the times the house was all lit up.

I stand in the front room and watch the cars drive past, their empty seats and their yellow headlights, their drivers and their boots, until each one becomes just another punter back from the red lights, back from Janice, their motors just another way to transport the killer from A to B, just another way to carry the dead back and forth, just another way to take her away.

And I swallow.

I walk back into the kitchen, legs weak, stomach empty.

I sit back down, tears on the evening paper and tears on Bobby's book and I open up his little book and I stare at the picture of the frog in galoshes but it doesn't help a bit because I don't live in a little damp house among the buttercups at the edge of the pond, I live here:

Yorkshire, 1977.

And I wipe my eyes but they won't dry because the tears won't stop and I know they'll never stop until I catch him.

Until I catch him.

Before he catches her.

Until I see his face.

Before he sees hers.

Until I say his name.

Before he says hers.

And I turn over the *Evening Post* and there he is, one step ahead, waiting for us both:

The Yorkshire Ripper.

Part 2
Police & thieves

Caller: You see this [reads]: *Men earn £72 gross a week on average.*

John Shark: *That you, is it Bob?*

Caller: *Course it's bloody not. Maybe down South, but no bugger round here.*

John Shark: *This is the same report that says there are 9,000,000 pensioners and three per cent of the population are immigrants.*

Caller: *Well, they got that wrong bloody way round for starters.*

The John Shark Show
Radio Leeds
Friday 3rd June 1977

Chapter 6

Jubela . . .

'Twice. He hit me twice, right on the top.'

Mrs Jobson leant forward, parting her grey hair to reveal the indentations in her skull.

'Go on, feel them,' urged her husband.

I reached across the room to touch the top of her head, the roots of her hair oily beneath my fingertips, the dents huge and hollow craters.

Mr Jobson was watching my face. 'Some hole isn't it?'

'Yes,' I said.

It was Friday, going up to eleven, and we were sitting in Mr and Mrs Jobson's homely front room at the bottom end of Halifax, sipping coffee and passing round photos, talking about the time a man hit Mrs Jobson twice on the head with a hammer, lifted up her skirt and bra, scratched her stomach once with a screwdriver and masturbated across her breasts.

And in amongst the photos, in amongst the ornaments, between the postcards and the empty vases, beside the pictures of royalty, there were bottles and bottles of pills because Mrs Jobson hadn't left the house since that night three years ago when she met the man with the hammer and the screwdriver coming back as she was from her weekly lasses' night out, lasses who've also stopped going out, lasses who got beatings from their husbands when the police suggested that Mrs Jobson liked to make a bit of pin money by sucking black men's willies down the bus station on her way back home from her weekly lasses' night out, Mrs Jobson who hasn't left the house since that last lasses' night out in 1974, not even to scrub the graffiti off the front door, the graffiti that said she liked to suck black men's willies down the bus station, graffiti that her husband, bad back or not, graffiti Mr Jobson painted over and had to paint over a second time, the same graffiti that made their Lesley never go to school because of all the things they were saying about her mum and the black men down the bus station, and it got to the point where Lesley came right out and asked her mum if she'd ever been down the bus station with a black man, standing there in her nightie at the bottom of these stairs having wet the bed for the third time that week and like Mrs Jobson said that night and many times since has said:

'There's times, times like that, when I wish he'd finished me off.'

Mr Jobson was nodding.

I put my cup down on the low coffee table next to the Philips Pocket Memo, the wheels turning.

'And how are you now?'

'Better. I mean, every time there's another and every time it's a prostitute, I know it starts folk talking again. I just wish they'd hurry up and catch the bastard.'

'You met Anita yet?' asked Mr Jobson.

'This afternoon.'

'Tell her Donald and Joyce said hello.'

'Of course.'

At the door Mr Jobson said, 'Sorry about the photographs, it's just we . . .'

'I know, don't worry. You've been more than kind just letting me in.'

'Well if it helps catch the . . .' Mr Jobson looked off down the street, then said quietly, 'Just ten minutes alone with the cunt, that's all I ask. And I wouldn't need no fucking hammer or screwdriver.'

I stood there on his front step, nodding.

We shook hands.

'Thank you again,' I said.

'You're welcome. Do call us if you hear owt.'

'Of course.'

I got in the Rover and drove away.

Jubelo . . .

*

Anita Bird lived in Cleckheaton in exactly the same kind of terrace as the Jobsons, both houses at the top end of steep inclines.

I knocked on the door and waited.

A woman with bleached blonde hair and heavy make-up answered the door.

'Jack Whitehead. We spoke on the telephone.'

'Come in,' she said. 'You'll have to excuse the mess.'

She cleared a pile of ironing off one end of the sofa and I sat down in her gloomy front room.

'Cup of tea?'

'I've just had one, thanks. Donald and Joyce Jobson said to say hello.'

'Right, of course. How is she?'

'I'd not met her before, so it's hard for me to say. She doesn't go out though.'

'I was same, me. Then I just thought, fuck him. Excuse my French, but why should he do that to me and leave me sat at home like it's me that's in prison while he walks round free as a bloody bird. No thank you. So one day I just said to myself, Anita, you're not staying locked up in here you silly cow or you might as well top yourself and have done with it, much use you are to anyone like this.'

I was nodding along, placing the tape recorder on the arm of the sofa.

'Sometimes it seems like a lifetime ago, other times like it was just yesterday.'

'You weren't living here, I understand?'

'No, I was staying with Clive, the feller I was seeing back then. Over on Cumberland Avenue. That was half the problem, him being black and all.'

'How do you mean?'

'Well they all thought it must have been him, didn't they.'

'Because he was black?'

'That and he'd battered me a couple of times and police had had to come down.'

'Was he ever charged?'

'No, he always talked me round, didn't he. Smooth he is, Clive.'

'Where is he now?'

'Clive? Armley, last I heard. GBH.'

'GBH?'

'Hit some bloke down International. Police hate him, always have. Daft bastard played straight into their hands.'

'When's he due out?'

'Twelfth of bloody never as far as I'm concerned. You sure you don't want that cup of tea?'

'Go on then. Twist my arm.'

She laughed and went off into the kitchen.

In the corner the TV was on with the sound off, lunchtime news with pictures from Ulster, changing to Wedgwood-Benn.

'Sugar?' Anita Bird handed me a cup of tea.

'Please.'

She brought a bag of sugar from the kitchen. 'Sorry,' she said.

'Thanks.'

We sat and sipped our teas, watching silent cricket from Old Trafford.

The Second Test.

I said, 'Do you mind telling me what happened again?'

She put down her cup and saucer. 'No.'

'It was August '74?'

'Yeah, the fifth. I'd gone down Bibby's to look for Clive but . . .'

'Bibby's?'

'It was a club. Shut down. And Clive wasn't there. Typical. So I'd had a drink, well more than one actually and then I'd had to go because one of his mates, Joe, he was drunk and trying to get me to go home with him and I knew if Clive had come in there'd have been trouble so I just thought I'd go back to Cumberland Avenue and wait for him there. So I came back and sat there and felt a bit of a lemon like and decided to go back down Bibby's again and that's when it happened.'

The room was dark, the sun gone.

'Did you see him?'

'Well, they reckon I did. Couple of minutes before it happened, some bloke passed me and said something like, "Weather's letting us down," and just kept going. Police reckoned it could have been him because he never came forward like.'

'Did you say anything back?'

'No, just kept going.'

'But you saw his face?'

'Yeah, I saw his face.'

She had her eyes closed, her hands locked together between her knees.

I sat there in her front room, another wicket down, like he was there on the sofa next to me, a big smile, a hand on my knee, a last laugh amongst the furniture.

She opened her eyes wide, staring past me.

'You OK?'

'He was well-dressed and smelt of soap. Had a neat beard and moustache. Looked Italian or Greek you know, like one of them good-looking waiters.'

He was stroking his beard, grinning.

'He have an accent?'

'Local.'

'Tall?'

'Nowt special. Could have been wearing boots and all, them Cuban type.'

He was shaking his head.

'And so he walked past you and . . .'

She closed her eyes again and said slowly, 'And then couple of minutes later he hit me and that was that.'

He winked once and was gone again.

She leant forward and pulled her blonde hair flat across the top of her head.

'Go on, feel it,' she said.

I reached across another room to touch the top of another head, through another set of damaged black roots, another huge and hollow crater.

I traced around the edges of the indentation, the smoothness beneath the hair.

'You want to see my scars?'

'OK.'

She stood up and pulled up her thin sweater, revealing broad red strokes across a flabby pale stomach.

They looked like giant medieval leeches, bleeding her.

'You can touch them if you want,' she said, stepping closer and taking my hand.

She ran my finger across the deepest scar, my throat dry and cock hard.

She held my finger in the deepest point.

After a minute she said, 'We can go upstairs if you want.'

I coughed and moved back. 'I don't think . . .'

'Married?'

'No. Not . . .'

She pulled down her sweater. 'You just don't fancy me, right?'

'It's not that.'

'Don't worry, love. There's not many that do these days. Attacked by that fucking maniac and known all over cos of her black fellers, that's me. Only fucks I get are from darkies and weirdos.'

'That why you asked me?'

'No,' she smiled. 'I like you, don't I.'

Collapsed in my car, picking through the fish and the chips, *the ones that got away*.

I looked at my watch.

It was time to go.

Underneath the arches, those dark, dark arches: Swinegate.

We'd said we'd meet at five, five while the light was still with us.

I parked down the bottom end but I could already see him, at the other end, up by the Scarborough Hotel, still wearing that

hat and coat, despite the weather, to spite the weather, still carrying that case, just like the last time:

Sunday 26 January 1975.

'Reverend Laws,' I said, my hand in my pocket.

'Jack,' he smiled. 'It's been too long.'

'Not long enough.'

'Jack, Jack. Always the same, always so sad.'

I was thinking, *not here, not in the street.*

I said, 'Can we go somewhere. Somewhere quiet?'

He nodded at the big black building looming over the Scarborough, 'The Griffin?'

'Why not.'

The Reverend Martin Laws led the way, walking ahead in his stoop, a giant too big for this world or the next, his grey hair protruding from under his hat, licking the collar of his coat. He turned to hurry me along, through the passers-by, past the shops, between the cars, under the scaffolding and into the dim lobby of the Griffin.

He waved at some seats in the far corner, two high-backed chairs under an unlit lamp, and I nodded.

We sat down and he took off his hat, placing it on his lap, his case at his calves.

He smiled at me again, through his long grey stubble and his dirty yellow skin, an old newspaper, just like mine.

He smelt of fish.

A Turkish waiter approached.

'Mehmet,' said Reverend Laws. 'How are you?'

'Father, so good to have you back. We are fine, all of us. Thank you.'

'And the school? The little one settled in?'

'Yes, Father. Thank you. It was just as you said.'

'Well, if there's ever anything more I can do, please . . .'

'You've been too kind, really.'

'It was nothing. My pleasure.'

I coughed, fidgeting in my jacket.

'Are you ready to order, Father?'

Reverend Laws smiled at me. 'Yes, I believe we are. Jack?'

'Brandy, please. And a pot of coffee.'

'Very good, sir. Father?'

'A pot of tea.'

'Your usual?'

'Thank you, Mehmet.'

He bowed quickly and was gone.

'Lovely, lovely man. Not been here that long, just since the trouble.'

'Good English.'

'Yes, exceptional. You should tell him, be your friend for life.'

'I wouldn't wish it on him.'

Reverend Laws smiled again, that same quizzical smile of faint disbelief that either melted or froze you. 'Come on now,' he said. 'You're being too hard on yourself. I enjoy being your friend.'

'It's hardly mutual.'

'Sticks and stones, Jack. Sticks and stones.'

I said, 'She's back.'

He looked down at the hat in his hands. 'I know.'

'How could you?'

'Your call the other night. I could feel . . .'

'Feel what? Feel my pain? Bollocks.'

'Is that why you wanted to meet me? To abuse me? It's OK, Jack.'

'Look at you, you hypocritical cunt, sat there all pompous and papal in your dirty old raincoat with your hat on your cock and your little bag of secrets, your cross and your prayers, your hammer and your nails, blessing the fucking wogs, turning the tea into wine. It's me Martin, it's Jack, not some lonely little old woman who hasn't had a fuck in fifty years. I was there, remember? The night you fucked up.'

I'd stopped and he was just sat there.

The night Michael Williams cradled Carol in his arms one last time.

Just sat there, the hat revolving in his fingers.

The night Michael Williams . . .

He looked up and smiled.

The night . . .

I opened my mouth to start up again, but it was the waiter he was smiling at.

Mehmet put down the drinks and then took a small envelope from his pocket and pressed it into the Reverend's hands.

'Mehmet, I couldn't. There's no need.'

'Father, I insist,' he said and was gone.

I looked round at the Griffin's lounge, watching the waiter scurry off back to his hole down below, an old woman with a walking stick trying to stand up from another high-backed chair, a child reading a comic, the dark yellow light at the front desk, the old brochures and paintings and lights almost gone, and it didn't seem such a mystery why the Reverend Martin Laws was drawn to the Griffin Hotel, looking as it did for all the world like an old church in need of repair.

He leant forward, the hat still between his fingers, and said, 'I can help you.'

'Like you helped Michael Williams?'

'I can make it go away.'

'Well you certainly got rid of Carol.'

'Make it stop.'

I looked down at his hat, at the long fingers white at the tips.

'Jack?'

I said, 'I want it to stop. To end.'

'I know you do. And it will, believe me.'

'Is there only that way. The one way.'

'I have a room. We can go upstairs right now and it'll all be over.'

I was staring at the old woman with the walking stick, at the child in the corner, the brochures and the paintings, the light fading.

Jubela, Jubelo . . .

'Not today,' I said.

'I'll be waiting.'

'I know.'

*

I walked back through City Square, the moon almost full up in the blue night sky, back through the Friday night boys and girls and the start of the Jubilee Weekend, its threat of rain and promise of a fuck, through City Square and back to the office, knowing what could have been in an upstairs room, back to what would be waiting in another, there on my desk in amongst the rain and the fucks.

It was already starting to spit a bit.

I put down the toilet lid and took the letter from my pocket.

I was thinking about fingerprints and what the police would say but then how would they expect me to know and I knew there wouldn't be any anyway.

I stared again at the postmark: *Preston.*

Posted yesterday.

First-class.

I used the end of my pen to slit the top of the envelope.

Still using the pen, I prised the paper out.

It was folded in two, the red ink leaking through the under-side, a lump between the sheets.

I opened it up and tried to read what he'd written.

I was shaking, vinegar in my eyes, salt in my mouth.

It wasn't going to end like this.

'I'll call George Oldman,' said Hadden, still staring at the piece of heavy writing paper on his desk, not looking at the contents to the side.

'Right.'

He swallowed, picked up the phone and dialled.

I waited, the moon gone, the rain here and the night out.

It was late in the evening, one hundred years too late in the evening.

A uniformed copper had come straight over to the Yorkshire Post Building, bagged the envelope and contents, and then driven Hadden and me straight here, to Millgarth, where we'd been ushered up to Detective Chief Superintendent Noble's office, George Oldman's old one, where they sat, Peter Noble and George, waiting for us.

'Sit down,' said Oldman.

The uniform put the clear plastic bags on the desk and made himself scarce.

Noble picked up a pair of tweezers and laid out the envelope and letter.

'You've both handled it?' he asked.

'Just me.'

'Don't worry about that. We'll take your prints later,' said Oldman.

I smiled, 'You've already got them.'

'Preston,' read Noble.

'Posted?'

'Looks like yesterday.'

Both of them looked like they were off somewhere deep.

Hadden was on the edge of his seat.

Noble placed the letter back in the clear bag and pushed it over to George Oldman, followed by the envelope and smaller parcel.

He read:

From Hell.

> *Mr Whitehead,*
> *Sir, I send you skin I took from one women, which I preserved for you. Other bits I fried and ate and it was very nise. I may send you the bloody knif that cut it off if you only wait a while longer.*
>> *You'd like that I know.*
>> *Catch me when you can.*
>> *Lewis.*

No-one spoke.

After a while Noble said, 'Lewis?'

'It wouldn't be his real name?' asked Hadden.

Oldman looked up and stared across his desk at me. 'What do you reckon, Jack? This genuine?'

'It's written as a pastiche of a letter sent to a man called George Lusk during the Ripper Murders in London.'

Noble shook his head. 'It was you who wrote the Yorkshire Ripper article, wasn't it?'

'Yeah,' I said quietly. 'It was me.'

'Marvellous. Bloody marvellous that was.'

Oldman: 'Leave it, Pete.'

'No, thank you.'

Hadden: 'Jack . . .'

'But we're going to get every fucking nut-job from here to Timbukbloodytu writing in. For fuck's sake.'

Oldman: 'Pete . . .'

'It's no nut-job. It's him.'

'No nut-job? Look at it. How the fuck can you sit there and say that?'

I pointed to the small parcel at his elbow, at the thin slice of skin cut from Mrs Marie Watts:

'How much proof do you want?'

On the steps outside, in the middle of the night, I lit up.

'What's with you and Noble?' Hadden asked.

'I don't care for him.'

'You don't care for him?'

'Nor him me.'

'You seem pretty bloody certain that letter's genuine.'

'What? You don't think so?'

'I wouldn't know, Jack. I mean, how the bloody hell do you know what a letter from a mass murderer looks like?'

I opened the door and there they were, standing with their six white backs to me.

I took off my jacket and poured myself a glass of Scotland, sat down and picked up *Edwin Drood*.

They kept their backs to me, looking up at the moon.

I smiled to myself and began to whistle:

'The man I love is up in the gallery . . .'

Whirling, Carol flew across the room, teeth bared and nails

out; out for my eyes, out for my ears, out for my tongue, wrenching me out from my chair to the floor.

Screaming: 'You think it's amusing? These things are amusing to you?'

'No, no, no.'

Laughing: 'Amusing?'

'Rest, I just want to rest.'

Hissing: 'Hell breaks loose and you want to rest. We should put you up against the wall.'

The others chanting: 'Up against the wall. Up against the wall with him.'

'Please, please. Let me be.'

Mocking: 'Let me be, let me be? And who will let us be, Jack?'

'I'm sorry, please . . .'

Taunting: 'Well sorry's just not good enough, is it?'

They'd opened the windows, the rain coming in, the curtains billowing.

Howling: *'The man I love is up in the gallery . . .'*

She took my hair and dragged my face out on to the ledge: 'He'll kill again and soon. See that moon?'

The rain in my face, a stomach full of night, the black moon in my eye: 'I know, I know.'

'You know but you won't stop him.'

'I can't.'

'You can.'

They had my tapes out of the drawers, spinning the reels, streamers in the wind, my books, my childhood crimes, tearing them to shreds –

Wailing: *'The man I love is up in the gallery . . .'*

'You know who he is.'

'I don't. He could be anyone.'

'No he couldn't. You know he couldn't.'

And then she put her mouth over mine, sucking out my breath, her tongue choking me.

'Fuck me, Jack. Fuck me like you used to.'

I broke away, screaming over and over: 'You're dead, dead, dead, dead, dead, dead, dead, dead, dead.'

Whispering: 'No, Jack. You are.'

They picked me up off the floor and carried me to my bed and laid me down, Carol stroking my face, Eddie gone and my Bible open, reading:

'This will happen in the last days: I will pour out upon everyone a portion of my spirit; and your sons and daughters shall prophesy; your young men shall see visions, and your old men shall dream dreams.'

'We love you, Jack. We love you,' they sang.

Don't lose yourself, not now.

In the last days.

Caller: This bloke Moody, he's the Head of Scotland Yard's
            Obscene Publications Squad right?

John Shark: Was, yeah.

Caller: And all the time he's accepting bribes and doing
            favours for these Porn Barons. Un-bloody-believable.

John Shark: All a far cry from Dixon of Dock Green.

Caller: Fuck, he was probably at it and all. Bloody coppers.
            Make you sick.

                                    The John Shark Show
                                    Radio Leeds
                                    Saturday 4th June 1977

Chapter 7

I wake alone from an empty sleep, alone in Janice's empty sheets, alone in her empty bed, in her empty room.

It's Saturday morning, 4 June, and I've had two hours fitful kip, hot sun coming up.

I lean over and switch on the radio:

Three policemen shot dead in Ulster, man on Nairac murder charge, ITV still on strike, Scotland fans arriving in London, Keegan joins Hamburg for half a million, temperatures expected to reach seventy.

Or more.

I sit on the edge of the bed, head waking:

Red lights, shotgun blasts, cancer wards, death camps, bodies under tan raincoats, terrible rooms peopled by the dead.

I put on my boots and walk across the hall and bang on Karen Burns' door.

Dragging the waters, drowning gulps from the black river:

Keith Lee, another Spencer Boy, bare-chested in jeans: 'What the fuck you want?'

'Seen Janice?'

Karen lying on her stomach on the bed, Keith glances round: 'This business or personal?'

I push him back into the room, 'That's not an answer Keith. That's a question.'

Karen raises her head, 'Fuck.'

'I know what you did to Kenny, man. Used up a lot of goodwill.'

I slap him and tell him: 'Kenny was sticking it into Marie Watts behind Barton's back. Fuck another man's woman you get everything that's coming to you.'

Karen pulls a dirty grey sheet over her head, white arse my way.

Keith rubs his face and points a finger: 'Yeah well, I'll remember that next time Eric Hall or Craven come knocking.'

I stare him down.

He looks round the room, nodding to himself.

Something's up with our Keith, something more than Kenny getting a slapping.

But *fuck him.*

I pull the sheet off Karen Burns, white, twenty-three, convicted prostitute, drug addict, mother of two, and slap her across the arse:

'Janice? Where the fuck is she?'

She rolls over, tits flat, one hand over her cunt, the other chasing the sheet: 'Fuck off, Fraser. I haven't seen her since Thursday night.'

'She wasn't working last night?'

'Fuck knows. All I'm saying is I didn't see her.'

I let the sheet drop over her and turn back to Keith: 'What about Joe?'

'What about him?'

'He's keeping a low profile.'

'Man hasn't left his room in a week.'

'Cos of that shit with Kenny?'

'Fuck that. Two sevens, man.'

'You believe that bollocks?'

'I believe what I see.'

'And what do you see, Keith?'

'A million little apocalypses and a lot of bloody reckonings.'

I laugh: 'Get a flag, Keith. It's the Jubilee.'

'Fuck off.'

I say, 'Very patriotic,' and shut the door on the pieces of shit and their shitty little world.

A key turns in the lock, the handle next.

And there she is, tired and full; tired from fucking, full from fucking.

'What you doing here?'

'I told you, I'm leaving her.'

'Not now, Bob. Not now,' and she goes into the bathroom, slamming the door.

I follow her.

She's sat on the toilet, lid down, crying.

'What's wrong?'

'Leave it, Bob.'

'Tell me.'

She's swallowing, trying to stop the sobs.

I'm on the toilet floor, holding up her chin, asking, 'What happened?'

In the backs of expensive motors, leather gloves gripping the back of her neck, cocks up her arse, bottles up her cunt . . .

'Tell me!'

She's shaking.

I hold her, kissing her tears.

'Please . . .'

She stands up, pushing me off, over to the mirror, wiping her face, 'Fuck it.'

'Janice, I need to know . . .'

She turns square, hands on her hips: 'All right. They picked me up . . .'

'Who?'

'Who do you fucking think?'

'Vice?'

'Yeah, Vice.'

'Who?'

'Fuck knows.'

'You saw their warrant cards?'

'Oh, for fuck's sake Bob.'

'You told them to call Eric?'

'Yeah.'

'And?'

'And Eric told them to call you.'

There are ropes around my chest, thick heavy ropes, getting tighter with every second, every sentence.

'What did they say?'

'They laughed and called the station. Called your house.'

'My house?'

'Yes, your house.'

'And then what?'

'They couldn't find you, Bob. You weren't there.'

'So what . . .'

'You weren't there, Bob?'

The ropes burning my chest, breaking my ribs.

'Janice . . .'

'You want to know what happened then? You want to know what they did next?'

'Janice . . .'

'They fucked me.'

Bile in my mouth, my eyes closed.

She's screaming: 'Look at me!'

I lift the lid and cough, her behind me.

'Look at me!'

I turn around and there she is:

Naked and bitten, red streaks across her breasts, across her arse.

'Who?'

'Who what?'

'Who was it?'

She slips down the wall and on to the bathroom floor, sobbing.

'Who?'

'I don't know. Four of them.'

'Uniforms?'

'No.'

'Where?'

'A van.'

'Where?'

'Manningham.'

'Fuck you doing in Bradford?'

'You said it wasn't safe round here.'

I've got her in my arms, cradling her, rocking her, kissing her.

'You want a doctor?'

She shakes her head and then looks up. 'They took photos.'

Fuck, Craven.

'One of them have a beard, a limp?'

'No.'

'You sure?'

She looks away and swallows.

There's bright sunlight on the window, creeping across the toilet mat, getting nearer.

'They're dead,' I hiss. 'All of them.'

And then suddenly there are car doors slamming outside, boots on the stairs, banging on the doors, banging on our door.

I'm out in the room, 'Who is it?'

'Fraser?'

I open the door and there's Rudkin, Ellis behind him.

Rudkin: 'Fuck you doing here? We've been looking for you everywhere.'

Visions of Bobby, broken eggs and red blood on white baby cheeks, cars braking too late.

Too late.

'What's wrong? What is it?'

But Rudkin's staring past me into the bathroom, at Janice on the floor:

Naked and bitten, red streaks across her breasts, across her arse.

Ellis has his mouth open, tongue out.

'What is it?'

'There's been another.'

I turn and close the door in their faces.

In the bathroom I say, 'I've got to go.'

She says nothing.

'Janice?'

Nothing.

'Love, I've got to go.'

Nothing.

I take a blanket off the bed and bring it into the bathroom and put it over her.

I bend down and kiss her forehead.

And then I go back to the door and when I open it they're still stood there, peering past me.

I close the door and push between them, down the stairs and into the car.

I sit in the back, heavy duty sunlight in my face.

Rudkin drives.

Ellis keeps turning round, grinning, desperate to start up but this is Rudkin's car and he's in the driving seat and he's saying nowt.

So I look out at Chapeltown, the trees and the sky, the shops and the people, and feel dull.

If it's him, it feels different.

Blank, my mind blank:

The trees are green, not black.

The sky blue, not blood.

The shops open, not gutted.

The people on the streets living, not dead.

Noon in a different world.

And then I think of Janice:

The trees black.

The sky blood.

The shops gone.

The people dead.

And we're back:

Millgarth, Leeds.

Saturday 4 June 1977.

Noon.

The gang's all here:

Oldman, Noble, Alderman, Prentice, Gaskins, Evans, and all their squads.

And Craven.

I catch his eye.

He smiles, then winks.

I could kill him now, here, in the briefing room, before lunch.

He leans over to Alderman and whispers something, patting his breast pocket, and they both laugh.

Three seconds later Alderman looks at me.

I stare back.

He looks away, a slight smile.

Fuck.

They're all whispering, I'm losing it:

Wasteground, a long black velvet dress on wasteground.

Oldman starts up:

'At a quarter to seven this morning a paper boy heard cries for help coming from wasteland beside the Sikh temple on Bowling Back Lane in the Bowling area of Bradford. He discovered Linda Clark, aged thirty-six, lying seriously injured with a fractured skull and stab wounds to her abdomen and back. A preliminary investigation suggests that her head injuries were caused by hammer blows. She was rushed to hospital and is now in Pinderfields Hospital, Wakefield, under twenty-four-hour guard. Despite the seriousness of her injuries, Mrs Clark has been able to give us some information. Pete.'

She's on her stomach on the wasteground, her bra up and her panties down, his trousers too.

Noble stands:

'Mrs Clark spent Friday night at the Mecca in the centre of Bradford. Upon leaving the Mecca, Mrs Clark went to queue for a taxi to her home in Bierley. Because the queue was too long, Mrs Clark decided to start walking and flag down a taxi on the way. At some point later, a car pulled up and offered Mrs Clark a lift, which she accepted.'

Noble pauses, shades of George.

He comes in his hand and then he cuts her.

'Gentlemen, we're looking for a Ford Cortina Mark II saloon, white or yellow, with a black roof.'

We're on our feet, practically out the door.

A triangle of skin, of flesh.

'Driver is white, approximately thirty-five, large build, about six foot, with light brown shoulder-length hair, thick eyebrows and puffed checks. With very large hands.'

For later.

The whole room is on fire:

WE'VE GOT HIM, WE'VE FUCKING GOT HIM.

I look at Rudkin, on the edge, impassive, miles, years away.
But it's not the same.

Alderman is saying, 'SOCO are checking tyre-marks as we speak, Bradford going door-to-door.'

The knock on the door, the thousand knocks on a thousand doors, a thousand wives with sideways eyes at husbands white as sheets, a thousand sheets.

Noble again: 'Forensics will be back within the hour, but Farley's already saying this is our man. Our *Ripper*,' he says, spitting the last words out.

Unending.

Oldman stands back up, pausing before his troops, his own private little army:

'He's fucked up lads. Let's get the cunt.'

We're all up, wired.

Noble's shouting over the electricity:

'Into your squads: DS Alderman and Prentice to Bradford, DI Rudkin upstairs, Vice and Admin here.'

I turn and see Detective Chief Superintendent Jobson at the door, *the Owl*, looking drained and old, eyes red under the thick frames.

I nod and he works upstream through the crowd in the doorway. 'How's Bill?' he's saying over the noise.

'Not good,' I say.

We're standing off to one side.

Maurice Jobson's got an arm on my elbow. 'And Louise and the little one?'

'OK, you know.'

'I've been meaning to drop by, but with all this . . .' he's looking round the room, the squads heading out, Vice and Admin standing about, Craven watching us.

'I know, I know.'

He looks at me. 'Must be tough on you?'

'Worse for Louise, with Bobby every day and having to go up to the hospital.'

'Least she's from a police family. Knows the score.'

'Yeah,' I say.

'Give them my love, yeah? And I'll try and get in to see Bill sometime this weekend. If I can,' he adds.

'Thanks.'

Then he looks at me again and says, 'You need anything, you let me know, yeah?'

'Thanks,' and we're gone; him over to George, me up the stairs thinking:

Uncle Maurice, the Owl, my guardian angel.

Rudkin and Ellis are sat in silence in Noble's office, waiting.

Ellis starts up the minute I come in: 'You think we'll have to go back to Preston?'

'Fuck knows,' I say, sitting down.

He keeps going, 'What you think Boss?'

Rudkin shrugs his shoulders and yawns.

Ellis: 'I reckon we'll have him by tomorrow.'

Rudkin and me say nothing.

Ellis keeps talking to himself: 'Maybe they'll send us down Mecca. That'd be all right, have a drink and chat up some birds . . .'

The door opens and in comes Noble with a file.

He sits down behind his desk and opens the file: 'Right. Donny Fairclough, white, thirty-six, lives in Pudsey with his old mum. Taxi driver. Drives a white Ford Cortina with a black roof.'

'Fuck,' says Ellis.

Noble's nodding, 'Exactly. His name came up last year with Joan Richards.'

'He likes to bite,' I add, thinking, *naked and bitten, red streaks across her breasts, across her arse.*

'Yeah, good,' says Noble, looking pleased. 'We've had him in a couple of times . . .'

Rudkin looks up. 'Blood group?'

'B.'

We pull up on Montreal Avenue, a hundred yards down from the rank.

There's a tap on the glass.

Rudkin winds down the window.

One of Vice leans in, big fat grin.

I've got him fucking Janice on the floor of a van, taking photos, sucking her tits . . .

'He's just come on.'

I come up behind them, pull him back by his hair, and slit his throat with a broken bottle . . .

'Owt else?' asks Rudkin.

'Fuck all.'

I drag him out the van, trousers round his ankles, and I get out my camera . . .

Ellis is saying, 'We should just nick the cunt. Kick it out of him.'

'You with us?' says Rudkin, turning round to me.

The bloke from Vice glances at me and then tosses the keys on to the back seat. 'It's the brown Datsun round on Calgary.'

'Least he'll never make us,' laughs Ellis.

'Off you go then,' grins Rudkin.

'Me?' says Ellis.

'Give him the keys,' Rudkin tells me.

I pass them forward, the Vice guy still staring in at me.

'You fucking fancy me or something?'

He smiles, 'You're Bob Fraser aren't you?'

I've got my hand on the handle, 'Yeah, why?'

Rudkin is saying, 'Leave it, Bob.'

The prick from Vice is backing away from the car, doing the usual, 'What's his problem?' speech.

Rudkin is out talking to him, glancing back.

Ellis turns round, sighs, 'Fuck,' and gets out.

I sit there in the back of the Rover, watching them.

The Vice copper walks off with Ellis.

Rudkin gets back in.

'What's his name?' I ask.

Rudkin's looking at me in the rearview mirror.

'Just tell me his name?'

'Ask Craven,' he says. Then, 'Fuck, get in the front. He's off.'

And I'm into the front, the car starting, and we're off.

I pick up the radio, calling Ellis.

Nothing.

'The cunt's still yapping,' spits Rudkin.

'Should've let me go solo,' I say.

'Bollocks,' he says, glancing at me. 'You've done enough bloody solo.'

We're at the junction with Harehills.

Fairclough's white Cortina with its black roof is turning left into Leeds.

I try Ellis again.

He picks up.

'Get your fucking finger out,' I'm shouting. 'He's heading into Leeds.'

I cut him off before he can piss off Rudkin any further.

Fairclough turns right on to Roundhay Road.

I'm writing:

4/6/77 16.18 Harehills Lane, right on to Roundhay Road.

Foot down, writing:

Bayswater Crescent.

Bayswater Terrace.

Bayswater Row.

Bayswater Grove.

Bayswater Mount.

Bayswater Place.

Bayswater Avenue.

Bayswater Road.

Then he's right on to Barrack Road and we keep straight on.

'Right on to Barrack Road,' Rudkin's shouting at me, me into the radio at Ellis.

I've got Ellis in the rearview, indicating right.

'He's on him,' I say.

Ellis's voice booms through the car: 'He's pulling up outside the clinic.'

We go right and pull up past the junction on Chapeltown Road.

'Just some fat Paki bitch with a ton of shopping,' says Ellis. 'Coming your way.'

We watch the Cortina pass us and turn back up the Roundhay Road.

'Proceeding,' I say into the radio and Rudkin pulls out.

'Tell Ellis to pick him up again at the next lights,' says Rudkin.

I do it.

And Rudkin pulls in.

We're at the entrance to Spencer Place, to Janice.

I look at him.

'You got some sorting out to do,' he says and leans across me, opening my door.

'What you going to say?'

'Nowt. Be here at seven.'

'What about Fairclough?'

'We'll manage.'

'Thanks, Skip,' I say and get out.

He pulls the door to and I watch him drive off up the Roundhay Road, radio in hand.

I check my watch.

Four-thirty.

Two and a half hours.

I knock on the door and wait.

Nothing.

I turn the handle.

It opens.

I step inside.

The window open, drawers out, bed stripped, radio on:

Hot Chocolate: *So You Win Again* . . .

The cupboards bare.

I pick a letter off the dresser.

To Bob.

I read it.

She's gone.

Caller: And thing is, more than half these Union Jacks, they're bloody upside-down.

John Shark: Disgusting.

Caller: No, you can laugh John, but imagine if it were a load of upside-down crosses hanging from everywhere.

John Shark: An upside-down Union Jack and an upside-down cross, they're hardly the same.

Caller: Course they bloody are, you daft bugger. There's a cross on flag isn't there?

The John Shark Show
Radio Leeds
Sunday 5th June 1977

Chapter 8

'There's been another,' Hadden had said.

But I'd just lain there, waiting, watching tiny black and white Scottish men on their knees, tearing chunks of turf out of the ground with their bare hands, the phone slipping in my own hand, thinking, *Carol, Carol, is this the way it will always be, forever and ever, oh Carol?*

'Press conference is tomorrow.'

'Sunday?'

'Monday's a Bank Holiday.'

'It's going to play hell with your Jubilee coverage.'

'She's not dead.'

'Really?'

'She got lucky.'

'You think so?'

'Oldman reckons he was disturbed.'

'Hats off to George.'

'Oldman says you should get in touch the minute you receive anything.'

'He took something then?'

'Oldman's not saying. And neither should you.'

Oh Carol, no wonders for the dead?

Jubelum . . .

There was another voice in the Bradford flat, there in the dark behind the heavy curtains.

Ka Su Peng looked up, lips moving, the words late:

'In October last year I was a prostitute.'

She had travelled ten thousand miles to be here, sat across a dim divide of stained chipped furniture, her skin grey, hair blue, ten thousand miles to fuck Yorkshire men for dirty five pound notes squeezed into damp palms.

Ten thousand miles to end up thus:

'I don't know many of the others so I'm usually alone. I do the early time on Lumb Lane, before the pubs close. He picked me up outside the Perseverance. The Percy they call it. It was a dark car, clean. He was friendly, quiet but friendly. Said he hadn't slept much, was tired. I said, me too. Tired eyes, he had such tired eyes. He drove us to the playing fields off White Abbey and he asked me how much and I said a fiver and he said he'd give it to me after but I said I wanted it first because he might not pay me after like happened before. He said OK but he wanted me to get into the back of the car. So I got out and so did he and that's when he hit me on the head with the hammer. Three times he hit me and I fell down on to the grass and he tried to hit me again but I closed my eyes and put up my hand and he hit that and then he just stopped and I could hear him breathing near my ear and then the breathing stopped and he was gone and I lay there, everything black and white, cars passing, and then I got up and walked to a phone box and called the police and they came to the phone box and took me to hospital.'

She was wearing a cream blouse and matching trousers, feet together, bare toes touching.

'Can you remember what he looked like?'

Ka Su Peng closed her eyes, biting her bottom lip.

'I'm sorry,' I said.

'It's OK. I don't want to remember, I want to forget, but I can't forget, only remember. That's all I do, remember.'

'If you don't want to talk about it . . .'

'No. He was white, about five feet six inches . . .'

I felt a hand on my knee and there he was again, as if by magic, *smiling through the gloom, meat between his teeth.*

'Stocky build . . .'

He patted his paunch, burped.

'With dark wavy hair and one of them Jason King moustaches.'

He primped at his hair, stroking his moustache, that grin.

'Did he have a local accent?'

'No, Liverpool perhaps.'

He arched an eyebrow.

'He said his name was Dave or Don, I'm not sure.'

He frowned and shook his head.

'He was wearing a yellow shirt and blue jeans.'

'Anything else?'

She sighed, 'That's all I can remember.'

He winked once and was gone again, as if by magic.

She said, 'Is that enough?'

'It's too much,' I whispered.

After the horror, tomorrow and the day after.

Suddenly she asked, 'You think he'll ever come back?'

'Has he ever gone away?'

'Sometimes, sometimes I can hear his breathing on the pillow next to me,' she said, her sad face hewn from violence with blunt tools, black and blue leaves of hair weeping across the damage.

I reached out across the dark, 'May I?'

She leant forward, parting her hair.

In the back room she drew the curtains.

I placed a ten pound note under the clock on the bedside table and then we sat with our backs to each other on opposite sides of the same single bed, unbuttoning our clothes on a Sunday morning in Bradford.

I stood up and lowered my trousers.

When I turned round she was lying on the bed, naked.

I laid down on top of her, my penis limp.

She moved her hand between my legs until she stopped and pushed me on to my back and leant over to the bedside table and took out a johnny.

She placed it over my cock and then straddled me, me inside her.

She began to move up and down, her tits just nipples, up and down, her sallow body bones, up and down, eyes closed, up and down, mouth open, up and down, up and down, up, down, up, down, up.

I closed my eyes.

Down.

We dressed in silence.
    At the door I said, 'Can I come again?'
    'Now?' she asked, and we both laughed, surprised.

Assistant Chief Superintendent George Oldman with a grave
smile:
    'Gentlemen, as you are aware, at approximately three a.m.
on Saturday morning, the 4th, Mrs Linda Clark, aged thirty-six,
of Bierley, was subjected to a violent assault on wasteland
behind the Sikh temple on Bowling Back Lane, Bradford. In the
course of the attack, Mrs Clark sustained a fractured skull and
stab wounds to her back and abdomen. On Saturday morning
Mrs Clark underwent surgery and will have to undergo another
operation later this week. However, despite the seriousness of
her injuries, Mrs Clark has been able to provide us with a
detailed account of the time leading up to her attack.'
    He paused, sipped a glass of water and continued:
    'Mrs Clark spent Friday night at the Mecca ballroom in the
centre of Bradford. She was wearing a long black velvet dress
and a green cotton jacket. At approximately two o'clock Mrs
Clark left the Mecca and made her way to Cheapside where she
began to queue for a taxi. About fifteen minutes later she
decided to start walking back towards Bierley. About thirty
minutes later Mrs Clark accepted a lift from the driver of a
white or yellow Ford Cortina Mark II with a black satin-look
roof which pulled up on the Wakefield Road. Mrs Clark was
then driven on to Bowling Back Lane where the assault took
place. Mrs Clark has been able to provide a detailed description
of the driver.'
    He paused again.
    'The man we would like to speak to is white, approximately
thirty-five years of age, about six feet and of a large build. He
is described as having light brown shoulder-length hair with
thick eyebrows and puffy cheeks. We would appeal for any
member of the public who knows a man fitting this description

and who drives a white or yellow Ford Cortina Mark II with a black roof, or who has access to such a vehicle, to please contact the Bradford Incident Room or their local police station as a matter of some urgency.'

Another sip of water, another pause.

'I would like to add that forensic evidence gathered at the scene of the attack leads me to believe that the man responsible for the assault upon Mrs Clark is the same man who murdered Theresa Campbell, Clare Strachan, Joan Richards, and Marie Watts, the same man who we believe assaulted Joyce Jobson in Halifax in 1974, Anita Bird in Cleckheaton also in 1974, and Miss Ka Su Peng in Bradford last October.'

Pause.

The whole room:

The Yorkshire Ripper.

I wrote: *Clare Strachan?*

I circled her name.

Oldman was asking for questions:

'Roger?'

'Would the Assistant Chief Constable care to elaborate on the forensic evidence that points to this latest attack being the work of the, the work of the Yorkshire Ripper?'

'At this point, no.'

He's getting away . . .

'Jack?'

'The description given by Mrs Clark seems to contradict previous descriptions that have been issued. For example, both Anita Bird and Ka Su Peng said that their attacker had dark curly hair and a beard or moustache . . .'

George, his knife out:

'Yes but Jack, the lady in Bradford, Miss Peng, she claimed her attacker also had a Scouse accent which contradicted Anita Bird and the description Miss Bird herself gave was based on the assumption that the man who passed her in the street was the same man who later attacked her.'

'An assumption you previously supported.'

'That was then, Jack. That was then.'

*

I walked back through the deserted Kirkgate Market, through the quiet Sunday city streets, through the bunting, all red, white, and blue, under the three o'clock sun.

I turned into a cobbled alley out of the heat, searching for the wall and a word written in red.

But the word was gone or the alley wrong and the only words were *Hate* and *Leeds*.

So I walked up Briggate and on to the Headrow, up to the Cathedral and went inside.

I sat down at the back, in the cold quiet black, sweating from the stroll, panting like a dog.

There was an old woman with a walking stick trying to stand up in the front pew, a child reading a prayer book, dark low lights at the altar, the statues and the paintings, their eyes on me.

I looked up, my sweat dry, my breathing slow.

And there I was before Him, before the cross, thinking about fucking and murders with hammers, seeing the nails in his hands, thinking about fucking and murders with screwdrivers, seeing the nails in his feet, the tears in their eyes, the tears in His, the tears in mine.

And then the child led the old woman by the hand down the aisle and when they reached my pew they paused under the statues and the paintings, the shadows against the altar, and the child held out his open prayer book and I took it from him and watched them walk away.

And I looked down and I read aloud the words I found:

Psalm 88

For my soul is full of troubles,
and my life draws near to Sheol.
I am counted among those who go down to the Pit;
I am like those who have no help,
like those forsaken among the dead,
like the slain that lie in the grave,
like those whom you remember no more,

for they are cut off from your hand.
You have put me in the depths of the Pit,
in the regions dark and deep.
Your wrath lies heavy upon me,
and you overwhelm with all your waves.

You have caused my companions to shun me;
you have made me a thing of horror to them.
I am shut in so that I cannot escape;
my eyes grow dim through sorrow.
Every day I call on you, O Lord;
I spread out my hands to you.
Do you work wonders for the dead?
Do the shades rise up to praise you?
Is your steadfast love declared in the grave,
or your faithfulness in Abaddon?
Are your wonders known in the darkness,
Or your saving help in the land of forgetfulness?

But I, O Lord, cry out to you;
in the morning my prayer comes before you.
O Lord, why do you cast me off?
Why do you hide your face from me?
Wretched and close to death from my youth up,
I suffer your terrors; I am desperate.
Your wrath has swept over me;
your dread assaults destroy me.
They surround me like a flood all day long;
from all sides they close in on me.
You have caused friend and neighbour to shun me;
my companions are in darkness.

Fucking and murders with hammers, the nails in His hand,
fucking and murders with screwdrivers, the nails in His feet,
fucking and murders, the tears in their eyes, fucking, the tears
in His, murders, tears in mine.

'We can go upstairs right now and it'll all be over.'

And I ran from the Cathedral, through the double wooden doors, running from the hammer, through the hot black streets, running from Him, through the red bunting, the white and blue all gone, running from them all, through 5 June 1977, running.

Oh Carol.

And then finally I stood before the Griffin, my clothes in flames, hands and eyes to the sky, shouting:

'*Carol, Carol, there's got to be another way.*'

The office was dead.

I sat down at my desk and I typed:

RIPPER STRIKES AGAIN

Police yesterday stepped up the hunt for the so-called Yorkshire Ripper, the man police believe could be responsible for the murders of four prostitutes and assaults upon three other women, following a fourth attack on Saturday morning.

Mrs Linda Clark, aged thirty-six of Bierley, Bradford, was attacked on wasteland off Bowling Back Lane, Bradford, following a night out at the city's Mecca Ballroom.

Mrs Clark suffered a fractured skull and stab wounds to her stomach and back, after accepting a lift from a driver on the Wakefield Road. Mrs Clark will undergo a second operation later this week.

The police issued the following description of the vehicle and the driver they would like to question in relation to the attack upon Mrs Clark:

The man is white, approximately thirty-five years old, about six feet tall and of a large build. He has light brown shoulder-length hair and thick eyebrows. He was driving a white or light-coloured Ford Cortina Mark II with a black roof. Police urged any member of the public with information to contact the Bradford Incident Room direct on 476532 or 476533 or their local police station as a matter of some urgency.

I stopped typing and opened my eyes.

I walked upstairs and placed the sheet of paper in Bill's tray.

I started to walk away but then I turned back, took out my pen and in red ink I wrote across the top:

It's not him.

*

I walked down the steps and out of the dark and into yet more.

The Press Club, Sunday-night busy.

George Greaves, head down on the table, the laces of his boots tied together, Tom and Bernard struggling to light their own fags.

'Busy day?' said Bet.

'Yep.'

'He's keeping you on your toes, this Ripper of yours.'

I nodded and tipped the Scotch down my throat.

Steph squeezed my elbow. 'Another?'

'Just to be sociable.'

'Not like you, Jack,' she laughed.

Bet filled the glass again. 'Don't know, he had a visitor earlier.'

'Me?'

'Young guy, skinhead.'

'Yeah?'

'Yeah. I've seen him before, but for life of me I can't remember his name.'

'Did he say what he wanted?'

'No. Another?'

'Only sociable, I suppose.'

'That's the spirit.'

'I'll say,' I said and downed the next one.

I paused upon the stair and then opened the door.

The room was empty, the windows open, my dirty curtains booming like grey sails on a big old Bride Ship bound for a New World, the warm night air fingering through me.

I sat down and poured myself another taste of Scotland, drank it, and picked up my book but began to drowse.

And that was when she came to me, there in the foothills I thought so fucking high, like I'd come so very, very far.

She put her hands over my eyes, cold as two dead stones:

'Did you miss me?'

I tried to look round but I was so weak.

'Did you miss me, Jackie boy?'

I nodded.

'Good,' and she put her mouth on mine.

I fled her tongue, her hard long tongue.

She stopped, her hand on my cock.

'Fuck me, Jack. Fuck me like you fucked that whore before.'

The road consists of six narrow garages, each splattered with white graffiti, the doors showing remnants of green paint. They lie off Church Street, the garages forming a passage to the multi-storey car park at the other end. All six garages are owned by a Mr Thomas Morrison who died intestate and the garages have thus fallen into disrepair and disuse. Number 6 has become a home of sorts for the homeless, destitute, alcoholics, drug-addicted and prostitutes of the area.

It's small, about twelve feet square, and entered through either of the double doors at the front. There are packing cases for tables, piles of wood and other rubbish. A fierce fire has been burning in a makeshift grate and the ashes disclose the remains of clothing. On the wall opposite the door is written The Fisherman's Widow *in wet red paint. In every other space are bottles, sherry bottles, bottles of spirits, beer bottles, bottles of chemicals, all empty. A man's pilot coat doubles as a curtain over the window, the only one, looking out on nothing.*

I woke, his breath still warm and rank upon my pillow.

They had my books off my shelves, strewn across the room, all my little Jack the Ripper books, the whole bloody lot of them, and my tapes too, they had them out of my bottom drawer, all of my little tapes in all of their little cases with all of their neat little dates and places, all of them strewn across the room, my cuttings too.

She flew across the room, a scrap of paper between her teeth:
Preston, November 1975.

I was on my feet on my bed then on the floor on my knees:
I suffer your terrors; I am
desperate.

A diary.

I suffer your terrors; I am
desperate.

There had been a diary.

I pulled the room apart, the six of them whirling and wailing in murderous cacophony, books in the air, tapes on the floor, cuttings to the wind, fingers in my ears, their hands across my eyes, their lies, my books, his lies, my tapes, her lies, my cuttings, her fucking diary:

I suffer your terrors; I am
desperate.

The telephone was ringing.

John Shark: *Well, Sir Robert Mark said and I quote [reads]: The cancer of corruption which existed in the Obscene Publications Squad has been exposed and exorcised.*

Caller: *Bollocks John, that's what it is.*

John Shark: *You're not impressed?*

Caller: *Course I'm not. He also said that none of it would have come to light if it hadn't have been for the bleeding press. Not very bloody reassuring that, is it? Relying on your lot.*

John Shark: *I believe Sir Robert said the whole country owes us a debt.*

Caller: *Not from me you don't. Not from me.*

The John Shark Show
Radio Leeds
Monday 6th June 1977

Chapter 9

Fuck Oldman.
   Fuck Noble.
   Fuck Rudkin.
   Fuck Ellis.
   Fuck Donny Fairclough.
   Fuck the fucking Ripper.
   Fuck Louise.
   Fuck them all.
   She's gone:
   I'm gone

In a hell.

Battering down doors, battering down people, kicking in doors, kicking in people, searching for her, searching for me.

In a hell of fireworks.

I'm out of her room and back across the hall, through the door, Keith gone, Karen looking up from the bed with a 'not again, the fuck . . .' and I pull her from the bed, across the floor, just a pair of pink knickers, tits out, shouting into her face, 'She's gone, taken her stuff, where she go?' and she's under me, hands across her face because I'm slapping the shit out of her because if anyone knows where Janice is it's Karen Burns, white, twenty-three, convicted prostitute, drug addict, mother of two, and I slap her again and then I look down at her bleeding lips and nose, the bloody smears on her chin and neck, her tits and arms, and I pull off her pink knickers and drag her back to the bed and pull open my trousers and push it into her and she's not even struggling, just shifting my weight on the bed so I come out and now she's looking up at me and I slap her again and turn her over and she starts struggling, saying we don't need to do it like this but I just push her face down into the dirty sheet and bring my cock up and stick it in her arse and she's screaming and it's hurting me but I keep going until I come and fall back on to the floor and she's lying there on the bed, semen and blood running down her thighs, her arse in my face, and I get up and do it again and this time it doesn't hurt and she's quiet and then I come and go.

In a hell of fireworks, she's gone.

I'm lying on the floor of the phone box, it's dark outside except for the bonfires and street lights, the fireworks and the head-lights, the big Chapeltown trees bending over me, the owls in the trees with their wide, wide fucking round eyes, and I'm cursing Maurice fucking Jobson, Uncle Maurice, the Owl, my guardian angel, with his *least she's from a police family. Knows the score* speech and all that *you need anything, you let me know* bollocks: well come down here to this fucking box and get me out of here and bring her back to me, come on cunt before I take a knife to those wings, those stinking black wings, those stinking black fucking wings of death, come on and bring her back to me, here in my little red box, here in my dark age, my stone age, the dead age, cradling the receiver, bring her back to see me crying, see me weeping, see me sobbing in a ball on a phone box floor, the hair in my hands, the bloody hair in my hands, the bloody clumps of hair in my hands.

In a hell of fireworks, she's gone and I'm alone.

'The fuck . . .'

I've got Joe fucking Rose by his throat, heavy smoke across the room, mattress against the window, two sevens painted on every surface, the dumb stoned fucking chimpanzee shitting his pants.

'I'll kill you.'

'I know, I know.'

'So tell me . . .'

He's shaking, white-ball-eyes to the ceiling, stuttering: 'Janice?'

'Tell me.'

'I don't know where she is, man. I swear.'

I've got my fingers up his nose, my keys to those big brown eyes of his.

'Please man, I swear.'

'I will kill you.'

'I know it man, I know it.'

'So tell me.'

'Tell you what? I don't know where she is.'

'You know she's gone?'

'Every fucker does.'

'So tell me something no fucker knows.'

'Like what?'

'Like who was pimping her?'

'Who was pimping her? You're joking right?'

'Do I look like I'm fucking joking?'

'Eric, man.'

'Eric Hall?'

'You didn't know?'

'She was his grass.'

'Fuck that. He was pimping her.'

'You're lying to me Joe.'

'You didn't fucking know?'

I grip his throat.

'I swear it, man. Eric Hall was pimping her. Ask anyone.'

I stare into those big brown eyes, those big brown blind eyes of his and wonder.

'Look, she'll be back,' he's saying. 'Like a boomerang, like the lot of them.'

I let go and he drops to the floor.

I walk towards what's left of the door, all shattered wood and splattered sevens.

'Cept the ones your Captain Jack gets,' he's still saying. 'Cept the ones that pirate takes.'

'You call me, Joe. The second you hear the slightest thing, you call me.'

He's nodding, rubbing his throat.

'Or I'll come back and I will fucking kill you.'

In a hell of fireworks, she's gone and I'm alone on the street.

I dial again, no Louise.

I dial again and again, no Louise.

I dial the hospital but they won't put me through.

I dial York and ten minutes later the Sister tells me Mr Ronald Prendergast died this morning of the haemorrhage caused by the injuries sustained during the robbery.

I look up and see the sky through the trees.

See more rain.

I dial again, no Louise.

I dial again and again, no Louise.

I dial the hospital but they hang up.

Fuck Karen Burns.

Fuck Joe Rose.

Fuck Ronald Prendergast.

Fuck the fucking Ripper.

Fuck Maurice.

Fuck Bill.

Fuck Louise.

Fuck them all.

She's gone:

I'm gone

In hell.

Battering down doors, battering down people, kicking in doors, kicking in people, searching for her, searching for me.

In hell in a stolen car.

*

Eric Hall, Detective Inspector Eric Hall, out of the Bradford HQ at Jacob's Well, and that's where I am, Jacob's Well, waiting in a stolen car, his car, Eric's car, the one I took from his drive out in Denholme:

No-one home, the taxi gone, my money with it.

Round the back of Eric's little castle, through the rain on the panes, the nets and the gaps in the curtains, kicking in his back door, through the stink of the family pets, the family photos, into his study with the big windows and views of the golf course, through his boxes of medals, his old coins, looking for anything, any piece of Janice, any little piece of her, finding nothing, taking the housekeeping and the keys to his brand new Granada 2000 in Miami fucking blue.

Cunt.

Down the Halifax Road, on to Thornton Road, through Allerton and into Bradford, one road straight to Jacob's Well.

Radio on:

'Mr Clive Peterson, the sub-postmaster at Heywood Road, Rochdale, was found unconscious early this morning after challenging intruders on his premises. Police on both sides of the Pennines were examining the possibility of a link to a similar series of crimes in the Yorkshire area.

'Mr Ronald Prendergast of New Park Road, Selby, died this morning having failed to regain consciousness after he disturbed intruders at his sub-post office on 4 June. Mr Prendergast is the second sub-postmaster to have been killed in as many months. A spokesman for the Post Office said . . .'

Cunts.

Foot down.

One road straight to him, to Eric Hall, Detective Inspector Eric Hall.

Cunt.

In an empty Bank Holiday car park, trying to think straight, trying to get some quiet in my brain, the rain drumming on the roof, the radio droning on:

'The RAC described conditions as the worst in years . . .'

Bitter winds and rain forecast.

'Weather is the only enemy to the biggest party in twenty-five years . . .'

Wanting a party of my own, getting out of Eric's car to find a phone box.

In hell in a stolen car, the lights all red.

I'm sat on the bonnet of his brand new Miami-blue Granada 2000, waiting for him.

He comes across the deserted car park, a sheepskin coat in summer, rain flattening his thin fair hair and crap 'tache, and he sees me, clocks the car, his car, and starts running, about to go fucking mental like I knew he would, and it hits me then how far I've come and it can't be more than 5 p.m. on Monday 6 June 1977, but it hits me then there's no way back from here.

This is where I am:

'You fucking cunt,' he's screaming. 'That's my fucking car. How you, what the . . .' and he pushes me off the bonnet on to the ground, jumping on top of me, the pair of us rolling about in the puddles, him punching me once in the side of the head.

But that's all he's getting.

I hit back, once, twice, getting him down, the side of his face flat on the car park tarmac:

'Fuck is she, Eric?'

He struggles, but when he speaks his lips bleed into the floor. I pull him up by the thin bits of shit he calls hair:

'Fuck is she?'

'How the fuck I know, you cunt. She's your fucking tart . . .'

I smash his skull down into the ground and pull it back and his eyes are rolling about and I'm thinking stop it, stop it, stop it, you can't do that again, you can't do that again, you cannot do that again or you'll kill him, you'll kill him, you will kill him, and there's blood pouring from his scalp and I'm fucked here and I grip his face between my hands until he focuses and I say:

'Eric, don't make me do that again.'

And he's nodding but I don't know what that means.

'Eric, I know you were pimping her.'

And he's still nodding but it could mean fucking anything.

'Eric, come on.'

And I slap him across his pink fat cheeks with the bits of car park stuck there between the broken blood vessels and fucked-up blood pressure.

'Eric . . .'

He's coming back, the nodding slowing.

'Eric, I know what you were doing, so just tell me where she is?'

He looks at me, the whites of his eyes red-streaked nicotine, the blacks wide in the blue, and through the spit he says:

'I pimped her before. She asked me . . .'

My fists clench, he flinches, but I stop:

'Eric, the truth . . .'

There are tears running down him.

'It's the truth.'

I pick him up, the pair of us falling about like a couple of ballroom drunks.

I lean him against the bonnet of his Miami-blue Granada 2000:

'So where is she?'

'I don't know. I haven't seen her in over six months.'

I dust down his coat, knocking the gravel and scraps of paper off him:

'You're a liar, Eric. And not a very good one.'

He's breathing heavily, sweating worse in that sheepskin coat of his.

I tell him:

'She got picked up on Friday night.'

He swallows, shaking.

'Here. In Manningham.'

'I know.'

'I know you know, cunt. Because she called you, didn't she Eric? Wanted to meet you.'

He's shaking his head.

'What did she want, Eric?'

I pick a piece of shit off his collar and wait.

He closes his eyes, nodding:

'Money, she wanted money.'

'And?'

'Said she had some stuff, information.'

'What kind?'

'She didn't say?'

'Eric . . .'

'Robberies, she didn't say anything else. She was on the phone.'

I stroke his cheek:

'And you arranged to meet her, didn't you?'

He's shaking his head.

'But you sent the Van, didn't you?'

He's shaking that head, faster.

'And they picked her up, didn't they?'

Faster.

'Thought you'd teach her a lesson, didn't you?'

Side to side, faster.

'And she told them to call you, didn't she?'

Faster.

'So they called you, didn't they?'

And faster.

'You could have made them go away, couldn't you?'

He's shaking.

'Could have made them stop it, couldn't you?'

And I grip that fat fucking face and an inch away I scream:

'So why the fuck didn't you, you piece of fucking fucking fucking shit!'

His eyes, his weak watery eyes, they frost over:

'She's yours, you took her.'

I have him now, in my hands, I have him, and I could kill him, batter his skull into the tarmac until it shattered, tip him into the boot of his brand new Miami-blue Granada 2000 and drive him up on to the Moors, or down into a quarry, or off into a lake, or over the edge and into the sea.

But I don't.

I push the fat fucking cunt off the bonnet of his car and I get inside.

And he just stands there, in front of his Miami-blue Granada 2000, staring through the windscreen at me sat behind the wheel, his wheel.

I start the car, his car, thinking, *move or I will kill you with your own car.*

He steps to the side, his mouth moving, a black slow-motion hole of threats and promises, treats and curses.

I put my foot down.

And I'm gone

In hell in a stolen car, the lights all red, the world lost.

Straight out of Bradford, the A650 Wakefield Road into Tong Street, Bradford Road, King Street, under the M62, under the M1 and into Wakefield, out on to the Doncaster Road, out to the one place left, the last place left:

The Redbeck Cafe and Motel.

I sit there, in another lonely car park, Heath Common before me, three big black unlit bonfires against the clearing evening, waiting for their witches.

I reach into my pocket and take out my keys.

And there it is, Room 27.

In hell in a stolen car, the lights all red, the world lost like us.

In my dream I was sitting on a sofa in a room. A nice sofa, three seats. A nice room, pink.

But I'm not asleep, I'm awake

In hell.

John Shark: You saw this, Bob? [reads]: *Among the jubilation there is a note of hostility from extreme left-wing groups who are busy printing anti-monarchist stickers and publishing articles describing the Jubilee as an appalling affront to the working population of 1977.*

Caller: *Bloody rubbish John, that's what it is. Working population? These people, they're not the working population. They're just a bunch of bloody students. Your working population are all for the Jubilee.*

John Shark: *You reckon?*

Caller: *Course they are, it's two days off bloody work and an excuse for a right old piss-up isn't it?*

The John Shark Show
Radio Leeds
Tuesday 7th June 1977

Chapter 10

It was pissing it down.

Real fucking sheets of the stuff, across six lanes of empty Jubilee motorway.

Over the Moors, across the Moors, under the Moors:

Fuck you then you sleep.

Kiss you then you wake.

No-one; no cars, no lorries, nothing:

Deserted spaces, these overground places.

The world gone in the flash of a bomb.

But if there's no-one here, no-one left, how is it I wake so bruised from sleep?

I switched off *Twenty-five Years of Jubilee Hits* and put my foot down, just the tapes in my head playing full blast:

DIARY MAY BE CLUE TO KILLER

A diary thought to be in her missing bag could hold the clue to a woman's killer.

Twenty-six-year-old Clare Strachan was found battered to death in a disused garage a quarter of a mile from Preston town centre, and last night police toured public houses in a bid to trace her killer.

Miss Strachan was last seen at 10.25 p.m. on Thursday when she left a friend's house.

A woman noticed her body as she passed the open doors of the garage in Frenchwood Street, Preston.

At a press conference today Detective Superintendent Alfred Hill said robbery was the likely motive behind the killing. He said a diary thought to be in her lost bag would hold a vital clue.

He said: 'I am anxious to hear about anyone who has been missing from Preston since Thursday.'

Det. Supt. Hill, second in command of Lancashire CID, is leading a team of eighty detectives hunting the killer.

Miss Strachan, originally from Scotland, lived in the Avenham area of Preston and also used the surname Morrison.

Hard bloody crime reporting from the wrong side of the hills, from the wrong year:

1975:

Eddie gone, Carol dead, hell round every corner, every dawn.

Dead elm trees, thousands of them.

Culled from clippings, torn from tape.

Two years going on two hundred.

The History Man.

Bye Bye Baby.

Start at the finish.

Begin at the end:

I slowed on Church Street, crawling up the road, looking for Frenchwood Street, looking for the garages, her garage.

I stopped by a multi-storey car park.

The car stank, my breath rank from no sleep, no breakfast, just a bellyful of bad dreams.

The clock on the dashboard said nine.

Rain, buckets of it drenching the windows.

I pulled the jacket of my suit over my head and got out and ran across the road to an open door swinging in the piss.

But I stopped before it, dead in my tracks, my jacket down, the rain in my face, flattening my hair, sick with the stench of dread and doom.

I stepped inside, out of the rain, into her pain.

Under my feet, under my feet I felt old clothing, a blanket of rags and paper, bottles brown and green, a sea of glass with islands of wood, crates and boxes, a workman's bench he surely used for that piece of work, his job.

I stood there, the door banging, everything before me, behind me, under me, over me, listening to the mice and the rats, the wind and the rain, a terrible soul music playing, but seeing nothing, blind:

'Your young men shall see visions, and your old men shall dream dreams.'

I was an old man.

An old man lost in a room.

*

'You look like a drowned rat. How long you been out here?'

'Not long,' I lied and followed the barmaid inside St Mary's, in out of the rain.

'What can I get you?' she asked, putting the lights on.

'A pint and a whisky.'

She went back behind the bar and started pulling my pint.

I took a stool at the cold early bar.

'There you go. Sixty-five, please.'

I handed her a pound note. 'Odd name for a pub.'

'That's what they all say, but place's more like a church anyway. I mean, just look at it.'

'Same name as that place down the road?'

'The hostel? Yeah, don't remind me.'

'Get a lot of them in, do you?'

'All we get,' she said, handing me my change. 'What line you in?'

'I work for *Yorkshire Post*.'

'Knew it. You're here about that woman who got done in a couple of years ago? What was her name?'

'Clare Strachan.'

She frowns. 'You sure?'

'Yeah. Knew her did you?'

'Oh yes. They reckon now it could have been this Yorkshire Ripper, don't they? Imagine if it was, I mean bloody hell, he was probably in here.'

'She came in a fair bit then, Clare?'

'Yeah, yeah. Gives you the creeps, doesn't it. Get you another?'

'Go on then. What was she like?'

'Loud and pissed. Same as rest of them.'

'Was she on game?'

She started wiping the top of the bar. 'Yeah. I mean, they all are from that place.'

'St Mary's?'

'Yeah. She was so out of it, I mean she probably gave it away.'

'Police talk to you about her?'

'Yeah. Talked to everyone.'

'What did you tell them?'

'Like I say, just that she came in here a lot, got pissed, didn't have a lot of brass and what she had she probably got from selling it up on French.'

'What did they say?'

'Police? Nothing, I mean like what would they say?'

'I don't know. Sometimes they tell you what they're thinking.'

She stopped wiping. 'Here, you're not going to put any of this in paper are you?'

'No, why?'

'I don't want that bloody Ripper reading my name, do I? Thinking I know more than I do, thinking he better silence me or something.'

'Don't worry, I'm not going to say anything.'

'Bet you always say that though, you lot, don't you?'

'As God is my witness.'

'Yeah, right. Another?'

'I'm sorry, I'm looking for a Roger Kennedy?'

The young man in the dim corridor, in the black glasses, he was shaking, sniffing, shitting himself.

I asked him again: 'Roger Kennedy?'

'He doesn't work here any more.'

'Do you know where I could find him?'

'No. You'll have to come back when the boss is here.'

'Who's that then?'

'Mr Hollis. He's the Senior Warden.'

'And what time will he be in?'

'He won't.'

'Right.'

'He's on holiday. Blackpool.'

'Nice. When does he get back?'

'Next Monday, I think.'

'Right. I'm sorry, my name's Jack Whitehead.'

'You're not a copper, are you?'

'No, why?'

'They were here a couple of days ago, that's all. So who are you?'

'I'm a journalist. For *Yorkshire Post*.'

That didn't seem to make him feel any better. 'This about Clare Strachan then? The woman who used to live here?'

'Yeah. Is that what the police wanted?'

'Yes.'

'You speak to them did you?'

'Yes. I wish Mr Hollis was here.'

'What did they say?'

'I think you better come back when Mr Hollis is here.'

'Well, actually you could save him some bother. I only want to ask a couple of questions. Nothing for the paper.'

'What kind of questions?'

'Just background. Is there anywhere we could sit down? Just for a couple of minutes?'

He pushed his glasses up his nose again and pointed to the white light at the end of the corridor.

'I'm sorry I didn't catch your name?' I said as I followed him into a dreary lounge, the rain in pools at the bottom of the old spoiled windowframe.

'Colin Minton.'

I shook his hand and said again, 'Jack Whitehead.'

'Colin Minton,' he repeated.

'Polo?' I offered and took a seat.

'No thanks.'

'So Colin, you worked here long?'

'About six months.'

'So you weren't here when it all happened?'

'No.'

'Is there anyone about who was? This Mr Hollis?'

'No. Just Walter.'

'Walter?'

'Walter Kendall, the blind bloke. He lives here.'

'He was here two years ago?'

'Yeah. He was one of her friends.'

'Would it be possible to have a word?'

'If he's in.'

I stood up. 'Get out much does he?'

'No.'

I followed Colin Minton out of the lounge and up two flights of dark stairs to a narrow corridor. We walked down the linoleum passageway to the room at the very end.

Colin Minton knocked on the door, 'Walter, it's Colin. I've got someone here to see you.'

'Bring him in,' came back a voice.

Inside the tiny room a man sat at a table before a window of running rain, his back to us.

Colin's face had gone red. 'I'm sorry, I've forgotten your name. Jack?'

'Jack Whitehead,' I said to the back of the man's head. 'From the *Yorkshire Post.*'

'I know,' said the man.

'You're Walter Kendall?'

'Yes, I am.'

Colin shifted from foot to foot, trying to smile.

'It's all right, Colin,' said Walter. 'You can leave us.'

'You sure?'

'Yes.'

'Thank you,' I said as Colin Minton made his exit, closing the door behind him.

I sat down on the small bed, Walter Kendall still facing the other way.

A train went past outside, shaking the window.

'Must be two o'clock,' said Walter.

I looked down at my watch. 'Unless it's late.'

'Be like you then,' said Walter, turning.

And for a moment that face, Walter Kendall's face, it was the face of Martin Laws, of Michael Williams, the face of the living, the face of the dead.

'What?'

'You're late, Mr Whitehead.'

That face, those eyes:

That grey unshaven face, those white unseeing eyes.

'I don't understand what you mean?'

'She's been dead almost two years.'

That tongue, that breath.

That white tongue, that black breath.

'I'm here following a remark made by the Assistant Chief Constable of West Yorkshire, when he recently suggested that Clare Strachan could have been murdered by the same man who has been murdering prostitutes in the West Yorkshire area.'

Mr Kendall said nothing, waiting.

So I said again, 'So I'm here to look into any connection there might be and any information you can give would be greatly appreciated.'

Another train, another shake.

And then he said: 'In the August we went into Blackpool, me and Clare. She'd heard her kids were coming down with her Aunty or someone. Scottish Week it was. So we got the first coach in and she could hardly sit still could Clare. Said she was going to wet herself, she was that excited. And it was a lovely day, wide blue sky, first thing, all clean as a new pin. And we met her daughters and her Aunty under the Tower and they were such lovely little things, all red hair and new teeth. About four and two I think they must have been. And there were a lot of tears because it had been a year or more and Clare, she had their Christmas presents from the year before and their smiles, Clare said it was almost worth the wait. And we went down on to the sands and it was still quiet, the tide just gone, the beach all engraved ridges and ripples and she took them down to the foam, the surf, and they took off their shoes and socks and kicked through the little waves the three of them, and me and the Aunty we just sat on the wall watching them, the Aunty crying and me too. Then we all five of us went to get ice-cream at some back-street place Clare knew and it was lovely stuff, Italian, and Clare had a Cappuccino with bits of chocolate flake on the top and because I liked look of it so much she bought me one as well as my ice-cream, then we went round some of the arcades and put the little ones on the donkeys even though Clare she thought that it was cruel, keeping the donkeys like they do but it was such a laugh because one of them donkeys he had a mind of his own he did and he sets off with the eldest one on board, sets off at a right pace, and she's loving it the little girl is, laughing her head off, but there's the donkey man and the rest of us chasing them up the beach, caught them in the end but it took some doing and I don't think donkey man thought it was so funny but we were in stitches we were. Then we had a lunch up in the Lobster Pot, bloody big fishes they do there, Moby Dicks Clare called them. Nice cup of tea too, strong as Scotch they say. Then we took a tram up to the Pleasure Beach and you should have seen them, Mr Whitehead, spinning around in them giant tea-cups, riding in flowers, wearing daft hats and sucking on huge pink sticks of rock, but I found Clare, outside the Gold Mine she was, big tears down her cheeks because they had to get the five o'clock train or something and the Aunty was saying that they'd maybe come down again for the Illumi-nations, get a special coach, but Clare was shaking her head, the little ones hanging off her neck, knowing that this was it and I couldn't watch at the station, it was too much, them all saying their goodbyes, the youngest not knowing what it was all about but the other one just sucking in her lips like her Mummy and not letting go of her hand, terrible it was, the heart's not built for that stuff and after, after we went to the Yates' and she got so pissed, so fucking pissed, but who can blame her Mr Whitehead, a day like that, living like she did, knowing what she did, eight weeks later fucked up the arse, her chest crushed by size ten boots, never to see those little girls again, their beautiful red hair, their new teeth, can you blame her?'

'No.'

'But they do, don't they?'

I stared past him, the rain on the window, an underwater cave, a chamber of tears.

'Are you going to print that?'

I stared at him, the tears on his cheeks, trapped in this underwater cave, this chamber of tears.

I swallowed, caught my breath at last and said: 'The night she died, who knew who she was going to meet?'

'Everybody did.'

'Who?'

'Mr Whitehead, I think you know who it was.'

'Tell me.'

Walter Kendall held his fingers up to the rain:

'Where you seek one there's two, two three, three four. Where you seek four there's three, three two, two one and so on. But you know this anyway.'

I was on my feet, shouting at the blind man with the white eyes and the grey face, shouting into those eyes, that face:

'Tell me!'

He spoke quickly, one finger in the air:

'Clare left the pub up the road, St Mary's, at ten-thirty. We told her not to go, told her she shouldn't, but she was tired Mr Whitehead, so fucking tired of running. They said, your taxi's here but she just walked up the street, up to French, up through the rain, rain worse than this, up to a car parked in the dark at the top, and we just watched her go.'

'Go to who?'

'A policeman.'

'A policeman? Who?'

Lancashire Police Headquarters, Preston.

A big plainclothes with a moustache showed me up to the second-floor offices of Detective Chief Superintendent Alfred Hill.

The big man knocked on the door, and I popped in another polo.

'You can go in,' said the plainclothes.

'Jack Whitehead,' I said, hand out.

The small man behind the desk put away his handkerchief and took my hand.

'Have a seat, Mr Whitehead. Have a seat.'

'Jack,' I said.

'Well Jack, can I get you anything to drink: tea, coffee, something stronger. Toast the Queen?'

'I'd better not. Got a long drive back.'

'Right, so what is it brings you over our way then?'

'Like I said on the telephone, it's the Clare Strachan murder and what George Oldman said a couple of days ago, about the possibility of there being a link . . .'

'With the Ripper?'

'Yes.'

'George was saying how it was you who coined that one.'

'Unfortunately.'

'Unfortunately?'

'Well . . .'

'I wouldn't say that, you should be proud. Good piece of journalistic licence like that, should be proud.'

'Thank you.'

'George thinks publicity will help him. You've done him a favour.'

'You don't agree?'

'Wouldn't say that, wouldn't say that at all. Case like this, you can't do anything without the public.'

'You got quite a bit with Clare Strachan at first.'

He'd taken out his handkerchief again, examining the contents, about to add some more, 'Not really.'

'Did you get anywhere with the diary?'

'The diary?'

'You seemed to think at the time that there was a diary in her missing bag.'

He was coughing hard, a hand on his chest.

'Did anything ever come of that?'

His face was bright red, panting into his hankie, whispering, 'No.'

'What made you think there was a diary?'

Detective Chief Superintendent Alfred Hill had his hand up: 'Mr Whitehead . . .'

'Jack, please.'

'Jack, I'm not quite sure what we're doing here. Is this an interview, is that what we're doing here?'

'No.'

'So you're not going to print any of this?'

'No.'

'So like, what exactly are we going through all this for? I mean, if you're not going to print anything?'

'Well, background. Given the possibility that it's the same man.'

He took a sip of water, disappointed.

I said, 'I don't mean to waste your time.'

'That wasn't what I meant, Jack. Not what I meant at all.'

'Can I ask you then, sir, do you think this murder, that it is the same man?'

'Off the record?'

'Off the record.'

'No.'

'And on the record?'

'There are certainly similarities,' he said, nodding at the window, 'similarities, as my erstwhile colleague across those hills has said.'

'So off the record, what makes you think it's not the same man?'

'We had over fifty men on her, you know.'

'I thought it was eighty?'

He smiled. 'All I'm saying is we did a thorough job on her, very thorough. It's been said that because of who she was, her history, what she was, that we didn't give it priority but I can tell you we worked flat out while we could. It's a lie, a complete lie to say that we don't take things like what happened to her seriously. Of course something like the murder of a kiddie, course it gets the headlines, gets the attention and keeps it, but I was one of first in that garage and I've seen some stuff, stuff like Brady and his, but what they'd done to her, slag or not, well no-one deserves that. No-one.'

He was away, far away, back in that garage, back with his own tapes.

And we sat there, in our silences, until I said:

'But it wasn't him.'

'No. From what George has shown us, what we've heard from the lads they sent over, no.'

'Can you be specific?'

'Look, George wants them linked. I'm not going to touch that.'

'OK. So how's George linked them?'

'Off the record?'

'Off the record.'

'Blood group, life-style of the victim, head injuries, and some positioning of the body, some arrangement that we're not publicising.'

'Blood group?'

'Same.'

'Which group?'

'B.'

'B. That's rare.'

'Ish. Nine per cent.'

'I'd call that rare.'

'I'd call it inconclusive.'

'So what makes you so conclusively against it?'

'Clare Strachan was penetrated, sodomised twice, once postmortem, hit on the head with a blunt instrument, but not fatally, throttled, but not fatally, and after all that she was finally killed, finally killed by a punctured lung which was caused by someone jumping up and down on her chest until one of her ribs snapped off and speared her lung, flooding it with blood so she choked, drowned.'

Again we sat in our silences, our desperate little silences, our nails down the window panes, our faces to the glass, wanting out out out.

'Can I ask you one more question then?'

He folded up the handkerchief again and nodded.

'You interviewed the people from the hostel?'

'St Mary's? Yes. Had them all in.'

I paused, my lips dry, a terrible vision on the hills out the window, above the room, a vision of the drunk and the mental, the drunk and the mental howling at a moon glimpsed through cell bars, bars high on a dark cell wall.

Eventually I said, 'And what did they tell you? What did they say?'

'Nothing.'

'Nothing?'

'Nothing.'

'Did you speak to a Walter Kendall?'

He rolled his eyes. 'The blind man? Repeatedly.'

'And what did he say?'

Alfred Hill, Detective Chief Superintendent Alfred Hill, he looked me dead for the first time and he said:

'Mr Whitehead, you have an extremely high reputation among the men of the West Yorkshire force, a high reputation as a diligent crime reporter who assists investigations and I'm prepared to give a lot of rope on that account, a lot of rope, but I must say I object to the insinuation.'

'What insinuation?'

'I am well, well aware of the things Mr Kendall has said, has said repeatedly, and I'm surprised that a journalist, a man of your reputation, surprised you would even credit such nonsense with a question.'

I smiled. 'So I'll take it that it's not a line of inquiry you are presently pursuing, shall I?'

Alfred Hill said nothing.

'One last question?'

He sighed.

'You said that Clare Strachan was a prostitute?'

He nodded.

'Did she have convictions?'

He was tired, wanted me gone and said, 'See for yourself,' and pushed an open file towards me.

I leant forward.

On a typed sheet, two dates:

23/08/74.

22/12/74.

Next to each date, letters and numbers:
See WKFD/MORRISON-C/CTNSOL1A.
See WKFD/MORRISON-C/MGRD-P/WSMT27C.
'What do they refer to?'
'One's a caution for soliciting, one a statement.'
'WKFD?'
'Wakefield.'

In the car, on the Moors, in tears, on my cheeks.
Laughing:
Big fucking howling gales of laughter, foot down through another bucket of Jubilee piss.
Laughing:
Thinking, *dumb, dumb, dumb.*
Looking in the rearview, asking myself:
'Do I look like a violin?'
Laughing:
Hell's teeth he was thick, thicker than I could have ever dreamt.
Laughing:
Because he was thick and he was mine.
Laughing:
Foot down, window open, head out in the rain, shouting:
'So fucking play me.'
Laughing:
'Go on cunt, play me!'

I pulled up just past a red box, put my jacket up over my ears and ran for it.
I dialled.
'I want to come over.'
'I'll look forward to it,' she half-laughed.

It had stopped raining just as it started to get dark, just to give them their street parties, just to let them light their stupid beacons.
Ka Su Peng was waiting at the corner of Manningham and

Queens, short black hair and dirty skin, in a black dress and tights, a bag and a jacket over her arm.

I pulled up and she got in.

'Thanks,' I said.

'How are you?'

'I'm OK.'

'You don't want to use the flat?'

'No, not if you don't mind.'

'It's your money,' she said and I wished she hadn't, really wished she hadn't said that.

So I turned left and left again until we were going down Whetley Hill and she said, 'Where are we going?'

'I want to do it here,' I said, turning on to the playing fields off White Abbey Road.

'But this is . . .'

I could feel her heart beating inside the car, feel her fear, but said, 'I know and I want you to show me where.'

'No,' she was twisting in her seat.

'You'll feel better after, much better.'

'The fuck you know.'

'It'll be over, finished.'

She was taking the money out of her bag, saying, 'Let me out, let me out right now.'

I pulled up on the grass before a line of trees and turned off the engine.

She darted for the door.

I held on to her arm.

'Ka Su Peng, please. I don't want to hurt you.'

'Then let me go. You're scaring me.'

'Please, I can help.'

She had the door open, one foot on the grass.

'Please.'

She turned and stared at me, black eyes in a ghost's face, a death mask made flesh, and said: 'What then?'

'Get in the back.'

We got out and stood in the night, looking across the roof of the car at each other, two white ghosts, death-made, black eyes on pale faces, masks flesh, and she went to open the back door but it was locked.

'Here,' I said, and I walked round the back of the car, a hand in my pocket, her face on mine, mine on hers, the moon in the trees, the trees in the sky, the sky in that black hell up, up above, looking down, down on the playing field, the field where the children played their games and their fathers murdered their mothers.

And I came up behind her and I unlocked the back door.

'Get in.'

She sat down on the edge of the back seat.

'Lie down.'

And she lay back on the black leather.

I stood by the door and undid my belt and buckle.

She watched me and raised up her arse to take down her black tights and white knickers.

I put one knee on the edge of the seat, the door still open.

She pulled up the black dress and reached up for me.

And then I fucked her on the back seat and came on her belly and wiped the come off the inside of her dress with my sleeve and held her there, held her in my arms while she cried, there on the back seat of my car with her tights and her pants hanging off one foot, there in the field, there in the night, under the Jubilee moon, watching the fireworks and the beacons light up the maroon sky, and as another silent firework span towards the earth, she asked:

'What does Jubilee mean?'

'It's Jewish. Every fifty years there was a year of emancipation, a time of remission and forgiveness from sin, an end to penance, so it was a time of celebration.'

'Jubilation?'

'Yeah.'

I drove her back to the flat where she lived and we parked outside in the dark, and I asked:

'Am I forgiven?'

'Yes,' she said and got out.

She had left the ten quid on the dashboard.

I drove back to Leeds with a warm stomach, a stomach like that time I'd dropped my fiancée back home and driven away with her waving, her parents too, that time twenty-five years ago, with a warm stomach.

A glow.

I took my time on the stairs, dreading them.

I turned the key in the lock and listened, knowing I could never bring her here.

The telephone was ringing on the other side.

I opened the door and answered it.

'Jack?'

'Yes.'

'It's Martin.'

'What do you want?'

'I was worried about you.'

'Well, don't be.'

From sleep I awoke into the darkest half of a silent night, the fireworks spent, drowning in sweat.

Kiss you then you wake.

Awoke to feel the softness of her kiss upon my brow, to see her sat upon the edge of my bed, legs apart, to hear her lullaby.

Fuck you then you sleep.

Awoke to fall back into sleep.

Dark panting streets, the leering terrace backs, surrounded by the silent stones, buried by the black bricks, through courtyards and alleyways where no trees grow, or grass too, foot upon brick, brick upon head, these are the houses that Jack built.

An adventure playground.

Ring-a-ring of roses, a pocket full of posies.

Mary-Ann, Annie, Liz, Catherine and Mary, hands together round the mulberry bush, singing:

'Where you seek one there's two, two three, three four.'

A shocking place, an evil plexus of slums that hide the human creeping things, where men and women live on penn'orths of gin, where collars and clean shirts are decencies unknown, where every citizen wears a black eye, and none ever combs his hair.

An adventure playground.

Ring-a-ring of roses, a pocket full of posies.

Theresa, Joan, and Marie, hands together round the mulberry bush, singing:

'Where you seek four there's three, three two, two one and so on.'

Within a short distance of the heart, a narrow court, a quiet thoroughfare, with two large gates, in one of which is a small wicket for use when the gates are closed, though at every hour these gates are open, indeed, according to the testimony of those living near, the entrance to the court is seldom closed.

An adventure playground.

Ring-a-ring of roses, a pocket full of posies.

Joyce, Anita, and Ka Su Peng, hands together under the mulberry bush, whispering in my ear:

'But you know this anyway.'

For a distance of 18ft or 20ft from the street there is a deadwall on each side of the place, the effect of which is to enshroud the intervening space in absolute darkness after sunset. Further back some light is thrown into the court from the window of a Working Men's club, which occupies the whole length of the court on the right, and from a number of terraces, all of which have been extinguished by this time.

An adventure playground.

Ring-a-ring of roses, a pocket full of posies.

I have my hand on the cold metal of the gate, staring dead ahead into the gloom, Carol beckoning me in.

An adventure playground.

Dead ahead.

Ripped from that hell into this:

Shrieking: HE'S COMING, HE'S COMING, HE'S COMING.

Howling: *Fuck you then you sleep.*

Shrieking: HE'S COMING, HE'S COMING, HE'S COMING.

Howling: *Kiss you then you wake.*

Shrieking: HE'S COMING, HE'S COMING, HE'S COMING.

Ripped from that into this, this into that, and back to this:
The dawn, the rattle of the flap, the letter on the mat.
HE WAS HERE.
Back.

Part 3
God save the queen

John Shark: Next caller?

Caller: I just want to say, she's a good Queen, she's Britain.

John Shark: Is that it?

Caller: Yes.

The John Shark Show
Radio Leeds
Wednesday 8th June 1977

Chapter 11

Leeds.

Wednesday 8 June 1977.

It's happening again:

When the two sevens clash . . .

Shot through another hot dawn to another ancient stage with her littered dead, from Soldier's Field to here, it's happening again.

Wednesday morning, doors wide open, *the morning after the night before*, the bunting tattered, the Union Jacks down.

Knuckles white and tight in prayer around the steering wheel, foot down.

The voices in my head, alive with death:

Wednesday morning – a jacket over her, her boots placed on her thighs, a pair of white panties left on one leg, a pink bra pushed up, her stomach and breasts hollowed out with a screwdriver, her skull caved in with a hammer.

Cars and vans screaming in from every direction, wailing:

Proceeding to Chapeltown.

I park, I pray, I make my deal:

Please God, dear God, please let her be safe, please let it be someone else and if she's safe and someone else, I'll let her be and go back to Louise and try again. Amen.

Me ditching Eric's Granada round the back, following the sirens down across Chapeltown.

Chapeltown – our town for one year; the leafy street with its grand old house, the shabby little flat which we filled full of sex, hiding out from the rest of the world, the rest of my world.

And I turn the corner on to Reginald Street, the blue lights spinning silently, the waking dead on every doorstep with their bottles of milk and their open mouths, and I walk up past the Community Centre, past the uniforms, under the tape and through the gates, into the adventure playground, this the ancient stage where we the players move our wooden limbs

and scratch our wooden heads with our wooden hands, and
Ellis looks up and says, 'Christ. The fuck . . .'

And they're all here:

Oldman, Noble, Prentice, Alderman, and Farley; Rudkin
sprinting across the playground towards me.

And I'm staring at the body on the floor under the jacket,
cursing God and all his fucking angels, tasting blood and the
end:

I can see black hair lying in the dirt.

Rudkin catches me, spins me round, and he's saying, 'The
fuck you been, the fuck you been, the fuck you been,' over and
over, again and again.

And I'm staring at the body on the floor under the jacket,
still cursing God and all his fucking angels, thinking:

There is no hell but this one.

Cursing all those false hells stuffed full of pretenders: those
generals and their witches.

I can see black hair.

And Rudkin is staring into my eyes, my eyes past him, and
I get free and I'm gone, away, across the playground, pushing
Prentice and Alderman to the ground, dropping on to my knees,
the jacket in my hands, the face between my fingers, the hair
blood not black, the prayers answered, the deal made, and
they're pulling me off, shouting:

'Get him fucking out of here.'

And Rudkin picks me up and leads me away into the path
of a man in his dressing gown and pyjamas clutching a bottle of
milk, walking across the playground towards us, *f-a-t-h-e-r*
tattooed across his face, eyes closed to the horror and death,
and he stares at us as he passes and we stop and we watch as
he gets nearer and nearer, until he drops the bottle of milk and
falls to the ground that killed his daughter and starts to dig
through the hard-packed dirt, searching for an exit which a year
from now he'll find, dead in the same pyjamas, his broken heart
unhealed, unmended, this unending.

My deal, my prayer; his hell.

Rudkin pushes my head down and into the back of the car and Ellis turns and is speaking to me but I can't hear him.

And they take me in.

They put me in a cell, chuck in some clean clothes, and bring in breakfast.

'Briefing's in ten minutes,' says Rudkin, sitting down opposite. 'They want you there.'

'Why?'

'They know fuck all. We covered for you.'

'You didn't need to do that.'

'I know, Mike kept saying.'

'What happens now?'

Rudkin leans across the table, hands together. 'She's gone, go back to your family. They need you, she doesn't.'

'I broke into Eric Hall's house, stole his car, beat him up.'

'I know.'

'You can't cover that up.'

'Word is they're sending in Peter Hunter to do the number on Bradford Vice.'

'You're fucking joking?'

'No.'

'What's going to happen to Eric?'

'He's been sent home for a bit.'

'Fuck.'

'Craven's shitting himself. Reckons Leeds'll be next.'

I start to smile.

'Don't think for a moment Eric'll forget.'

I nod.

Rudkin stands up.

I say, 'Thanks, John.'

'You won't thank me, not when see what he did last night.'

'But thanks for helping me.'

'She's gone, Bob. Go back to your family and everything'll be all right.'

I nod.

'I can't hear you,' he says.

'OK,' I say.

Oldman stands up, looks at us, like this is all he ever sees.

No days off.

We wait, but it's not like before.

The game's over.

'At about 5.45 a.m. this morning, the body of Rachel Louise Johnson, sixteen years of age, shop assistant, of 66 St Mary's Road, Leeds 7, was found in the adventure playground compound, between Reginald Terrace and Reginald Street, Chapeltown, Leeds. She was last seen at 10.30 p.m. Tuesday 7th June in the Hofbrauhaus in the Merrion Centre, Leeds.

'She is described as follows: five feet four inches with proportionate build, shoulder-length fair hair and wearing a blue-and-yellow check gingham skirt, a blue jacket, dark blue tights and high-heeled clog-fronted shoes in black and cream with brass studs around the front.

'A post-mortem is being carried out by the Home Office Pathologist, Professor Farley. So far as can be ascertained the deceased had been subjected to violent blows about the head with a blunt instrument and had not been sexually assaulted.

'The body had been dragged a distance of some fifteen or twenty yards from where the initial assault took place. Her assailant's clothing will be heavily bloodstained, particularly the front of any jacket, shirt, or trousers worn by him.

'There is no evidence that Rachel Louise Johnson was an active prostitute.'

Assistant Chief Constable George Oldman sits down, his head in his hands, and we say nothing.

Nothing.

Nothing until Detective Chief Superintendent Noble stands up in front of the board, the board that says in big bold letters:

Theresa Campbell.

Clare Strachan.

Joan Richards.

Marie Watts.

Until he stands there and says, 'Dismissed.'

*

Noble looks up and says, 'What about Fairclough?'

'We lost him,' says Rudkin.

'You lost him?'

Ellis is burning a hole into the side of my face.

'Yes.'

'That's my fault, sir,' I say.

Noble has his hand up, 'Whatever. Where is he now?'

Ellis says, 'At home. Asleep.'

'Then you'd better go and fucking wake him up, hadn't you.'

He's on his knees, on the floor, in the corner, hands up, nose bloody.

My body weak.

'Come on,' shouts Rudkin. 'Where the fuck were you?'

I was battering down doors, battering down people, kicking in doors, kicking in people.

'Working,' he screams.

Ellis, fists into the wall, 'Liar!'

I was raping whores, fucking them up the arse.

'I was.'

'You murdering bastard. You tell me now!'

I was breaking into houses, stealing cars, beating up cunts like Eric Hall.

'I was working.'

'The fucking truth!'

I was searching for a whore.

'Working, I was fucking working.'

Rudkin picks him up off the floor, rights the chair and sits him in it, nodding at the door.

'You fucking sit here and you think about where the fuck you were at two o'clock this morning and what you were bloody doing?'

I was on the floor of the Redbeck, in tears.

We're standing outside the Belly, Noble staring through the peephole into the cell.

'What's the cunt doing?' asks Ellis.

'Not much,' says Noble.

Rudkin looks up from the end of his cigarette, asks, 'What next?'

Noble comes away from the hole, the four of us in a prayer circle. He looks up at the low ceiling, eyes wide like he's trying not to cry, and says:

'Fairclough's the best we got for now. Bob Craven's out pulling in witnesses, Alderman's door-to-door, Prentice is down the cab firm. Just keep at him.'

Rudkin nods and stamps out his cigarette, 'Right then. Back to work.'

Rudkin and I sit down across the table from Donny Fairclough, Ellis leaning against the door.

I sit forward, elbows on the table: 'OK, Don. We all want to go home, right?'

Nothing, head down.

'You do want to go home, don't you?'

A nod.

'That makes four of us. So help us out, will you?'

Head still down.

'What time did you clock on yesterday?'

He looks up, sniffs, and says: 'Just after lunch. One-ish.'

'And what time did you finish?'

'Like I said, about one in morning.'

'And what did you do then?'

'I went to a party.'

'Where? Whose?'

'Chapeltown, one of them kind. I don't know whose it was.'

'You remember where?'

'Off Leopold Street.'

'And this was?'

'About half-one.'

'Till?'

'Two-thirty, three o'clock.'

'See anyone you know?'

'Yeah.'

'Who?'

'I don't know their names.'

Rudkin looks up, 'That's unfortunate that is, Donald.'

I say, 'Would you know them again, if you saw them?'

'Yeah.'

'Men or women?'

'A couple of the black lads, couple of the girls.'

'The girls?'

'You know?'

'No, I don't. Be more specific.'

'Prostitutes.'

'Whores, you mean?' says Rudkin.

He nods.

I ask, 'You go with whores, do you Donny?'

'No.'

'So how come you know they're prostitutes?'

'I pick them up, don't I? Get talking.'

'They offer you discounts, do they? For cheap lifts?'

'No.'

'Right, so you're at the party. What did you?'

'Had a drink.'

'You always go to a party after work?'

'No, but it's Jubilee, isn't it?'

Rudkin smiles, 'Bit of a patriot are you, Don?'

'Yeah I am, as a matter of fact.'

'Fuck you drink with wogs and whores for then?'

'I told you, I just wanted a drink.'

I say, 'So you just sat there in the corner, sipping a half did you?'

'Yeah, that was about it.'

'Didn't have a dance or a bit of a cuddle?'

'No.'

'Smoke a bit of the old wog weed, did you?'

'No.'

'So then you just went home?'

'Yeah.'

'And what time was that then?'

'Must have been about three-ish.'

'And where's home?'

'Pudsey.'

'Nice place, Pudsey.'

'It's all right.'

'Live alone do you Donny?'

'No, with my mum.'

'That's nice.'

'It's all right.'

'Light sleeper is she, your mum?'

'What do you mean?'

'Well, did she hear you come in?'

'Doubt it.'

Rudkin, big fat fucking grin: 'So you don't sleep in the same fucking bed or anything daft like that?'

'Fuck off.'

'Here,' spits Rudkin, the hard stare in Fairclough's face. 'The shit you're in, you'll wish you had been fucking your mum. Understand?'

Fairclough's eyes drop, nails up to his mouth.

'So,' I say, 'what we got is this: you knocked off work about one, went down to a party on Leopold Street, had a couple of drinks, drove home to Pudsey for about three. Right?'

'Right,' he's nodding. 'Right.'

'Says who?'

'Says me.'

'And?'

'And anyone who was at that party.'

'Whose names you don't know?'

'Just ask anyone who was there. They'll pick me out, I swear.'

'Let's hope so. For your fucking sake.'

Upstairs, out of the Belly.

No sleep.

Just coffee.

No dreams.

Just this:

Shirtsleeves and smoke, grey skins with big black rings crayoned across our faces:

Oldman, Noble, Prentice, Alderman, Rudkin, and me.

On every wall, names:

Jobson.

Bird.

Campbell.

Strachan.

Richards.

Peng.

Watts.

Clark.

Johnson.

On every wall, words:

Screwdriver.

Abdomen.

Boots.

Chest.

Hammer.

Skull.

Bottle.

Rectum.

Knife.

On every wall, numbers:

1.3"

1974.

32.

1975.

239 + 584.

1976.

X3

1977.

3.5.

And Noble is saying:

'We got a witness, this Mark Lancaster, who says he saw a white Ford Cortina, black roof, on Reginald Street about two this morning. Fairclough's motor. No question.'

We're listening, waiting.

'Right, Farley is saying that this is definitely the same man. No question. And Bob Craven's lads have turned up another witness who saw this guy, this *Dave*, the night Joan Richards was murdered. Description's a ringer for Fairclough. No question.'

Listening, waiting.

'I say we stick the cunt in a line-up, see if this witness'll pick him out.'

Waiting.

'No alibi, motor spotted at the time of death, witness has him for Joan Richards, same blood group, what you reckon?'

Oldman:

'Cunt's going down.'

The magnificent seven.

We're standing there, in the line-up, in the room we use for press conferences, the chairs all folded up at the back, Ellis and me either side of Fairclough, two guys from Vice and a couple of civilians making up the numbers and a fiver each.

The coppers, we all look alike.

The civilians are both over forty.

No-one looks like Donny.

And there we stand, in the line-up, numbers three, four, and five. Number four shaking, stinking, smelling like FEAR, HATE, and DIRTY THOUGHTS.

'This isn't right,' he's moaning. 'I should have a lawyer.'

'But you haven't done anything, Donny,' says Ellis. 'Or so you keep saying.'

'But I haven't.'

'We'll see,' I say. 'We'll see who's not done anything.'

Rudkin sticks his head in, 'Right, quiet now ladies. Eyes front.'

He opens the door wider and Oldman, Noble, and Craven lead in Karen Burns.

Karen fucking Burns.

Fuck.

She looks down the line, looks at Craven, who nods, and steps towards us.

Noble puts a hand on her arm to hold her back.

He turns to Rudkin, 'Where are the bloody numbers?'

'Shit.'

Noble rolls his eyes and turns to Karen Burns and says in a low voice, 'When you see the man you saw last year on the night of 6th February please stand before him and touch his right shoulder.'

She nods, swallows, and steps towards the first man.

She doesn't even look at him.

Past the second, straight to us.

She stands before Ellis, and I'm wondering if he's ever fucked her, if there's a man in this room who hasn't.

Ellis is almost smiling.

She glances down the line at me.

I fix on the wall ahead, the white patches where the pictures were.

She moves on.

Fairclough coughs.

She's standing in front of him.

He's staring at her.

'Eyes front,' hisses Rudkin.

She's staring back.

He's smiling.

She moves her hand.

The whole row turns.

She adjusts the strap of her bag and turns to me.

I can see the teeth of Fairclough's grin out the corner of my eye, in my face.

He's laughing.

I swallow.

She's before me, smiling.

I pull her from the bed, across the floor.

My eyes dead ahead.

Just a pair of pink knickers, tits out.

Staring me up and down.

And she's under me, hands across her face because I'm slapping the shit out of her.

I can feel myself start to rock, a mouth full of sand.

And I slap her again and then I look down at her bleeding lips and nose.

She won't stop staring.

The bloody smears on her chin and neck, her tits and arms.

I've got sweat running down my face, down my neck, down my back, down my legs, rivers of salt.

And I pull off her pink knickers and drag her back to the bed and pull open my trousers and push it into her.

She doesn't move.

And I slap her again and turn her over.

Rudkin's next to her, Ellis turning sideways back down the line.

And she starts struggling, saying we don't need to do it like this.

She moves her arm, her hand coming up.

But I push her face down into the dirty sheets and bring my cock up.

I step back.

And stick it in her arse and she's screaming.

She sniffs, wipes her nose, and she smiles.

And she's lying there on the bed, semen and blood running down her thighs.

I look down.

And I get up and do it again and this time it doesn't hurt.

'He's not here,' she says, not even looking at six and seven.

I look up.

'Would you like to go through them one more time? Just to be sure,' says Noble.

'He's not here.'

'I think you should take one more . . .'

'He's not here. I want to go home.'

'The fuck was that?' Noble's shouting at Craven. 'You said you could fucking deliver her . . .'

'Ask fucking Fraser.'

'Fuck off,' says Rudkin. 'Nowt to do with us.'

Craven's spewing, spit in his beard, the lot of us jammed into Noble's office, Oldman wedged behind the desk, pitch black outside, same inside:

'She grasses for you, doesn't she?'

'So fucking what,' says Ellis and I know then he's been shagging her.

And so does Craven: 'You fucking her Mike? Taking a leaf out of his book,' he yells, pointing my way.

Me with a feeble: 'Fuck off.'

Noble's shaking his head, staring round the room at us, 'Right fucking balls-up.'

'OK. Now what?' asks Rudkin, looking from Noble to Oldman.

'Total fucking cock-up.'

'We can't let the cunt just walk. He's our man, I know it,' says Ellis.

'He's not going anywhere but down,' says Noble.

'Fucking know it,' Ellis is saying.

Rudkin looking to George, 'So what then?'

Oldman:

'Do it the hard way.'

He's naked on his knees, on the floor, in the corner, holding his balls, body bloody.

My arms are weak.

'Come on,' Rudkin is screaming, over and over, again and again, screaming, 'Where the fuck were you?'

I was searching for a whore.

He's crying.

Ellis, fists into Fairclough's face, 'Tell us!'

I was searching for a whore.

He's crying.

'You murdering fucking cunt. She wasn't a slag. She was a good girl. Sixteen fucking years old. From a good Christian family. Never even had a bloody fuck! A child, a bloody child.'

I was searching for a whore.

He just keeps crying, face like Bobby, no noise, just tears, mouth open, crying, like a child, a baby.

'The truth. Give us the fucking truth!'

I was searching for a whore.

Just crying.

Rudkin picks him up off the floor, rights the chair and ties him to it with our belts, taking out his cigarette lighter.

'You fucking sit here and you think about where the fuck you were at two o'clock yesterday morning and what you were bloody doing.'

I was on the floor of the Redbeck, in tears.

Crying.

Rudkin flicks the lighter open and Ellis and me, we take a leg each and keep his knees apart as Rudkin puts the flame to Donny's tiny little balls.

I was on the floor of the Redbeck, in tears.

Screaming.

The door flies open.

Oldman and Noble.

Noble: 'Let him go!'

Us: 'What?'

Oldman: 'It's not him. Let him fucking go.'

Caller: You saw this about that four-year-old, this little lass? Taken from a bloody Jubilee party, raped and murdered in a graveyard while her parents are toasting Queen.

John Shark: What a Jubilee for them.

Caller: Then there's that woman who was pushed off cliffs at Botany Bay after another Jubilee party.

John Shark: And that's on top of bloody Ripper.

Caller: You said it, John; some bloody Jubilee.

The John Shark Show
Radio Leeds
Thursday 9th June 1977

Chapter 12

Silence.

A hot, dirty, red-eyed silence.

Twenty-four hours for the four of us.

Oldman was staring at the letter in his hands, the piece of flowered cloth in another plastic envelope on the desk, Noble avoiding me, Bill Hadden biting a nail in his beard.

Silence.

A hot, dirty, yellow, sweaty silence.

Thursday 9 June 1977.

The morning's headlines stared up from the desk at us:

RIPPER RIDDLE IN MURDER OF RACHEL, 16.

Yesterday's news.

Oldman put the letter flat on the desk and read it aloud again:

> *From Hell.*
>
> *Mr Whitehead,*
> *Sir, this is a little something for your drawer, would have been a bit of stuff from underneath but for that dog. Lucky cow.*
>
> *Up to four now they say three but remember Preston 75, come my load up that one. Dirty cow.*
>
> *Anyway, warn whores to keep off streets cause I feel it coming on again.*
>
> *Maybe do one for queen. Love our queen.*
> *God saves*
> *Lewis.*
>
> *I have given advance warning so its yours and their fault.*

Silence.

Then Oldman: 'Why you Jack?'

'What do you mean?'

'Why's he writing to you?'

'I don't know.'

'He's got your home address,' said Noble.

Me: 'It's in the book.'

'It's in his, that's for sure.'

Oldman picked up the envelope: 'Sunderland. Monday.'

'Took its time,' said Noble.

Me: 'Bank Holiday. The Jubilee.'

'Last one was Preston, right?' said Hadden.

Noble sighed, 'He gets about a bit.'

Hadden asked, 'Lorry driver?'

I said, 'Taxi driver?'

Oldman and Noble just sat there, mouths shut.

'That last one,' said Hadden. 'That stuff he sent, that was from Marie Watts?'

'No,' said Noble, looking at me.

Hadden, eyes wide: 'What was it then?'

'Beef,' smiled Noble.

'Cow,' I said.

'Yeah,' said Noble, the smile gone.

I asked Oldman, 'But this must match what Linda Clark was wearing?'

'It would appear to,' stressed Noble.

I repeated, 'Appear to?'

'Gentlemen,' said Oldman, hands up, looking at Hadden and me. 'I'm going to be frank with you, but I must insist that this remain completely off the record.'

'Understood,' said Hadden.

Noble was looking at me.

I nodded.

'Yesterday was about the worst day of my career as a police officer. And this,' said Oldman, holding up the plastic envelope with the letter, 'this didn't help. As Pete says, the jury was still out on the last letter but this one, the tests are more conclusive.'

I couldn't help myself: 'Conclusive?'

'Yes, conclusive. One, it's the same bloke as before. Two, the contents are genuine. Three, initial saliva tests indicate the blood group we're interested in.'

'B?' said Hadden.

'Yes. The tests on the first letter were spoiled. Four, there are traces of a mineral oil on both letters that have been present at each of the crime scenes.'

I was straight in: 'What kind of oil?'

'A lubricant used in engineering,' said Noble, clear this was as specific as he was going to get.

'Finally,' said Oldman. 'There's the content: the threat to kill just days before Rachel Johnson, the Queen and the Jubilee, and the reference to Preston and him *coming his load.*'

Hadden said, 'That wasn't in any of the papers?'

'No,' said Noble. 'And that's what distinguishes that crime from the others.'

I was straight at Oldman: 'So you think he did it?'

'Yes.'

'Alf Hill's sceptical.'

'Not any more,' said Oldman, nodding at the letter.

WKFD.

Wakefield.

'Would it be possible for me to take a look at the Preston file?'

'Talk to Pete later,' shrugged Oldman.

Bill Hadden, on the edge of his seat, eyes on the letter: 'Are you going to go public with it?'

'Not at this stage, no.'

'And so we're not to print anything?'

'No.'

'Are you going to brief the other editors, Bradford, Manchester?'

'Not unless they start getting fan mail like this, no.'

I said, 'It'll put a few noses out of joint if it gets out.'

'Well, let's see that it doesn't then.'

Assistant Chief Constable George Oldman picked up his glass of water and stared out at the pack.

Millgarth, 10.30 a.m.

Another press conference.

Tom from Bradford: 'At this stage do you have a picture in your mind of the kind of man you're looking for?'

Oldman: 'Yes, we now have a very clear picture in our minds of the type of man we are looking for, and obviously no woman is really safe until he is found. We are looking for a psychopathic killer who has a pathological hatred of women he believes are prostitutes. We believe he is probably being protected by someone because on several occasions he must have returned home with heavily bloodstained clothing. This person is in urgent need of help, and anyone who leads us to him will be doing him a service.'

Gilman from Manchester: 'Would the Assistant Chief Constable be prepared to describe the type of weapons members of the public should be on the lookout for?'

'I believe I know the weapons that have been used but no, I am not prepared to say what, other than that they include a blunt instrument.'

'Have any weapons been recovered?'

'No.'

'Have any eye-witnesses come forward in connection to the murder of Rachel Johnson?'

'No. As yet we have not had any detailed descriptions of this man.'

'Have you got any suspects?'

'No.'

'What have you got?'

Back in the office, the sun on the big seventh-floor windows, burning paper under glass.

Leeds on fire.

I got out my fiddle:

NO WOMAN SAFE WITH RIPPER FREE, SAY POLICE

Detectives hunting West Yorkshire's Jack the Ripper killer finally established last night that the same man had brutally murdered five women in the North of England.

Forensic scientists at the Home Office laboratories, Wetherby, yes-

terday managed to link the sadistic attacks on four prostitutes with that on Rachel Johnson, a sixteen-year-old shop assistant.

Her mutilated body was found in an adventure playground alongside Chapeltown Community Centre on Wednesday morning.

Last night the police officer who has taken charge of the biggest multiple murder hunt in the North since the M62 coach-bomb explosion described the wanted man:

'We are looking for a psychopathic killer who has a pathological hatred of women who he believes are prostitutes. It is crucial that this man is found quickly,' said Mr George Oldman, Assistant Chief Constable of the West Yorkshire Police.

Throughout yesterday, as the striking similarities between the five murders were matched up, Mr Oldman and other senior detectives spent time discussing the mind of the killer with psychiatrists.

'We now have a clear picture in our minds of the type of man we are looking for, and obviously no woman is safe until he is found.

'We believe he is probably being protected by someone because on several occasions he must have returned home with heavily blood-stained clothing. This person is in urgent need of help, and anyone who leads us to him will be doing him a service,' added Mr Oldman.

Police believe the man is from West Yorkshire, certainly with good knowledge of Leeds and Bradford, and has possibly developed a psychological hang-up about prostitutes, either at the hands of one or because his mother was one.

Mr Oldman said that as well as forensic evidence, the details of which he was not prepared to discuss, other similarities included:

all the victims were 'good time girls' except Rachel Johnson, who could have been attacked by mistake as she made her way home late on Tuesday night.

no evidence of sexual assault or robbery on any of the victims apart from one.

all suffered horrific head injuries and other injuries to their bodies, including frenzied knife wounds.

Last night Rachel Johnson's Chapeltown neighbours were collecting signatures on a petition calling on the Home Secretary Mr Merlyn Rees to restore the death penalty for murder.

One of the organisers, Mrs Rosemary Hamilton, said: 'We're going *to go round every house in Leeds if necessary. This kid never did anyone any harm in her life and when they catch her killer he won't get what he deserves.'*

The Press Club.

Dead, but for George, Bet, and me.

'Some of the things they say he does,' Bet was saying.

George, nodding along, 'Slices their tits off, right?'

'Takes out their wombs, this copper was saying.'

'Eats bits and all.'

'Another?'

'And keep them coming,' I said, sick.

I staggered round the corner of my road and there he was, under the streetlight.

A tall man in a black raincoat, a hat, and a battered briefcase.

He was standing motionless, staring up at my flat, frozen.

'Martin,' I said, coming up behind him.

He turned, 'Jack. I was getting worried.'

'I told you, I'm fine.'

'Been drinking?'

'About forty years.'

'You need some new jokes, Jack.'

'Got any?'

'Jack, you can't keep running.'

'You going to exorcise my demons, are you? Put me out of my fucking misery?'

'I'd like to come up. To talk.'

'Another time.'

'Jack, there might not be another time. It's running out.'

'Good.'

'Jack, please.'

'Goodnight.'

The telephone was ringing on the other side.

I opened the door and answered it.

'Hello.'

'Jack Whitehead?'

'Speaking.'

'I've got some information concerning one of these Ripper murders.'

A man's voice, young and local.

'Go on.'

'Not on the phone.'

'Where are you?'

'Not important, but I can meet Saturday night.'

'What kind of information?'

'On Saturday. Variety Club.'

'Batley?'

'Yeah. Between ten and eleven.'

'OK, but I need a name?'

'No names.'

'You want money I suppose?'

'No money.'

'Then what do you want?'

'You just be there.'

At the window, the Reverend Laws still under the streetlight, a lynched East End Jew in his black hat and coat.

I sat down and tried to read, but I was thinking of her, thinking of her, thinking of her, praying Carol stayed gone, thinking of her hair, thinking of her ears, thinking of her eyes, praying Carol stayed gone, thinking of her lips, thinking of her teeth, thinking of her tongue, praying Carol stayed gone, thinking of her neck, thinking of her collarbone, thinking of her shoulders, praying Carol stayed gone, thinking of her breasts, thinking of the skin, thinking of her nipples, praying Carol stayed gone, thinking of her stomach, thinking of her belly, thinking of her womb, praying Carol stayed gone, thinking of her thighs, thinking of the skin, thinking of the hair, praying Carol stayed gone, thinking of her piss, thinking of her shit, thinking of her hidden bits, praying Carol stayed gone, thinking of her, thinking of her, thinking of her, and praying.

I stood up and turned to the bed, to be under the sheets, thinking of her, touching me.

I stood up, I turned, and there she was.

Ka Su Peng gone.

Carol home.

'Did you miss me?'

John Shark: *I like this [reads]: According to Mr James Anderton, the Chief Constable of Greater Manchester, an increase in violence has put police forces' backs to the wall, and the burden may get worse before it gets better.*

Caller: *I think he's right.*

John Shark: *I don't. I blame the police for the increase in violence. Fear and bloody indecision? That's their doing.*

Caller: *You're talking bollocks John, utter bollocks. Your posh house got robbed, who you going to call?*

The John Shark Show
Radio Leeds
Friday 10th June 1977

Chapter 13

In my dream I was sitting on a sofa in a pink room. A dirty sofa with three rotting seats, smelling worse and worse, but I couldn't stand.

And then in the dream I was sitting on a sofa in a playing field. A horrible sofa with three rusty springs, cutting into my arse and thighs, but I couldn't stand, couldn't get up.

Someone's tapping on my face.

I open my eyes.

It's Bobby.

He smiles, eyes alive, teeth tiny and white.

He pushes a book on to my chest.

I close my eyes.

He taps on my face again.

I open my eyes.

It's Bobby, in his blue pyjamas.

I'm on the settee in the front room, the radio on in the back, the smell of breakfast in the house.

I sit up and pick up Bobby and his blue pyjamas, put him on my knee and open his book.

'Once upon a time there was a rabbit, a magic rabbit who lived on the moon.'

And Bobby's got his hands up, pretending they're rabbit's ears.

'And the rabbit had a giant telescope, a magic telescope that looked down on the earth.'

And Bobby's making a telescope out of his hands, turning round to stare up at me, hands to his eye.

'One day the magic rabbit pointed his magic telescope at the world and said: "Magic telescope, magic telescope, please show me Great Britain."

'And the magic rabbit put his eye to the magic telescope and looked down on Great Britain.'

And suddenly Bobby jumps down from my knee and runs

to the lounge door, arms flapping in his blue pyjamas, shouting, 'Mummy, Mummy, Magic Rabbit, Magic Rabbit!'

And Louise is standing there, behind us, watching, and she says, 'Breakfast's ready.'

I sit down at the table, the neat cloth and three places, Bobby between us, and look out on the back garden.

It's seven, and the sun is on the other side of the house.

Louise is pouring milk on Bobby's Weetabix, her face fresh, the room slightly cold in the shadow.

'How's your Dad?' I say.

'Not good,' she says, mashing the cereal for Bobby.

'I'm off today. We can go up together if you want?'

'Really? I thought they'd have cancelled all days off.'

'They have, but I think Maurice must have swung me a day.'

'He was at the hospital Tuesday.'

'Yeah? Said he was going to try and get up.'

'John Rudkin and all.'

'Yeah?'

'He's kind, isn't he? What did your Uncle John buy you?' she asks Bobby.

'Car, car,' and he tries to get down.

'Later, love,' I say. 'Eat your Weetabix first.'

'Peace car. Peace car.'

I look at Louise, 'Peace car?'

'Police car,' she smiles.

'What's Daddy's job?' I ask him.

'Peace Man,' he grins, a mouth full of milk and cereal.

And we laugh, all three of us.

Bobby's walking between us, one hand for Mummy, one for Daddy.

It's going to be really hot and all the gardens on the street smell of cut grass and barley water, the sky completely blue.

We turn into the park and he slips out of our hands.

'You've forgotten the bread,' I shout, but he just keeps on running towards the pond.

'It's the slide he likes,' says Louise.

'He's getting big, isn't he?'

'Yeah.'

And we sit on the swings among the quiet and gentle nature, the ducks and the butterflies, the sandstone buildings and black hills watching us from above the trees, waiting.

I reach across and take her hand, give it a squeeze.

'Should have gone to Flamingo Land or somewhere. Scarborough or Whitby.'

'It's difficult,' she says.

'Sorry,' I say, remembering.

'No, you're right. We should do though.'

And Bobby comes down the slide on his belly, his shirt all up and his tummy out.

'Getting a paunch like his dad,' I say.

But she's miles away.

Louise is in the queue for the fish stall, Bobby tugging my arm to come and look in the toy shop window, to come and look at the Lone Ranger and Tonto.

All around us, a Friday.

And the sky is still blue, the flowers and the fruit bright, the telephone box red, the old women and the young mothers in their summer dresses, the ice-cream van white.

All around us, a market day.

Louise comes back and I take the shopping bags and we walk back up Kingsway, Bobby between us, a hand for both of us, back home.

All around us, a summer's day.

A Yorkshire summer's day.

Louise cooks the lunch while Bobby and I play with his car and bricks, his Action Man and Tonka Toy, his Lego and teddies, the Royal Flotilla coming down the Thames on the TV.

We eat fish in breadcrumbs, drenched in parsley sauce and ketchup, with chips and garden peas, and jelly for pudding, Bobby wearing his dinner medals with pride.

After, I do the dishes and Louise and Bobby dry, the TV off before the news.

Then we have a cup of tea and watch Bobby showing off, dancing on the settee to an LP of Bond themes.

On the drive over to Leeds, Louise and Bobby sit in the back and Bobby falls asleep with his head in her lap, the sun baking the car, the windows open, listening to Wings and Abba, Boney M and Manhattan Transfer.

We park round the back and I lift Bobby out and we walk round to the front of the hospital, the trees in the grounds almost black in the sun, Bobby's head hanging over my shoulder.

In the ward we sit on tiny hard chairs, Bobby still asleep across the bottom of his Grandad's bed, as Louise feeds her father tinned tangerines on a plastic spoon, the juice dribbling down his unshaven face and neck and over his striped Marks & Spencer pyjamas, while I make aimless trips to the trolley and the toilet and flick through women's magazines and eat two Mars Bars.

And when Bobby wakes up about three, we go out into the grounds, leaving Louise with her father, and we run across the bouncy grass playing Stop and Go, me shouting, 'Stop,' him shouting, 'Go,' the pair of us laughing, and then we go from flower to flower, sniffing and pointing at all the different colours, and when we find a dandelion clock we take it in turns to blow away the time.

But when we go back upstairs, tired and covered in grass stains, she's crying by the bed, him asleep with his mouth open and his dry cracked tongue hanging out of his bald shrunken head, and I put my arm round her shoulder and Bobby rests his head upon her knees and she squeezes us tight.

On the drive back home, we sing nursery rhymes with Bobby and it's a pity we had fish for lunch because we could have stopped at Harry Ramsden's for a fish supper or something.

*

We bath Bobby together, him splashing about in the bubbles, drinking the bathwater, crying when we take him out, and I dry him and then carry him up to our room and I read him a story, the same story three times:

'*Once upon a time there was a rabbit, a magic rabbit who lived on the moon.*'

And half an hour later I say:

'*Magic telescope, magic telescope, please show me Yorkshire . . .*'

And this time he doesn't make a telescope with his hands, this time he just makes wet smacking sounds with his lips, and I kiss him night-night and go downstairs.

Louise is sitting on the settee watching the end of *Crossroads*.

I sit down next to her, asking, 'Anything good on?'

She shrugs, '*Get Some In*, that *XYY Man* thing you like.'

'Is there a film?'

'Later, I think,' and she hands me the paper.

'*I Start Counting*?'

'Too late for me.'

'Yeah, should have an early night.'

'What time you on tomorrow?'

'John was going to call.'

Louise looks at her watch. 'You going to call him?'

'No, I'll just go in for seven.'

We sit and watch Max Bygraves, Bobby's toys between us.

And later, in the adverts before *World in Action*, I say, 'Do you think we can get over this?'

'I don't know love,' she says, staring at the TV. 'I don't know.'

And I say, 'Thanks for today.'

I must have fallen asleep because when I wake up she's gone and I'm on the settee alone, *I Start Counting* ending, and I turn off the TV and go upstairs, get undressed and get into bed, Bobby and Louise beside me, sleeping.

In my dream I was sitting on a sofa in a pink room. A dirty sofa with three rotting seats, smelling worse and worse, but I couldn't stand.

And then in the dream I was sitting on a sofa in a playing field. A horrible sofa with three rusty springs, cutting into my arse and thighs, but I couldn't stand, couldn't get up.

And then in the dream I was sitting on a sofa on wasteground. A terrible sofa thick with blood, seeping up into my palms and nails, but I still couldn't stand, still couldn't get up, still couldn't walk away.

Caller: *That little girl in Luton, the four-year-old that was raped and murdered? You see they got a lad of twelve for it? Bloody twelve years old.*

John Shark: *Unbelievable.*

Caller: *And all papers can go on about is the Royal bloody Flotilla and Yorkshire Ripper.*

John Shark: *There's no end to it is there?*

Caller: *Yeah there is. There's the end of the world, that's what there is. The end of the bloody world.*

The John Shark Show
Radio Leeds
Saturday 11th June 1977

Chapter 14

I swung my legs over the edge of the bed and started to pull on my trousers.

It was dawn, grey and wet, Saturday 11 June 1977.

The dream hung like a lost ghost across her gloomy backroom, a dream of bloodstained furniture and fair-haired coppers, crime and punishment, holes and heads.

Again, bruised from sleep.

The windows rattled with the rain, my stomach with them.

I was an old man sitting on a prostitute's bed.

I felt a hand on my hip.

'You don't have to go,' she said.

I turned back round to the bed, to the sallow face on the pillow, and I leant in to kiss her, taking off my trousers again.

She pulled the sheet over us and opened her legs.

I put my left thigh between them, her damp on the skin and hair of my leg as I ran my hand through her hair, feeling again for the mark that he'd left.

I drove back to Leeds through morning traffic and continued showers, the radio keeping her at bay:

Widespread flooding expected, John Tyndall – the leader of the National Front – punched, 3,287 policemen left without a pension or gratuity, journalists' strike to intensify.

When I reached the dark arches, I switched off the engine and sat in the car thinking of all of the things I wanted to do to her, a cigarette burning down to the skin just below my nail.

Bad things, things I'd never thought of before.

I stubbed out the cigarette.

The office, empty.

Bored, I picked up today's paper and re-read my inside piece:

THE VICTIMS OF A BURNING HATE?
Background by Jack Whitehead

It's becoming an all-too-familiar scene for the luckless residents of the so-called 'red light' district of Chapeltown, Leeds:

A mobile police command post, a towering radio mast, a noisy generator, cordoned-off roads, detectives with clipboards knocking on doors, and children peeping through curtains at endless blue lights.

The fifth woman savagely murdered in the middle of the night in the last two years, the fourth within a two-mile radius, was immediately marked down as the latest victim of a killer who has become known as Yorkshire's own 'Jack the Ripper'.

Rachel Johnson, sixteen, like the others, was savagely attacked. Like two of the earlier victims her body was found in a playground-type area, a place for fun and games, and Rachel was also only a few hundred yards from her home.

The major difference between Rachel, who only left school at Easter, and the previous victims was that the others were known prostitutes operating in the Chapeltown area.

But Rachel may have made the same fatal mistake as the others – accepting a lift in a stranger's car after an evening out – something the police say they have repeatedly warned against since the first of the murders in June 1975.

The first prostitute victim of a man the police believe is a psychopath with a burning hatred of women was a 26-year-old mother of three, Mrs Theresa Campbell, of Scott Hall Avenue, Chapeltown.

A milkman on his early morning rounds found Mrs Campbell's partly-clothed bloodstained body on the Prince Philip Playing Fields, only 150 yards from her home where her three young children were anxiously waiting for their mummy to return from 'work'.

She had been savagely stabbed to death.

Five months later on the other side of the Pennines, Clare Strachan, a 26-year-old mother of two, was brutally beaten to death in Preston, a crime police now consider to be the work of the same psychopath.

Just three months later, in February 1976, Mrs Joan Richards, a 45-year-old mother of four, also met a brutally violent death, this time in a little-used Chapeltown alley.

Mrs Richards, who lived at New Farnley, had been beaten brutally about the head and repeatedly stabbed.

Then, less than two weeks ago, 32-year-old Marie Watts of Francis Street, Chapeltown, was found dead on Soldier's Field, Roundhay Park, with her throat cut and several stab wounds to her stomach. She had been depressed and was running away from her boyfriend.

Mrs Campbell was last seen trying to thumb a lift in Meanwood Road, Leeds, just after 1 a.m. on the morning of her death. She is known to have visited earlier the Room at the Top club in Sheepscar Street.

On the night Mrs Richards was murdered she had visited the Gaiety Public House, Roundhay Road, with her husband. She left him in the early evening and he never saw her again.

The Gaiety was also one of the last places Marie Watts was seen alive.

Yesterday, police again renewed their appeal for any member of the public with information to come forward.

The telephone numbers of the Murder HQ at Millgarth Police Station are Leeds 461212 and 461213.

'Happy?'

I turned round, Bill Hadden in his Saturday sports jacket was looking over my shoulder.

'Butchered. And I never used *savagely* and *brutally* so many times, did I?'

'More.'

I handed him a folded piece of paper from my pocket. 'You going to do the same to this?'

Millgarth, about ten-thirty.

Sergeant Wilson on the desk:

'Here comes trouble.'

'Samuel,' I nodded.

'And what can I do you for this fine and miserable June morning?'

'Pete Noble in, is he?'

He looked down at the log on the counter.

'No. Just missed him.'

'Fuck. Maurice?'

'Not these days. What was it about?'

'I'd arranged with George Oldman to see some files. Clare Strachan?'

Wilson looked down at the book again. 'Could try John Rudkin or DS Fraser?'

'They about, are they?'

'Hang on,' he said and picked up the phone.

He came down the stairs to meet me, young, blond and from before.

He paused.

'Jack Whitehead,' I said.

He shook my hand. 'Bob Fraser. We've met before.'

'Barry Gannon,' I said.

'You remember?'

'Hard to forget.'

'Right,' he nodded.

Detective Sergeant Fraser looked short of sleep, lost for words, old before his time, but mainly just plain lost.

'You've done well for yourself,' I said.

He looked surprised, frowning, 'How do you mean?'

'CID. Murder Squad.'

'Suppose so,' he said and glanced at his watch.

'I'd like to talk to you about Clare Strachan, if you have time?'

Fraser looked at his watch again and repeated, 'Clare Strachan?'

'See, I spoke with George Oldman a couple of days ago and we arranged for Chief Superintendent Noble to show me the files, but . . .'

'They're all in Bradford.'

'Right. So they said if John Rudkin or yourself wouldn't mind . . .'

'Yeah, OK. You better come up.'

I followed him up the stairs.

'It's all a bit chaotic,' he was saying, holding open the door
to a room of metallic filing cabinets.

'I can imagine.'

'If you want to wait here for a minute,' he pointed at two
chairs under a desk, 'I'll just go and get the files.'

'Thanks.'

I sat down facing the cabinets, the letters and the numbers,
and I wondered how many of the enclosed I'd written about,
how many I'd filed away in my own drawer, how many I'd
dreamt about.

Fraser came back kicking open the door with his foot, a large
cardboard box in his arms.

He put it down on the table:

Preston, November 1975.

'This is everything?' I said.

'From our end. Lancashire have the rest.'

'I spoke with Alf Hill. He seems sceptical?'

'About a link? Yeah, I think we all were.'

'Were?'

'Yeah, were,' he said, knowing we both knew about the
letters.

'You're convinced?'

'Yeah.'

'I see,' I said.

He nodded at the box, 'You don't want me to talk you
through all this, do you?'

'No, but I was hoping you might know what these mean?'
and I handed him the two file references from Preston:

23/08/74 – WKFD/MORRISON-C/CTNSOL1A

22/12/74 – WKFD/MORRISON-C/MGRD-P/WSMT27C

He stared down at the letters and the numbers, pale, and
said, 'Where did you get these?'

'From the Clare Strachan file in Preston.'

'Really?'

'Yes. Really.'

'I've never seen them before.'

'But you know what they refer to?'

'No, not specifically. Just that they're file references from
Wakefield, to a C. Morrison.'

'You don't know any C. Morrison then?'

'Not off the top of my head, no. Should I?'

'Just that Clare Strachan sometimes went by the name
Morrison.'

He stood there, staring down at me, cold blue eyes drowning
in hurt pride.

'I'm sorry,' I said, watching the walls come up, keys turn in
the locks. 'I didn't mean to . . .'

'Forget it,' he muttered, like he never would.

'I know I'm pushing it, but would it be possible for you to
check on these?'

He pulled the other chair out from under the table, sat down
and picked up the black phone.

'Sam, it's Bob Fraser. Can you put us through to Wood
Street?'

He put the phone down and we sat in silence, waiting.

The phone rang and Fraser picked it up.

'Thanks. This is Detective Sergeant Fraser at Millgarth, I'd
like a check on two files please.'

A pause.

'Yes, Detective Sergeant Fraser at Millgarth. Name's Morrison, initial C. First one is 23–8–74, Caution for Soliciting 1A.'

Another pause.

'Yep. And the next one is Morrison, C again. 22–12–74,
Murder of a GRD-P, Witness Statement 27C.'

Pause.

'Thanks,' and he hung up.

I looked up, the blue eyes staring back.

He said, 'They'll call me back in ten minutes.'

'Thanks for doing this.'

Fiddling with the paper, he asked, 'You got these from
Preston?'

'Yeah, Alf Hill showed me a file. He said she was a prostitute,
so I asked him if she'd had any convictions and he showed me
a typed sheet. Just this written on it. You been over there?'

'Last week. And he told you she went by the name Morrison?'

'No, only time I ever saw it was in the *Manchester Evening News*, said she was originally from Scotland and also went by the name Morrison.'

'*Manchester Evening News*?'

'Yeah,' and I handed him the cutting from my pocket.

The phone rang and we both jumped.

Fraser put the cutting on the desk and read as he picked up the receiver.

'Thanks.'

Pause.

'Speaking.'

Another pause, longer.

'Both of them? Who was that?'

Pause.

'Yeah, yeah. Our arse from our elbow. Thanks.'

He hung up again, still staring down at the cutting.

'No luck?' I said.

'They're here,' he said, looking up at the box. 'Or at least they should be. Can I keep this?' he asked, holding up the cutting.

'Yeah, if you want.'

'Thanks,' he nodded and upended the box, files spilling over the desk.

I said, 'You want me to go?'

'No, be my guest,' he said, adding, 'Eventually all this'll be on the National Police Computer, you know?'

'Think it'll make a difference?'

'Bloody hope so,' he laughed, taking off his jacket as we started the search until, ten quiet minutes later, everything was back inside the box and the desk was bare.

'Fuck,' and then, 'Sorry.'

'Don't worry,' I said.

'I'll call you if anything comes of it,' he said and stood up. 'It was just a bit of background, that was all.'

We walked back downstairs and at the bottom he said again, 'I'll give you a ring.'

At the door we shook hands and he smiled and suddenly I said, 'You knew Eddie didn't you?'

And he dropped my hand and shook his head, 'No, not really.'

Back across the haunted city, ghosts on every corner, drinking in working-class packs, the morning gone, the day sliding away.

I stood before the Griffin and looked up at her scaffold face, at the dark windows in the grey floors above, wondering which black hole was his.

I went inside, into the lounge with its empty high-backed chairs and dim light, and I went up to the front desk and rang the bell and waited, heart beating heavy and fast.

In the mirror above the desk I watched a little boy lead an old woman with a walking stick across the lounge.

I'd seen them before.

They sat down in the same two chairs that Laws and I had seven days before.

I went over and pulled up a third chair.

They said nothing but rose as one to sit at the next table.

I sat alone in my silence and then stood up and went back to the desk and rang the bell for a second time.

In the mirror I watched the child whisper to the old woman, the pair of them staring at me.

'Can I help you?'

I turned back to the desk, to the man in the dark suit.

'Yes, I was wondering if Mr Laws, Martin Laws is in?'

The man glanced at the wooden boxes behind him, at the dangling keys, and said, 'I'm afraid Reverend Laws is out at the moment. Would you care to leave a message?'

'No, I'll come back later.'

'Very good, sir.'

'I'd met him before.'

'When was that?' asked Hadden.

'He was the one who was here over Barry.'

'Right,' sighed Hadden, right back there. 'What a terrible time.'

'Not like now,' I said, and we both said nothing until he handed me a piece of paper.

'I think you'll find I spared the knife,' he smiled.

I sat down across the desk from him and read:

AN OPEN LETTER TO THE RIPPER

Dear Ripper

You have killed five times now. In less than two years you have butchered four women in Leeds and one in Preston. Your motive, it is believed, is a dreadful hatred of prostitutes, a hate that drives you to slash and bludgeon your victims. But, inevitably, that twisted passion went terribly wrong on Tuesday night. An innocent sixteen-year-old lass, a happy, respectable, working-class girl from a decent Leeds family, crossed your path. How did you feel when you learned that your bloodstained crusade had gone so horribly wrong? That your vengeful knife had found so innocent a target? Sick in mind though you undoubtedly are, there must have been some spark of remorse as you tried to rid yourself of Rachel's bloodstains.

Don't make the same mistake again, don't put another innocent family through this hell.

End it now.

Give yourself up now, safe in the knowledge that only care and treatment awaits you, no rope or electric chair.

Please, for Rachel's sake, turn yourself in and stop these terrible, terrible murders.

From the People of Leeds.

'What do you think?'

'George seen it?'

'We spoke on the phone.'

'And?'

'Worth a shot he said.'

'He's not had a change of heart about publishing the other half of the correspondence?'

Hadden shrugged, 'What do you think?'

'I've thought about it a lot actually, and I think he's making a mistake. One that'll come to haunt him. And us.'

'In what way?'

'The last one, it contained a warning right?'

'Yes.'

'Well, when he kills again and it comes out that we had a letter, a fucking warning letter, I don't think the Great British Public'll be too impressed that we didn't see fit to share that warning with them.'

'He's got his reasons.'

'Who? George? Well I hope they're bloody good ones.'

Bill Hadden was staring at me, pulling at his beard. 'What is it Jack?'

'What do you mean?'

'What is it?'

'Just his fucking arrogance.'

'No, it's not. I know you too well. There's something else.'

'Just this whole business. Just the Ripper. The letters . . .'

'Seeing Sergeant Fraser can't have helped?'

'No, it was good actually.'

'Brings it all back though?'

'It never goes away, Bill. Never goes away.'

It was night when I left the office and went for the car, a black wet summer's night.

I drove over the Tingley Roundabout and down through Shawcross and Hanging Heaton, down to the Batley Variety Club.

It was Saturday night and the best they could come up with were the New Zombies, unable to compete with the shows on the piers.

I parked, wished I was drunk, and walked across the car park to the canopy that covered the entrance.

I paid and went inside.

It was half-empty and I stood at the bar with a double Scotch, watching the long dresses and cheap tuxs and checking the time.

Down the front a skinny woman in a low-cut pink dress that swept the floor was already drunk and arguing with a fat man and his moustache, leaning in to shout and show a bit of tit.

The man slapped her arse and she threw a drink and tipped a plate down him.

It was ten-thirty.

'Enjoying the wildlife, Mr Whitehead?'

A young man in a black suit and skinhead was at my elbow, a carrier bag in his left hand.

'You're one up on me,' I said.

I'd seen him before, but I was fucked if I knew where.

'Sorry. No names.'

'But we've met before, I think?'

'No, we haven't. You'd remember.'

'OK, whatever you say. Do you want to sit down?'

'Why not?'

I ordered a round and we went over to a booth near the back.

He lit a cigarette and tilted his head back, sending smoke up to the low ceiling tiles.

I sat there, watching the crowd until I asked him: 'Why here?'

'Police eyes can't see me.'

'They looking?'

'Always.'

I took a big bite out of my Scotch and waited, watching him twisting his jewellery, making smoke rings, the carrier bag on his lap.

He leant forward, a smile wet on his thin lips, and hissed, 'We can sit here all night. I'm in no hurry.'

'So why are the police looking?'

'What I got in here,' he said, patting the plastic bag. 'What I got here is big fucking news.'

'Well, let's have a look . . .'

He pressed the palm of his hand into his forehead, 'No. And don't fucking rush me.'

I sat back in my seat. 'OK. I'm listening.'

'I hope so, because when this thing breaks it's going to rip the fucking lid off this whole place.'

'You mind if I take some notes then?'

'Yes, I do. I do fucking mind. Just listen.'

'OK.'

He stubbed out his cigarette, shaking his head to himself. 'I've had dealings with you people before and, believe me, I had some serious doubts about meeting you, about giving you this stuff. I still do.'

'You want to talk money first?'

'I don't want any fucking money. That's not why I'm here.'

'OK,' I said, sure he was lying, thinking *money, attention, revenge*. 'You want to tell me why you are here then?'

His eyes were moving through the people as they came in, saying, 'When you listen to what I'm going to say, when you see what's in here, then you'll understand.'

Attention.

I pointed to the empty glasses. 'You want another?'

'Why not?' he nodded and I signalled to the barmaid.

We sat there, saying nothing, waiting.

The barmaid brought over the drinks.

The house lights dimmed.

He leant forward, glancing at his watch.

I leant in to meet him, like we were going to kiss.

He spoke quickly but clearly:

'Clare Strachan, the woman they say the Ripper did in Preston, well I knew her. Used to live round here, called herself Morrison. She was mixed up with some people, not very nice people, people I am very fucking afraid of, people I never ever want to meet again. Understand?'

I sat there nodding, saying nothing, nodding, thinking lots:
Revenge.

The lights at the front changed from blue to red and back again.

His eyes danced across the room and back to me.

'I made a lot of mistakes, got in way over my head, I think she must have done the same.'

I stared straight ahead, the band about to come on.

He tipped his Scotch into his pint.

'You say, she must have. Why?' I said. 'What makes you think that?'

He looked up from his pint, head on his lips, and smiled. 'She's dead, isn't she?'

From the front of the stage a man in a velvet dinner jacket bellowed into a loud microphone:

'Ladies and gentlemen, boys and girls, they say we're dying, say we're dead and buried, well they said the same about these boys but here to prove them wrong, back from the dead, from beyond the grave, the living dead themselves, please give a big Yorkshire Clubland welcome to the New Zombies!'

The blue curtain went up, the drums started, and the song began.

'*She's Not There,*' said the skinhead, looking at the stage.

'I wouldn't know,' I said.

He turned back to me. 'Spot of late night reading,' he said and passed the bag under the table.

I took it and started to open it.

'Not here,' he snapped, nodding to the side: 'Bogs.'

I got up and walked through the empty tables, glancing back at the pale youth in the black suit, head bobbing to the keyboards from the stage.

'Give you hand if you want,' he called after me.

I shut the cubicle door and closed the toilet lid, sat down and opened the plastic bag.

Inside was another bag, a brown paper bag.

I opened the brown bag and pulled out a magazine.

A nack mag, pornography.

Cheap pornography.

Amateurs:

Spunk.

The corner of one page was folded down.

I turned to the marked page and there she was:

White hair and pink flesh, wet red holes and dry blue eyes, legs spread and flicking her clit.

Clare Strachan.

I was hard.

I was hard and she was dead.

I came out of the toilets, back into the ballroom, the skinny woman in the long pink dress dancing alone in front of the stage, one hundred stark albino faces staring back at the bar where four coppers were talking to the barmaid, pointing at our empty table.

Two of the police suddenly ran outside.

The other two were looking at me.

I had the bag in my hands.

I was afraid, really fucking scared, and I knew why.

The policemen walked through the tables, coming towards me, getting nearer.

I started back the other way towards my table.

I felt a hand on my elbow.

'Can I help you?' I asked.

'The gentleman who was at your table, do you know where he might have gone?'

'I'm sorry, no. Why?'

'Would you mind stepping outside for a moment, sir?'

'No,' I nodded, letting myself be led through the tables, the band still playing, the pink lady still dancing, the ghosts still watching me.

Outside it was raining again and we stood together, the three of us under the canopy.

The two policemen were both young and nervous, unsure: 'May I have your name please, sir?'

'Jack Whitehead.'

The one looked at the other. 'From the papers?'

'Yep. Do you mind if I ask what this is about?'

'The man who was at your table, we believe he may have stolen that Austin Allegro over there.'

'Well I'm sorry Officer, but I wouldn't know anything about that. Don't even know his name.'

'Anderson. Barry James Anderson.'

Bells ringing, peeling back the years.

The two other policemen were coming back across the car park, wet and out of breath.

'Fuck,' said the older of the two, head down, hands on his knees.

'Who we got here?' asked the other.

'Says he's Jack Whitehead from the *Post*.'

The fat, older copper looked up, 'Fuck me it is and all. Talk of the bloody devil.'

'Don,' I said.

'Been a while,' he nodded.

Not nearly fucking long enough, I was thinking, the day complete; this plagued day of blighted visions and wretched memory, no stones unturned, no bones still sleeping, the dead abroad, wrought from the living.

'This is Jack Whitehead,' Sergeant Donald Humphries was saying, the rain heavy on the canopy above our heads. 'It was him and me who found that *Exorcist* job that night I was telling you about.'

Yeah, I thought, like he ever talked about anything but that night, like for a moment he understood the things we saw that night, that night we stood before the hills and the mills, before the bones and the stones, before the living and the dead, that night Michael Williams lay naked in the rain upon his lawn and cradled Carol in his arms and stroked her bloody hair for one last time.

But maybe I was doing him a disservice, for the smile went behind a clouded face and he shook his head and said, 'How've you been Jack?'

'Never better. And yourself?'

'Can't complain,' he said. 'What brings you to this neck of the woods?'

'Bit of supper,' I said.

He pointed to the bag in my hand and smiled, 'Spot of shopping and all?'

'Less than 200 days to Christmas, Don.'

I drove back, hitting eighty.

I did the steps in a heartbeat, opened the door, boots off and on to the bed, opened the mag, glasses on and into Clare:

Spunk.

Issue 3 – January 1975.

I turned it over, nothing.

I opened up the inside, something:

Spunk is published by MJM Publishing Ltd. Printed and Distributed by MJM Printing Ltd, 270 Oldham Street, Manchester, England.

I went over to the telephone and dialled Millgarth.

'Detective Sergeant Fraser please.'

'I'm afraid Sergeant Fraser went off – '

Telephone down, back to the bed, back to – Carol, striking Clare's pose.

'This what you like?'

'No.'

'This what your dirty little Chinese bitch does?'

'No.'

'Come on, Jack. Fuck me.'

I ran into the kitchen, opened the drawer, took out the carving knife.

She had her fingers up her cunt, 'Come on, Jack.'

'Leave me alone,' I shouted.

'You're going to use that are you?' she winked.

'Leave me alone.'

'You should take it Bradford,' she laughed. 'Finish what he started.'

I flew across the room, the knife and a boot in my hands, on to the bed, battering her head, her white skin streaked red, her fair hair dark, everything sticky and black, laughter and screams until there was nothing left but a dirty knife in my hand, grey hairs stuck to the heel of my boot, drops of blood across the crumpled colour spread of dear Clare Strachan, fingers wet and cunt red.

My fingers were turning cold, dripping blood.

I'd cut my hand on the carving knife.

I dropped the knife and boot and put a thumb to my skull and felt the mark I'd made:

I suffer your terrors; I am
desperate.

I turned and there she was.

'I'm sorry,' I wept.

Carol said, 'I love you, Jack. I love you.'

John Shark: *So you didn't reckon much to Royal Flotilla then Bob?*

Caller: *Bloody weather let us down and all.*

John Shark: *But them fireworks. They were a bit special . . .*

Caller: *Oh aye, but my point is how many folks these days, how many remember King George's Jubilee?*

John Shark: *When was that then Bob?*

Caller: *See what I mean? Nineteen-thirty-five it was John, nineteen-bloody-thirty-five.*

The John Shark Show
Radio Leeds
Sunday 12th June 1977

Chapter 15

In the dream I was sitting on the sofa again, on the wasteground, the sofa thick with blood, the blood seeping into my clothes and into my skin and next to me, sat beside me, was that journalist Jack Whitehead, blood running down his face, and I looked down and Bobby was on my knee in his blue pyjamas holding a big black book and he started to cry, and I turned to Jack Whitehead and said, 'It wasn't me.'

She's asleep on the big hard chair next to mine, Bobby back home with next doors.

I get up to go, knowing he's going to die, knowing it'll be the minute I'm gone, but knowing I can't stay, can't stay knowing:

Knowing I've got to find those files, find those files to find him, find him to stop him, stop him to save her, save her to end these thoughts.

Knowing I've got to end these thoughts of Janice.

Knowing I've got to end these thoughts of Janice, end these thoughts of Janice to end everything, end everything to start again HERE.

Here with my wife, here with my son, here with her dying father.

My new deal, new prayer:

Stop him to save her,

Save her to start again.

To start again.

HERE.

She opens her eyes.

I nod morning and apologies.

'What time did you get here?' she whispers.

'After I knocked off, about eleven.'

'Thanks,' she says.

'Bobby with Tina?' I ask.

'Yeah.'

'She mind?'

'She'd say if she did.'

'I've got to go,' I say, looking at my watch.

She moves to let me pass, then catches my sleeve and says, 'Thanks again, Bob.'

I bend down and kiss the top of her head. 'See you later,' I say.

'See you,' she smiles.

I drive from Leeds to Wakefield, the M1 Sunday morning quiet, radio loud:

Eighty-four arrested outside the Grunwick Processing Laboratories in Willesden. The Metropolitan Police accused of unnecessary brutality, aggressive and provocative tactics.

I park on Wood Street, another shower starting, not a soul to be seen.

'Bob Fraser, from Millgarth.'

'And what can I do for you, Bob Fraser from Millgarth?' asks the Sergeant on the desk as he hands back my card.

'I'd like to see Chief Superintendent Jobson, if he's about?'

He picks up the phone, asks for Maurice, tells him it's me, and sends me up.

I knock twice.

'Bob,' says Maurice, on his feet, hand out.

'Sorry to barge in like this, without ringing.'

'Not at all. It's good to see you Bob. How's Bill?'

'Just come from the hospital actually. Not much change though.'

He shakes his head. 'And Louise?'

'Bearing up as ever. Don't know how she does it.'

And we slip into a sudden silence, me seeing that taut boned body in its striped pyjamas sipping tinned fruit off a plastic spoon, seeing him and Maurice, the Owl, with his thick lenses and heavy rims, the pair of them taking thieves, pulling villains, breaking skulls, cracking the A1 Shootings, getting famous,

Badger Bill and Maurice the Owl, like something out of one of Bobby's books.

'What's on your mind, Bob?'

'Clare Strachan.'

'Go on,' he says.

'You know Jack Whitehead? He gave me these, got them off Alf Hill in Preston,' and I hand him the Wakefield file references.

Maurice reads them, looks up and asks, 'Morrison?'

'Clare Strachan's other name.'

'Right, right. Her maiden name, I think.'

'You knew?'

He pushes the frames up the bridge of his nose, nodding. 'You pulled them?'

Less sure, I hesitate and then say, 'Well, that's half of why I'm here.'

'What do you mean?'

'They've been pulled.'

'And?'

I swallow, fidget, and say, 'This is between us?'

He nods.

'John Rudkin took them.'

'So?'

'They're not in her file at Millgarth. And he's never even mentioned them.'

'You spoken to him?'

'I haven't had chance. But there's another thing as well.'

'Go on.'

I take another deep one. 'I went over to Preston with him a couple of weeks ago, and we went through all the files.'

'About Clare Strachan?'

'Yeah, and we were to take copies back. Anything we didn't have, anything we might have missed. And, anyway, I saw one of the files he was taking back and he'd taken the originals, not copies.'

'Could've been a mistake?'

'Could have been, but it was the Inquest.'

'The Coroner's Report?'

'Yeah, and the blood grouping looked wrong. Like it had been typed in later.'

'What did it say?'

'B.'

'And you think Rudkin had altered it?'

'Maybe, I don't . . .'

'When you were over there the last time?'

'No, no. He went over after we got Joan Richards.'

'But why would he want to change it? What would be the point?'

'I don't know.'

'So what are you saying?'

'I'm just saying it looked wrong. And one way or another he knows it's wrong.'

Maurice takes off his glasses, rubs his eyes, and says, 'This is serious, Bob.'

'I know.'

'Really bloody serious.'

He picks up the phone:

'Yes. I'd like a check on two files, both Morrison, initial C. First one is 23rd August 1974, Caution for Soliciting 1A. Second one is 22nd December 1974, Witness Statement 27C, Murder of GRD initial P.'

He puts down the phone and we wait, him cleaning his specs, me biting a nail.

The phone rings, he picks it up, listens and asks:

'OK. Who by?'

The Owl is staring at me as he speaks, unblinking:

'When was that?'

He's writing on the top of his Sunday paper.

'Thanks.'

He puts down the phone.

I ask, 'What did they say?'

'A DI Rudkin signed them out.'

'When?'

'April 1975.'

I'm on my feet: 'April 1975? Fuck, she wasn't even dead.'

Maurice stares down at his newspaper, then looks up, eyes rounder and wider and larger than ever:

'GRD-P,' he says. 'You know who that is?'

I slump back down in my chair and just nod.

'Paula Garland,' he says to himself, the mind behind the glasses off and scuttling along the corridors down to his own little hells.

I can hear the Cathedral bells.

Palms up, I ask, 'What are we going to do?'

'We? Nothing.'

I start to speak, he raises a hand and gives me a wink: 'Leave it to your Uncle Maurice.'

For the second time in a week I park between the lorries of the Redbeck car park, though I can't remember much about the last time I was here.

Just the pain.

Now I just feel hungry, starving.

That's what I'm telling myself it is.

I go into the cafe, buy a sausage and chip sandwich and two cups of hot sweet tea.

I take them out and round to Room 27.

I open the door and go inside.

The air is old and cold, the smell of sweat and fear, death everywhere:

I stand in the dark centre of the room and I want to rip the soiled grey sheets down, pull the mattress from the window, burn the photos and the names from the walls, but I don't.

I sit on the base of the bed and think about the dead and the missing, the missing and the dead:

Missing the dead.

I drive back to Leeds with a splitting headache, the sandwich cold and uneaten on the passenger seat.

I switch on the radio:

Yes Sir I Can Boogie.

I think about what I want to say to Rudkin, think about all

the weird shit he's said that now makes sense, think about all the shit I think he's done, all the shit I know he's done.

I park and walk into Millgarth –

into running bodies, shouts and boots, jackets on and tearing off, thinking:

There's been another:

JANICE.

'Fraser! Thank fucking Christ,' shouts Noble.

'What?'

'Get over to Morley, Gledhill Road.'

'What?'

'There's been another.'

'Who?'

'Another fucking post office.'

'Shit.'

And bang, just like that I'm back on Robbery.

Mr Godfrey Hurst looks like someone's sewn oranges into his skin, all the holes in his face swollen shut.

'Heard the knock,' he's trying to say. 'Came down the stairs and I opened the back door and thwack! Reckon they must have shoved door back in my face. Next news I'm on the floor then thwack! Reckon they must have kicked me in the head.'

'That's when I came down,' says Mrs Doris Hurst, bird-thin, sheet-white, still stinking of piss. 'I screamed and then one of them slapped me right hard across my face and then he put bag on my head and tied me up.'

Around us, parents are bringing in children with broken limbs and bleeding skins, nurses leading the injured and the worried back and forward through Casualty, everyone crying.

'Believe it or not,' I say as I take down what they're saying. 'Believe it or not, you're both very lucky.'

Mr Hurst squeezes his wife's hand and tries to smile, but he can't, he can't because of the stitches, all thirty-five of them.

I ask, 'How much did they get away with?'

'About seven hundred and fifty quid.'

'Is that a lot for you?'

'We never used to have anything at all over weekend, but Post Office they've stopped collecting on Saturdays.'

'Why's that then?'

'Cuts, I suppose.'

I turn back to Mrs Hurst. 'You get a look at them?'

'Not really, they were wearing masks.'

'How many were there?'

She shakes her head and says, 'I just saw two, but I had feeling there were more.'

'Why did you think that?'

'Voices, the light.'

'This was about what time?'

Mr Hurst says, 'About seven-thirty. We were getting ready for Church.'

'And you said there was something about the light, Mrs Hurst?'

'Just that kitchen looked dark, so I thought maybe there were more than two.'

'And can you remember what they were saying?'

'One was telling other to go upstairs.'

'Did you hear any names or anything?'

'No, but after they'd put bag on my head and tied me up, they seemed angry like, that there wasn't more money, angry with someone.'

'Can you remember exactly what they said?'

'Just that . . .' she purses her lips. 'Exactly?'

'I'm sorry. It's important.'

'One of them said that someone had, you know, *fucked up*,' Mrs Hurst blushes and then adds, 'Excuse me.'

'And what did the other one say?'

'Well, that's what I mean. I think there was a third voice and he said that they'd deal with it later.'

'A different voice?'

'Yes, deeper, older. You know, like he was boss.'

I look at Mr Hurst, but he shrugs, 'I was out cold. Sorry.'

I turn back to Mrs H and ask her, 'These voices, where do reckon they were from?'

'Local, definitely local.'

'Anything else?'

She looks at her husband and then, slowly, shaking her head, says, 'I think they were, you know, black men.'

'Black men?'

'Mmm, I think so.'

'Why's that?'

'Size. They were big and their voices, they just sounded like black men's voices.'

I keep writing, wheels turning.

Then she says, 'That or they were gypsies.'

I stop writing, wheels braking.

A nurse comes up, plain but pretty. 'The doctor says you can both go home now if you want.'

Mr and Mrs Hurst look at each other and nod.

I close my notebook and say, 'I'll give you a lift.'

We turn into Gledhill Road, Morley, my old stomping ground and I'm thinking Victoria Road's not far, wondering if they remember Barry Gannon, certain they remember that Clare Kemplay lived on Winterbourne Avenue, wondering if they were out that night looking for her, then thinking I must remember to call Louise, tell her I'll probably be late, thinking maybe we can work this out, and that's what I'm thinking when I see the squad cars parked in front of the post office, still thinking that when I see Noble and Rudkin getting out of the first car, that's what I'm thinking when I turn to Mr Hurst and say, 'It wasn't me,' that's what I'm thinking when it gets really fucked up, forever, and –

Part 4
What's my name?

Caller: *And all the cannabis they were taking off darkies they were nicking, this other copper he was selling back to other dealers, and I read this copper who was doing it, he was something to do with A10, that lot that are now Complaints Division.*

John Shark: *Hold on, hold on. What's this got to do with the man with the baboon's heart?*

Caller: *Nothing, I suppose.*

John Shark: *Fair enough. All right, seeing as how you're on the line, is there anything you want to say about this man, the one in South Africa who's been given a baboon's heart?*

Caller: *No, not really. Except I think it's not right and he's going to die.*

The John Shark Show
Radio Leeds
Sunday 12th June 1977

Chapter 16

– I turn and ask Mr Hurst where it's best to park and the wife is looking sideways at him, us pulling up next to the squad cars, the Hursts looking at the three big men coming towards our car, us stopping there in the middle of the street, me getting out, Mr Hurst too, Mrs Hurst her hand to her mouth and me turning, straight into Rudkin's fist, Noble and Ellis pulling him off, me reeling, coming back, him another arm loose and smashing it into me with a low kick to my balls and then there are some uniforms dragging me back by my jacket and bundling me into the back of a tiny Panda, Rudkin still screaming, 'You cunt, you fucking cunt!' and our car pulls off and I turn and watch them push Rudkin head down into a car, Ellis and Noble in behind him, my car sitting there in the middle of Gledhill Road, doors open, Mr and Mrs Hurst shaking their heads, hands on hips or at their lips.

The uniforms drive me into Leeds, into Millgarth, no-one speaking, lots of glances in the mirror, me with a wink, wondering what the fuck Maurice must have said, bracing myself for Complaints and the love of my Brother Officers.

Inside, the uniforms take me straight down to the Belly, the whole station deserted. They sit me down in one of the cells we use for interrogations and close the door. I look at my watch, it's gone six, Sunday 12 June 1977.

Thirty minutes later I get up and try the door.
It's locked.

Another thirty minutes later and the door opens.
Two uniforms who I've never seen before come in.
One of them hands me a pale blue shirt and pair of darker blue overalls and says, 'Can you change into these please, sir.'
'Why?'

'Can you just do it, sir.'

'Not until you tell me why.'

'We need your clothes to run some tests.'

'What kind of tests?'

'I'm sorry, sir, but I don't know.'

'Well, can you please get someone who does.'

'I'm afraid there are no senior officers on duty.'

'I'm a bloody senior officer.'

'I know, sir.'

'Well then, until someone can be good enough to tell me why I should hand over my bloody clothes to you, you can go and fuck yourself.'

The uniforms shrug and leave, locking the door behind them.

Ten minutes later the door opens again and four uniforms come in, grab my arms and legs, gag me and strip me.

Then they remove the gag and toss the shirt and overalls at me and leave, locking the door behind them.

I lie naked on the floor and look at my watch, but it's gone.

I get up and put on the shirt and overalls, sit down at the table and wait, aware something's gone wrong.

Very wrong.

I look up, the door opening.

Detective Superintendents Alderman and Prentice come in.

They pull up two chairs and sit down opposite me:

Dick Alderman and Jim Prentice.

They don't look well.

Not happy.

'Bob?' says Prentice.

'What's going on?' I ask.

'Thought you might be able to tell us that?'

'Come on,' I say, looking from one to the other. 'You here to question me?'

'Chat,' winks Prentice.

'Fuck off,' I say. 'This is me, Bob Fraser. If something's going down, just tell me.'

'It's never as simple as that though, is it Bob?' says Jimmy Prentice and he offers me a fag.

I shake my head: 'I don't know, Jim. You tell me.'

They look at each other and sigh.

I say, 'This is to do with John Rudkin, isn't it?'

Dick Alderman shakes his head. 'All right, Bob. Cut the crap and just tell us what happened to you between six o'clock the night of Saturday 4 June and six o'clock on the morning of Wednesday 8 June?'

'Why?'

He smiles, 'You do remember?'

'Of course I fucking remember.'

'Well that's a bloody start, because up to now no other cunt seems to have a fucking clue.'

I pause and then say, 'I was with Rudkin and Ellis.'

Prentice smiles. 'That's what they said.'

I start to speak, smiling, relieved and eager to expand.

But Alderman leans forward, 'Yeah, that's what they *said*. Up until about half-three this afternoon, that is. Just before they were both suspended from their duties. Just before they vowed to kick your fucking head in, next time they see you.'

I stare at him, at the face full of pride at the way he's stuck the boot in, and I shrug my shoulders.

He smiles, a bloated smile: 'What you say now, Bobby?'

I turn to Prentice. 'You think I need someone from the Fed here?'

He shrugs: 'Depends what you been up to Bob, depends what you done.'

'Nothing.'

Alderman stands up. 'You might want to have a think about that,' he says. 'Before we come back.'

And they leave, locking the door behind them.

The door opens, I look up.

Detective Superintendents Alderman and Prentice come in.

They sit down in the two chairs opposite me.

Dick and Jim.

They look better.

But not happy.

'Bob?' nods Prentice.

I say, 'Just tell us what's going on, will you?'

'We don't know, Bob. That's why we're here.'

'To find out,' adds Alderman.

'Find out what?'

'Find out what you got up to between Saturday night and Wednesday morning.'

'What if I was to tell you that I went home? That I was with my wife?'

Alderman looks at Prentice.

Prentice says: 'Is that what you're saying?'

'Yeah,' I nod.

And they leave again, locking the door behind them.

The door opens.

Detective Superintendents Alderman and Prentice come in.

They don't sit down.

Richard Alderman and James Prentice.

They look really fucked off.

Not happy.

'Fraser,' says Alderman. 'I'm going to ask you for the last time: what you did, where you went, and who you saw between Saturday night and Wednesday morning?'

'And don't fucking lie to us, Bob,' Prentice is saying. 'Please, Bob?'

I look at them, the pair of them leaning over me, staring down at me, knowing they'd have beaten the truth out of me by now if I wasn't who I was, what I was.

'I was drinking,' I say, say quietly and slowly.

They pull the chairs back and sit down.

'And what should you have been doing?' asks Alderman.

'I was supposed to be on surveillance with Rudkin and Ellis.'

'OK. So what were you doing?'

'Like I say, I was drinking.'

'Where?'

'In my car, in the park.'

'You see anyone?'

'No.'

But I'm starting to see Karen Burns and Eric Hall, knowing I'm fucked.

'I'm going to ask you again,' says Alderman. 'You see anyone, anyone at all during this time?'

'No.'

'OK,' nods Alderman. 'You want to tell us why you were drinking when you were supposed to be watching a suspect in a murder investigation; an investigation into the murders of four women that now, on one of the nights that you were supposed to be tailing our prime fucking suspect, now has risen to include the murder of a sixteen-year-old virgin.'

I'm staring at the table-top.

'You going to tell me why you were drinking?'

'Domestic problems,' I whisper.

'Would you care to elaborate?'

'Not really, no.'

Prentice says, 'It goes no further, Bob.'

'Bollocks,' I laugh. 'It'll be on other side of Moors before breakfast.'

'You got no bloody choice,' says Alderman.

'The fuck I have. I want to know what this is about?'

'You can fuck off,' spits Alderman. 'I am asking you as a senior officer, asking you why you were drinking for eighty-four hours, eighty-four fucking hours when you were supposed to be on duty?'

'And I've already told you, I had domestic problems.'

'And I'm telling you that answer will not suffice. So I'll ask you one last time, what kind of fucking domestic problems?'

We stare into each other's purple faces, eyes wide and teeth barred.

Prentice leans forward, tapping the table-top: 'Come on, Bob. This is us.'

'And this is me, Jim. This is me.'

He nods and Alderman follows him out, locking the door behind them.

About another half-hour later, the door opens.

Detective Superintendents Alderman and Prentice come in, three teas between them.

They sit down and push a tea across the table.

They look tired.

Not happy, resigned.

Jim Prentice says, 'Bob? I'm going to ask you again just to give us a bit more about this domestic problem. It'd help us a lot. Help you.'

'How?'

'Bob, we're all policemen here. All on the same side. If you don't start helping us out a bit, then we'll have to turn it over to another crew. And no-one wants that, do they?'

'But you're not going to tell us what this is about?'

'Bob, how many more times? We already have. It's about what you were up to in them "missing hours"?'

I pick up the cigarette Alderman's chucked down beside my tea and lean forward to let him light it.

I sit back in the chair, the smoke curling up to the low ceiling, my head with it, until finally I say:

'I was having an affair with another woman.'

Alderman sniffs up, disappointed: 'Was? Past tense?'

'Yeah.'

'Why's that?' he asks.

'She left.'

'What's her name, this woman?'

I look up at the ceiling again and weigh up the odds.

'Janice Ryan,' I say.

'When did you last see her?'

'Saturday morning.'

'What time?'

'About eight.'

'And that's why you were drinking?'

'Yeah.'

'Because she left you?'

'Yeah.'

'Does your wife know?'

'Know what?'

'That you had a bit on the side?'

'No.'

'Is there anything more you want to tell us about your relationship with this other woman?'

'No.'

'Thanks, Bob,' says Jim Prentice and they leave, locking the door behind them.

I look up, the room dark.

The door opens, men rush in and hood me and handcuff me.

They take me from the room, up the stairs, out to the night, into the back of a car, and then we go for a drive.

No-one's speaking and the car smells of alcohol and cigarettes.

I'm guessing, but I think there are three other men in the car; two in the front and one next to me on the back seat.

About thirty minutes later we leave the road and pull up on what feels like wasteland.

The door opens and they take me out of the car, leading me across uneven ground.

I stumble once and someone hooks an arm through mine.

We stop and stand still for a moment, then they take off the hood.

Blinded by lights, I blink, blink, blink.

It's night at the edges, white light at the core.

Noble, Alderman, and Prentice are standing before me, under the floodlights, the bright alien floodlights.

Centre-stage, a sofa.

A horrible, terrible, rotting, eaten, bloody sofa.

'You been here before?' asks Noble.

I'm staring at the sofa, the rusted metal springs sharpened to spikes, the velvet almost gone.

'You know where you are?' Prentice asks.

I look up at them, the angel glow around their faces, and I shake my head.

Again Alderman asks, 'You been here before or not?'

And I have; in those nightmares, this is where I'd come, and so I'm nodding, saying, 'Yes.'

And Noble lunges forward and punches me in the jaw and I fall to my knees, tears running down my cheeks, blood filling my mouth, the lights out.

Dark eyes, dark eyes that would not open.

Indian skin painted red, white, and blue, with welts, pus, and bruises.

Dark eyes, dark eyes turned back in death.

Indian skin painted murder, lonely murder.

A slap and I'm awake, sat in a chair in a cell, hood and handcuffs gone.

'Look at her!' Noble is yelling.

I try and focus on the table-top.

'Look at her!'

Noble is standing, Alderman seated.

I pick up the photograph, the enlarged black and white photograph of her face, her swollen lids and risen lips, her blackened cheeks and matted hair, and I'm shaking, shaking, then puking, puking across the table, hot yellow bile all over the room.

'Aw Christ, for fuck's sake.'

I'm in a clean pair of overalls and shirt.

Noble and Alderman are sat across from me, three hot teas on the table.

Alderman sighs and reads from a piece of typed A4:

'At 12 noon Sunday 12th June, the body of Janice Ryan, twenty-two years old, a convicted prostitute, was found secreted under an old settee on wasteground off White Abbey Road, Bradford.

'A post-mortem has been carried out and death was due to

massive head injuries caused by a heavy blunt instrument. It is thought that death occurred some seven days before due to the partial decomposition of the body.

'It is also thought from the pattern of the injuries that this death is not connected, repeat not connected, with the other murders publicly referred to as the *Ripper Murders*.'

Silence.

Then Noble says, 'She was found by a kid. Saw her right arm sticking out from under the couch.'

Silence.

Then I say, tears not dry, 'And you think I did it?'

Silence.

Then Noble nods and says, 'Yeah, and this is how I think you did it: I think you drove her out to Bradford, took her on to wasteground, hit her on head with a rock or stone, then you jumped up and down on her until you broke her ribs and ruptured her liver. You didn't have a knife on you, but you thought you'd try and make it look like a Ripper job, so you pulled up her bra and pulled down her panties, took off her jeans, then dragged her by her collar over to couch and dumped it on top of her, then you threw her handbag away and pissed off.'

Silence.

Then I say, 'But why?'

'Forensics, Bobby,' says Alderman. 'We got her all over your clothes, you all over hers, you're in her flat, under her fucking nails and up her bloody cunt.'

'But why? Why would I kill her?'

Silence.

'Bob, we know,' says Alderman, glancing at Noble.

'Know what?'

'She was pregnant,' he winks.

Silence, until Noble says:

'And it was yours.'

I'm screaming, my hands pinned to the table, Alderman and Prentice trying to sit me back down, Noble walking away.

Screaming over and over, again and again:

'Ask him, ask Eric fucking Hall. Get him in here. It wasn't me. It wasn't fucking me. I'd never.'

Cuts that won't stop bleeding, bruises that won't heal.

'Ask him, ask that fucking cunt. He did it, I know he fucking did. It wasn't me. I'd never. I couldn't.'

Screaming over and over, again and again.

I'm choking, head in an arm-lock, Alderman and Prentice trying to sit me down, Noble gone.

'Thing is,' says Noble, 'Eric says that Janice called him for protection. Protection from you.'

'Bollocks.'

'OK, so how come he knows she's pregnant by you if she never called him?'

'She called him for money. She was his grass until he started pimping her.'

'Bobby, Bobby, Bobby. This is going in fucking circles.'

'Look, I've told you. You're not listening. That last Saturday I saw her, the 4th, she'd been over to Bradford and was supposed to meet Eric but he sent a van for her and they picked her up and fucking did her didn't they?'

'Did her?'

'Raped her. Ask Rudkin and Mike. They came round her place to pick me up, they saw state she was in.'

'Yeah, yeah, and they seem to think that it was you who did it.'

'Did what?'

'Beat the fucking living shit out of her.'

'Bollocks. Fucking bollocks.'

'You're all over her, mate.'

'Course I am, I fucking loved her.'

'Bob . . .'

'Listen to me, I'd wake up in bed next to my wife with come in my pyjamas, come all over me because I couldn't stop fucking dreaming about her.'

'Jesus Christ, Fraser.'

*

Alone –
> *Alone together:*
> *I shut my eyes, you call my name.*
> *A cigarette, a plastic cup, a porno mag.*
> *The shoes on the wrong feet, the laces gone.*
> *Fingers round my throat, fingers down my throat.*
> *Fingers under skull skin, fingers at my temple bones.*
> *You shut your eyes, I call your name:*
> *Alone together –*
> *Alone.*

'You going to charge me?'

Prentice pushes the tea towards me, 'Drink it, Bob.'

'Just tell me.'

'It doesn't look good, not good at all.'

'I didn't do it, Jim. I didn't do it.'

'Drink your tea, Bob. Before it gets cold.'

Black piss-holes stained with sleep, down white corridors stuffed full of memories to a bloody pillow stuffed full of albatross feathers, glimpsing happy days through windows and doors as they closed, to a table and three chairs beneath a bulb caged in mesh.

'Let's start at the beginning again.'

I push the plastic cup forward and sigh, 'Whatever.'

'When did you meet her?' asks Noble, lighting up.

'Last year.'

'When?'

'4 November.'

'Mischief Night?'

I nod, no smiles.

'Where?'

'She was in middle of road outside Gaiety, pissed. She looked to be soliciting, so we picked her up.'

'We?'

'Me and Rudkin.'

'Detective Inspector Rudkin?'

'Yeah, Detective Inspector Rudkin.'

'And?'

'Brought her in here. Found out she was covered by Eric Hall over at Jacob's Well and . . .'

'Detective Inspector Eric Hall?'

'Yeah, Detective Inspector Eric Hall.'

'So what did you do when you found that out?'

'I drove her home.'

'Alone?'

'Yeah.'

'And that's when it started?'

'Yeah.'

'And how often did you see her?'

'Often as I could.'

'Which was?'

I shrug: 'Every other day. Got easier when Eric set her up over here in Chapeltown.'

'So you're saying Eric Hall, Detective Inspector Eric Hall, set up a convicted prostitute in a flat in Leeds?'

I nod.

'Why the fuck would he do that?'

'Ask him.'

Noble slams his palm down on to the table. 'Fuck off, Fraser. I'm asking you.'

'She told me it was like a thank you. Golden handshake.'

'And you believed her?'

'At the time.'

'But . . .'

'But I've since heard that he was pimping her and he'd got her the flat to set her up over here.'

'How did you find that out?'

'Joseph Rose, he's listed on record as my P.I.'

Noble glances at Alderman.

Alderman nods at Prentice.

Prentice gets up and leaves the room.

Noble looks up from his notes. 'OK. So for almost a year, beginning last November, you continued to meet Ryan?'

'Yes.'

'And this was usually at her flat on Spencer Place?'

'From January, yeah.'

'And during this time you were unaware that she was working for DI Hall?'

'As a prostitute, yes. But I knew she still phoned him.'

'But you knew she was working as a prostitute?'

'Yeah, just not for him.'

'So who did you think she was working for?'

'Kenny D.'

'Kenny D? That fucking nig-nog we had in here over Marie Watts, you're taking piss?'

'No.'

'Jesus Christ, Fraser. You thought your girlfriend was working for him?'

'Yeah.'

'Why?'

'What she said. What he said.'

Noble pauses, swallows, and says, 'So if you thought she was working for Kenny D, why did you think she kept phoning DI Hall?'

'To get money out of him.'

'How?'

'Selling stuff she'd heard.'

'Did she try and sell you stuff?'

'No. She wasn't that well connected round here.'

'Did she get money off him?'

'I don't know. Ask him.'

Noble is staring at me, eyes locked again. 'So you're saying your relationship with this woman, Janice Ryan, it was purely for sex?'

I look up at the ceiling, the earth tilting.

Cuts that won't stop bleeding, bruises that won't heal.

I stare back at Noble and I shrug my shoulders and I tell him how it was: 'Yes,' I say.

'Did you pay for it?'

Eyes locked, I tell him how it is: 'Looks that way,' I say. 'Fucking looks that way now.'

Silence.

Prentice comes back in and the three of them go into a huddle.

I wonder what time it is, unable even to guess what fucking day it is.

They return to their places and Noble says, 'OK, who else knew about this relationship?'

'Me and Janice?'

'Yes.'

'I don't know. I didn't tell folk, but did you know? Did you Jim? Did you Dick?'

They don't smile, they just keep it shut.

'OK,' says Noble again. 'But by the start of this month you say your relationship with Ryan had deteriorated?'

'Yeah.'

'In what way?'

'I hadn't been able to see so much of her, what with Ripper and everything, and I wanted her to stop working.'

'Why was that?'

'I didn't want her fucking dead, did I?'

'Why was that?'

'Fuck off.'

'But you didn't mind her fucking other blokes?'

'Course I fucking did.'

'So why didn't you do owt about it?'

But I catch myself, just in time:

Cuts that won't stop bleeding, bruises that won't heal.

And I smile, 'I couldn't say so bloody much could I?'

'Why was that?'

'I'm married, aren't I?'

'But you were arguing a lot, you and Ryan?'

'On and off, yeah.'

'OK, so tell us about that last Saturday, the 4th.'

'I've told you a million times.'

'Well it won't hurt to tell us one last time then, will it Bob?'

'I went round on Friday and she wasn't in. I was knackered, put my head down for a bit at her place, and waited.'

'So you had a key?'

'You know I did. You fucking took it, didn't you?'

'OK, go on.'

'About 7, maybe 8, she came home . . .'

'In the morning?'

'Yeah, in the morning. She was in a bad way, she'd been tied up, whipped, bitten. There were marks across her breasts, her stomach, her backside. She said she'd been over to Bradford, Manningham, to meet Eric Hall. Said she got picked up by Vice, or that's what she thought. There were four of them; they raped her, took photos.'

'And did they, these men, they know anything about you or DI Hall?'

'Apparently.'

'Apparently?'

'She said they called Eric Hall, tried to call me. Whatever Eric said, it didn't stop them.'

'And she told you all this on the Saturday morning at her flat?'

'Yes.'

'Then?'

'Then DI Rudkin and DC Ellis came and picked me up, because of the attack on Linda Clark, and they brought me here.'

'They picked you up at her place?'

'Yeah.'

'Right, so how come they knew where to find you?'

'I don't know. I presume because they knew about me and Janice.'

'But you'd never told them?'

'No.'

'And that was the last time you saw Ryan?'

'Yes.'

'But you went back to the flat?'

'Yeah, a couple of times.'

'On the Saturday?'

'Yeah, I went back to the flat straight after the briefing.'

'And?'

'And she'd gone.'

'Gone for good?'

'Mmm.'

'How did you know?'

'She'd taken most of her gear.'

'She leave a note?'

Cuts that won't stop bleeding, bruises that won't heal.

'No,' I lie.

'And what time was that?'

'About five on the Saturday afternoon.'

'And so you were upset?'

'Yes, I was.'

'So instead of returning to your assigned duties and your colleagues, you decided to drown your sorrows.'

'Yeah.'

'And during this time who did you see?'

'I saw Joseph Rose.'

'And this was when he told you about Detective Inspector Eric Hall pimping Janice?'

'Yes.'

'So what did you do?'

'I went over to Bradford to see him.'

'And when was this?'

'I'm not sure, but I think it was Monday.'

'And that was when you assaulted DI Hall?'

'That's when we had the fucking fight, if that's what you mean?'

'About Ryan?'

'Yes.'

'Then what did you do?'

'I took his car . . .'

'DI Hall's car?'

'Yeah.'

'And where did you go?'

'I just drove around, I don't remember where exactly.'

'But eventually you ended up back in Chapeltown, just as the body of Rachel Johnson was discovered?'

'Yeah, I think I went back to Janice's flat, and when I woke up there was all the shit going on because of the Johnson girl.'

'OK. One last thing; until today you're saying you had no idea that Ryan was pregnant and that you were the father?'

'That's correct.'

'And that the reason forensics have got you all over her, it's because of the last time you had sexual relations with her, with Ryan?'

'Yes.'

'Which would have been when?'

'Possibly Thursday 2nd June.'

'But you have no alibi for anytime between 5 p.m. on Saturday 4th June and the morning of Wednesday 8th?'

'Except for when I saw Joseph Rose and later Eric Hall, no.'

'But you're unsure exactly when it was you saw them?'

'Yes.'

Silence.

Noble is staring at me.

'You do realise the fucking shit you're in?'

I look up, the veins in my eyes shards.

'Yes,' I say.

He doesn't blink.

'The shit we're all in?'

I nod.

'All right then,' he sighs. 'It's your call.'

I weigh it up, the arms of my body dead.

Cuts that won't stop bleeding, bruises that won't heal.

'I'd like to see my solicitor, please.'

John Shark: *See John Poulson got himself an early parole?*

Caller: *And on same day George Davis ends up back inside.*

John Shark: *One law for them, one law for us, eh Bob?*

Caller: *No, John. There's no bloody law for them, that's trouble.*

The John Shark Show
Radio Leeds
Monday 13th June 1977

Chapter 17

'There's something strange going on,' said Hadden.

'Like what?'

'They reckon there's been another and that they've only bloody got someone for it. Holding them.'

'You're joking?'

'No.'

'Ripper?'

'What it looks like.'

'Bollocks. Who told you this?'

'A little bird.'

'How little?'

'Stephanie.'

'And she got it from?'

'Desk at Bradford.'

'Fuck.'

'That's almost what I said.'

'What do you want me to do?'

'Make some calls.'

Fuck.

Back at the desk, I picked up the telephone and dialled Millgarth.

'Samuel?'

'Jack?'

'What's going on?'

'I don't know what you could mean.'

'Oh yes you do.'

'Oh no I don't.'

'OK. What time you going to stop playing silly buggers and start earning yourself a bit of what makes you happy?'

'In about half an hour?'

I looked at my watch.

Shit.

'Where?'

'The Scarborough?'

'It's a date,' and I hung up.

I looked at my watch again, checked my briefcase, and left.

I was the first in the Scarborough.

I put my pint on top of the telephone and dialled.

'It's me.'

'Just can't keep away, can you?' she laughed.

'Not if I can help it.'

'It's only been a couple of hours.'

'And I miss you.'

'Me too. Thought you were going to Manchester?'

'I am, maybe. Just thought I'd give you a ring.'

'That'd be nice.'

I laughed and said, 'Thanks for the weekend.'

'No, thank you.'

'I'll call you when I get back.'

'I'll be waiting.'

'Bye then.'

'Bye, Jack.'

She hung up first and then I put down the telephone, picked up my pint and went to a copper-topped table over in the corner.

I had a hard-on.

I looked at my watch, wanting to make the twelve-thirty train at the latest.

If they hadn't caught the cunt, that was.

I could hear the rain lashing the windows.

'Call this bloody summer,' said the barman across the room.

I nodded, drained my pint and went back to the bar and ordered two bitters and a packet of salt and vinegar.

Back at the table I looked at my watch again.

'Best not be flat,' said Sergeant Samuel Wilson, sitting down.

'Fuck off,' I said.

'And a merry bloody Christmas to you too,' he laughed, then said, 'What fuck happened to your hand?'

'Cut myself.'

'Fuck were you doing?'

'Cooking.'

'Fuck off.'

I offered him a crisp. 'So?'

'What?'

'Samuel?'

'Jack?'

'Fuck off, it's not *Come* bloody *Dancing* is it?'

He sighed. 'Go on, what you heard?'

'You got a body in Bradford and a bloke for it over here.'

'And?'

'It's Ripper.'

Wilson killed his pint and grinned, cream on his lips.

'Samuel?'

'How about another, Jack?'

I finished mine and went back to the bar.

When I sat back down, he'd taken off his raincoat.

I glanced at my watch.

'Not keeping you am I, Jack?'

'No, got be over in Manchester this afternoon though.' Then I added, 'Depending on what you tell me. If you're going to tell me anything that is?'

He sniffed up, 'So how much is a busy man like you prepared to give a poor working man like myself?'

'Depends what you got, you know how it works.'

He took out a piece of folded paper and waved it in front of me. 'Internal memo from Oldman?'

'Twenty?'

'Fifty.'

'Fuck off. I'm just confirming what I've already heard. If you'd come straight to your old mate Jack yesterday, then that'd be a different story wouldn't it?'

'Forty.'

'Thirty.'

'Thirty-five?'

'Show us.'

He handed me the paper and I read:

At twelve noon Sunday 12 June, the body of Janice Ryan, twenty-two years old, a convicted prostitute, was found secreted under an old settee on wasteground off White Abbey Road, Bradford.

A post-mortem has been carried out and death was due to massive head injuries caused by a heavy blunt instrument. It is thought that death occurred some seven days before due to the partial decomposition of the body.

It is also thought from the pattern of the injuries that this death is not connected, repeat not connected, with the other murders publicly referred to as the Ripper Murders.

At the present time no information is to be given to the press in regard to this crime.

I stood up.

'Where you going?'

'It's him,' I said and walked over to the telephone.

'What about my thirty-five quid?'

'In a minute.'

I picked up the telephone and dialled.

Her telephone rang, and rang, and rang:

Warn whores to keep off streets cause I feel it coming on again.

I hung up and then dialled again.

Her telephone rang, and rang, and –

'Hello?'

'Where were you?'

'In the bath, why?'

'There's been another.'

'Another?'

'Him. In Bradford. Same place.'

'No.'

'Please, don't go out. I'll be over later.'

'When?'

'As soon as I can. Don't go out.'

'OK.'

'Promise?'

'Promise.'

'Bye.'

And she hung up.

I walked back across the pub, visions of bloodstained furniture, holes and heads:

I have given advance warning so its yours and their fault.

I sat down.

'You all right?'

'Fine,' I lied.

'Don't look it.'

'So they got someone?'

'Yep.'

'Who?'

'Fuck knows.'

'Come on?'

'Straight up. No-one knows, just brass.'

'Why all the secrecy?'

'I tell you, fuck knows.'

'But they're saying it's not Ripper?'

'That's what they're saying.'

'What you reckon?'

'Fuck knows, Jack. It's weird.'

'You heard owt else? Anything?'

'How much?'

'Call it an even fifty if it's good.'

'Couple of lads reckon some blokes have been suspended, but you didn't hear that from me.'

'Over this?'

'Aye, that's what a couple of lads here said.'

'From Millgarth?'

'That's what they said.'

'Who?'

'DI Rudkin, your mate Fraser, and DC Ellis.'

'Ellis?'

'Mike Ellis. Fat twat with a big gob?'

'Don't know him. And they reckon they did this woman in Bradford?'

'Now Jack, I didn't say that. They've just been suspended, that's all I know.'

'Fuck.'

'Aye.'

'You surprised?'

'Rudkin, no. Fraser, yes. Ellis, yeah but everyone hates him anyway.'

'Cunt?'

'Complete and utter.'

'But everyone knew Rudkin was dirty?'

'Lads don't call him Harry for nowt.'

'Fuck. What way?'

'When he worked Vice he was keeping more than streets clean.'

'And Fraser?'

'You met him; he's Mr fucking Clean. Owl's always helped him along and all.'

'Maurice Jobson? Why?'

'Fraser's married to Bill Molloy's daughter, isn't he?'

'Fuck,' I sighed. 'And Badger Bill's got cancer, yeah?'

'Aye.'

'Interesting.'

'If you say so,' shrugged Wilson.

I looked at my watch.

'Best put that away,' he said, pointing at the piece of paper on the table.

I nodded and put it in my pocket, taking out my wallet.

I counted out the notes under the table and handed him fifty.

'That'll do nicely, sir,' he winked and stood up to go.

'Anything at all, Samuel, give us a call?'

'You bet.'

'I mean it. If this is him, I want to know first.'

'Got you,' and he buttoned up his coat and was gone.

I looked at my watch and went to the telephone.

'Bill? Jack.'

'What you got?'

'It's strange, all right. Dead prostitute under a sofa in Bradford.'

'Told you, Jack. I told you.'

'But they're saying it's not a Ripper job.'

'So why are they keeping it from us?'

'I don't know but, and this is just what I reckon, somehow some of brass have fucked up and there's been some suspensions.'

'Really?'

'That's what rumour is round Millgarth.'

'Who?'

'That Sergeant Fraser for one. John Rudkin and someone else.'

'Detective Inspector John Rudkin? Over what?'

'Don't know. Might be nowt to do with this, but seems odd yeah?'

'Yeah.'

'I've got a bloke going to let us know first thing he hears.'

'Good. I'll have Front Page on standby.'

'But you best not say why.'

'You still going to Manchester?'

'I think so, yeah. But I'll come back via Bradford.'

'Keep in touch, Jack.'

'Bye.'

I sat on the train and smoked and drank a warm can, picked at a sandwich and flicked through a paperback book, *Jack the Ripper: the Final Solution.*

After Huddersfield I just dozed, bad ale and sleep to match, waking to the hills and the rain, hair stuck against a dirty window, drifting:

I look at my watch, it's 7.07.

I'm on the Moors, walking across the Moors, and I come to a chair, a high-backed leather chair, and there's a woman in white kneeling before the chair, hands in angel prayer, hair across her face.

I lean down to scoop the hair away and it's Carol, then Ka Su Peng. She stands up and points to the middle of the long white dress and a word in bloody fingerprints there writ:

livE.

And there on the Moors, in the wind and in the rain, she pulls the white dress up over her head, her yellow belly swollen, and then puts

*the dress back on, inside out, the word in bloody fingerprints there
writ:*

Evil.

*And a small boy in blue pyjamas comes out from behind the high-
backed leather chair and leads her away across the Moors and I stand
there in the wind and in the rain and I look at my watch and it's
stopped:*

7.07.

I woke, my head against the window, and looked at my
watch.

I picked up my briefcase and locked myself in the toilet.

I sat on the rocking bog and took out the porno mag.

Spunk.

Clare Strachan in all her bloody glory.

Hard again, I checked the address and went back to my seat
and the half-eaten cheese sandwich.

From Stalybridge into Manchester I tried to put all of
Wilson's shit together, re-reading Oldman's memo, wondering
what the fuck Fraser could have done, knowing suspensions
could be anything these days:

Back-handers and one-handers, dodgy overtime and faked
expenses, sloppy paperwork, no paperwork.

John bloody Rudkin leading Mr fucking Clean astray.

Clueless, I went back to the window, the rain and the fac-
tories, the local horror movies, remembering the photographs
of death camps my uncle had brought back from the war.

I'd been fifteen when that war ended and now, in 1977, I
was sat on a train, head against the black glass, the bloody rain,
the fucking North, wondering if this one ever would.

I was thinking of Martin Laws and *The Exorcist* when we
pulled into Victoria.

In the station, straight to a telephone:

'Anything?'

'Nothing.'

Out of Victoria, up to Oldham Street.

*

270 Oldham Street, dark and rain-stained, rotting black bin bags heaped up outside, MJM Publishing sat on the third floor.

I stood at the foot of the stairs and shook down my raincoat.

Soaked through, I walked up the stairs.

I banged on the double doors and went inside.

It was a big office, full of low furniture, almost empty, a door to another office at the back.

A woman sat at a desk near the back door, a bag, typing.

I stood at the low counter by the door and coughed.

'Yes?' she said, not looking up.

'I'd like to talk to the proprietor please?'

'The what?'

'The owner.'

'Who are you?'

'Jack Williams.'

She shrugged and picked up the old telephone on her desk:

'There's a man here wants to see the owner. Name's Jack Williams.'

She sat there, nodding, then covered the mouthpiece and said, 'What do you want?'

'Business.'

'Business,' she repeated, nodded again, and asked, 'What kind of business?'

'Orders.'

'Orders,' she said, nodded one last time, and then hung up.

'What?' I said.

She rolled her eyes. 'Leave your name and number and he'll call you back.'

'But I've come all way over from Leeds.'

She shrugged her shoulders.

'Bloody hell,' I said.

'Yep,' she said.

'Can I at least have his name?'

'Lord High and Bloody Mighty,' she said, ripping the piece of paper out of the typewriter.

I went for it: 'Don't know how you can work for a bloke like that.'

'I don't intend to for much longer.'

'You out of here then?'

She stopped pretending to work and smiled, 'Week next Friday.'

'Good on you.'

'I hope so.'

I said, 'You want to earn yourself a couple of quid for your retirement?'

'My retirement? You're no spring chicken yourself, you cheeky sod.'

'A couple of quid to tide you over?'

'Only a couple?'

'Twenty?'

She came over to the front of the office, a little smile. 'So who are you really?'

'A business rival, shall we say?'

'Say what you bloody well want for twenty quid.'

'So you'll help me out?'

She glanced round at the door to the back office and winked, 'Depends what you want me to do, doesn't it?'

'You know your magazine *Spunk*?'

She rolled her eyes again, pursed her lips, and nodded.

'You keep lists of the models?'

'The *models*?'

'You know what I mean.'

'Yeah.'

'Yeah?'

'Yeah.'

'Addresses, phone numbers?'

'Probably, if they went through the books but, believe me, I doubt they all did.'

'If you could get us names and anything else on models that'd be great.'

'What you want them for?'

I glanced at the back office and said, 'Look, I sold a job lot of old *Spunks* to Amsterdam. Got a bloody bomb for them. If

your Lordship is too busy to earn himself a cut, then I'll see if
I can't set myself up.'

'Twenty quid?'

'Twenty quid.'

She said, 'I can't do it now.'

I looked at my watch. 'What time you finished?'

'Five.'

'Bottom of stairs at five?'

'Twenty quid?'

'Twenty quid.'

'See you then.'

I stood in a red telephone box in the middle of Piccadilly Bus
Station and dialled.

'It's me.'

'Where are you?'

'Still in Manchester.'

'What time you coming home?'

'Soon as I can.'

'I'll wear something pretty then.'

Outside, the rain kept falling, the red box leaking.

I'd been here before, this very box, twenty-five years before,
my fiancée and I, waiting for the bus to Altrincham to see her
Aunt, a new ring on her finger, the wedding but one week away.

'Bye,' I said, but she'd already gone.

I stepped back into the sheets of piss and walked about
Piccadilly for a couple of hours, going in and out of cafés, sitting
in damp booths with weak coffees, waiting, watching skinny
black figures dancing through the rain, the lot of us dodging
the raindrops, the memories, the pain.

I looked at my watch.

It was time to go.

Going up to five, I found another telephone box on Oldham
Street.

'Anything?'

'Nothing.'

*

At five to five I was huddled at the bottom of the steps, ringing wet.

Ten minutes later she came down the stairs.

'I've got to go back up,' she said. 'I'm not finished.'

'Did you get the stuff?'

She handed me an envelope.

I glanced inside.

She said, 'It's all there. What there is.'

'I believe you,' I said and handed her twenty folded quid.

'Pleasure doing business with you,' she laughed, walking back upstairs.

'Bet it was,' I said. 'Bet it was.'

I went down to Victoria where they told me the Bradford train went from Piccadilly.

I ran up through the cats and the dogs and caught a cab for the last bit.

It was almost six when we got there, but there was a train on the hour and I caught it.

Inside, the carriage stank of wet clothes and stale smoke and I had to share a table with an old couple from Pennistone and their sweating sandwiches.

The woman smiled, I smiled back and the husband bit into a large red apple.

I opened the envelope and took out tissue-thin pieces of duplicate paper, three in all.

There were lists of payments, cash or cheque for February 1974 through to March 1976, payments to photoshops, chemists, photographers, paper mills, ink works, and models.

Models.

I ran down the list, out of breath:

Christine Bowen	*Teresa Lane*	*Mary Shore*
Catherine Macey	*Alison Wilcox*	*Marcella Oldroyd*
Susan Baker	*Jane O'Neill*	*Carolyn Ellis*
Tracy Olsen	*Sharon Pearson*	*Gaye Catton*
Nicola Knox	*Liz McDonald*	*Helen Mills*

Fiona Sutton	Heidi Toyer	Patricia Oscroft
Linda Shay	Michelle May	Mona Balston
Stephanie White	Melanie Freeman	Julie Toy
Jane Hogan	Emily Radford	Grace Dalgliesh
Barbara Miller	Jane Dixon	Sarah Raine
Clare Morrison	Jane Ryan	Sue Penn

Everything stopped, dead.
Clare Morrison, known to be Strachan.
Everything stopped.
I took out Oldman's memo:
Jane Ryan, read Janice.
Everything –
Sue Penn, read Su Peng.
Stopped –
Read Ka Su Peng.
Dead.
There on that train, that train of tears, crawling across those undressed hells, those naked little hells, those naked little hells all decked out in tiny, tiny bells, there on that train listening to those bells ring in the end of the world:
1977.
In 1977, the year the world broke.
My world:
The old woman across the table finishing the last sandwich and screwing up the silver foil into a tiny, tiny ball, the egg and cheese on her false teeth, crumbs stuck in the powder on her face, her face smiling at me, a gargoyle, her husband bleeding his teeth into that big red apple, this big red, red, red world.
1977.
In 1977, the year the world turned red.
My world:
I needed to see the photographs.
The train crawled on.
I had to see the photographs.
The train stopped at another station.
The photographs, the photographs, the photographs.

Clare Morrison, Jane Ryan, Sue Penn.

I was crying and I wanted to stop, wanted to pull myself together but, when I tried, the bits didn't fit.

Pieces missing.

1977.

In 1977, the year the world fell to bits.

My world:

Going under, to the sea-bed, better off dead, that evil, evil bed, those secret underwater waves that floated me up bloated, up from the sea-bed.

Beached, washed up.

1977.

In 1977, the year the world drowned.

My world:

1977 and I needed to see the photographs, had to see the photographs, the photographs.

In 1977, the year –

1977.

My world:

An imagined photograph.

Wear something pretty . . .

I didn't stop in Bradford, just changed trains for Leeds and sat on another slow train through hell, hell:

Hell.

In Leeds I ran through the black rain along Boar Lane, stumbling, through the precinct, tripping, on to Briggate, falling, into Joe's Adult Books.

'*Spunk*? Back issues?'

'By the door.'

'You got every issue?'

'I don't know. Have a look.'

On my knees, through the pile, stacking doubles to one side

and holding on to every different issue I came to, clutching their plastic wrappings.

'This it?'

'Maybe some in the back.'

'I want them.'

'All right, all right.'

'All of them.'

I stood there while Joe went into the back, stood there in the bright pink light, the cars outside in the rain, the blokes browsing, giving it to me sideways.

Joe came back, six or seven in his hands.

'That it?'

'You must have them all.'

I looked down and saw I'd got a good thirteen or fourteen.

'It still going?'

'No.'

'How much?'

He tried to take them from me but then said, 'How many you got there?'

I counted, dropping them and then picking them up, until I said, 'Thirteen.'

'Eight forty-five.'

I handed him a tenner.

'You want a bag?'

But I was gone.

In the Market toilets, the cubicle door locked, on the floor, ripping open plastic bags, tearing through the pages, through the pictures and the photographs, the photographs of bums and tits, cunts and clits, the hairy bits, the dirty bits, the bloody, bloody red bits, until I came – came to the yellow bits.

This is why people die.

This is why people.

This is why.

I stood upright in another box and dialled.

'George Oldman, please.'

'Who's calling?'

'Jack Whitehead.'

'Just a moment.'

I stood and waited inside the box.

'Mr Whitehead?'

'Yes.'

'Assistant Chief Constable Oldman's office is not accepting any more calls from the press. Could you please call Detective Inspector Evans on – '

I hung up and puked down the inside of the red telephone box.

On my bed, a bed of paper and pornography, in prayer, the telephone ringing and ringing and ringing, the rain against the windows falling and falling and falling, the wind through the frames blowing and blowing and blowing, the knocks on the door knocking and knocking and knocking.

'What happened to our Jubilee?'

'It's over.'

'To remission and forgiveness, an end to penance?'

'I can't forgive the things I don't even know.'

'I do, Jack. I have to.'

The telephone was ringing and ringing and ringing and she was still beside me on the bed.

I lifted up her head to free my arm, to stand.

Barefoot, I went to the telephone.

'Martin?'

'Jack? It's Bill.'

'Bill?'

'Christ, Jack. Where you been? All bloody hell's broken loose.'

I stood there in the dark, nodding.

'Turns out the dead prostitute in Bradford, it's only Fraser's bloody girlfriend and that it's him they're holding.'

I looked back over at the bed, at her still on the bed.

Jane Ryan, read Janice.

Bill was saying, 'Then Bradford got a letter from Ripper and they didn't say anything to Oldman or anyone and they've only gone and fucking printed it in the morning edition, and sold it on to *The Sun*.'

I stood there, in the dark.

'Jack?'

'Fuck,' I said.

'Shit creek, mate. You better come in.'

I dressed in the dawn light, the dim light, and left her still on the bed.

On the stairs, I looked at my watch.

It had stopped.

Outside, I walked down the road to the Paki shop on the corner and bought a *Telegraph & Argus*.

I sat on a low wall, my back in a hedge, and read:

RIPPER LETTER TO OLDMAN?

Yesterday morning the Telegraph & Argus received the following letter from a man claiming to be Yorkshire's Jack the Ripper killer.

Tests carried out by independent experts and information from reliable police sources lead us here at the Telegraph & Argus to believe that this letter is genuine, and not the first such letter this man has sent.

We here at the Telegraph & Argus, however, believe the British Public should have the right to judge for yourselves.

From Hell.

Dear George
I am sorry I cannot give my name for obvious reasons. I am the Ripper. I've been dubbed a maniac by the Press but not by you, you call me clever cause you know I am. You and your boys haven't a clue that photo in the paper gave me fits and that bit about killing myself, no chance. I've got things to do.

My purpose is to rid streets of them sluts. My one regret is that young lassie Johnson, did not know cause changed routine that nite but warned you and XXXX XXXXXXXXX at Post.

Up to number five now you say, but there's a surprise in Bradford, get about you know.

Warn whores to keep off streets cause I feel it coming on again.

Sorry about young lassie.

Yours respectfully

Jack the Ripper.

Might write again later I not sure last one really deserved it. Whores getting younger each time. Old slut next time hope.

The next headline:

DID THE POLICE AND THE POST KNOW?

I sat on the low wall, bile in my mouth, blood on my hands, crying.

This is why people die.

This is why people.

This is why.

Caller: They're going to let that bloody Neilson bloke, that Black Panther, going to let him appeal aren't they?

John Shark: You're against that are you Bob?

Caller: Well makes me laugh, it does. They're locking up all the sodding coppers and setting free bloody criminals.

John Shark: You reckon you'll notice?

Caller: Fair point, John. Fair point.

The John Shark Show
Radio Leeds
Tuesday 14th June 1977

Chapter 18

I open my eyes and say:

'I didn't do it.'

And John Piggott, my solicitor, stubs out his cigarette and says, 'Bob, Bob, I know you didn't.'

'So get me fucking out of here.'

I close my eyes and say:

'But I didn't do it.'

And John Piggott, my solicitor, a year younger and five stone fatter, says, 'Bob, Bob, I know.'

'So why the fuck do I have to report to Wood Street bloody Nick every fucking morning?'

'Bob, Bob, let's just take it and get you out of here.'

'But this means they can just pick me up any fucking time they want, haul me back in here.'

'Bob, Bob, they can anyway. You know that.'

'But they're not going to charge me?'

'No.'

'Just suspend me without pay and have me report in every fucking morning until they find a way to fit me up?'

'Yes.'

The Sergeant on the desk, Sergeant Wilson, he hands me my watch and the coins from my trousers.

'Don't be buying no tickets to Rio now.'

I say, 'I didn't do it.'

'No-one said you did,' he smiles.

'So keep it fucking shut, Sergeant.'

And I walk away, John Piggott holding the door open for me.

But Wilson calls after me:

'Don't forget: ten o'clock, tomorrow, Wood Street.'

*

In the car park, the empty car park, John Piggott unlocks the car door.

'Take a deep breath,' he says, doing just that.

I get into the car and we go, Hot Chocolate on the radio again.

John Piggott pulls up on Tammy Hall Street, Wakefield, just across from the Wood Street Police Station.

'I've just to nip in and get something,' he says and heads into the old building and up the stairs to his first-floor office.

I sit in the car, the rain on the windscreen, the radio playing, Janice dead, and I feel like I've been here before.

She was pregnant.

In a dream, in a vision, in a buried memory, I don't know which or where, but I know I've been here before.

And it was yours.

'Where to?' asks Piggott as he gets back in.

'The Redbeck,' I say.

'On the Doncaster Road?'

'Yeah.'

She lay down beside me on the floor of Room 27 and I felt grey, finished.

I close my eyes and she's under them, waiting.

She stood before me, her cracked skull and punctured lungs, pregnant, suffocated.

I open my eyes and rinse cold water over my face, down my neck, grey, finished.

John Piggott comes in with two teas and a chip sandwich.

It stinks out the room, the sandwich.

'Fuck is this place?' he asks, eyes this way and that.

'Just somewhere.'

'How long you had it?'

'It's not really mine.'

'But you got the key?'

'Yeah.'

'Must cost a bloody fortune.'

'It's for a friend.'

'Who?'

'That journalist, Eddie Dunford.'

'Fuck off?'

'No.'

I stepped out of the old lift and on to the landing.

I walked down the corridor, the threadbare carpet, the dirty walls, the smell.

I came to a door and stopped.

Room 77.

I wake and Piggott's still sleeping, wedged under the sink.

I count coins and head out into the rain, collar up.

In the lobby, under the on/off strip lighting, I dial.

'Speak to Jack Whitehead, please?'

'One moment.'

In the lobby, under the on/off lighting, I wait, everything gone quiet.

'Jack Whitehead speaking.'

'This is Robert Fraser.'

'Where are you?'

'The Redbeck Motel, just outside Wakefield on the Doncaster Road.'

'I know it.'

'I need to see you.'

'Likewise.'

'When?'

'Give us half an hour?'

'Room 27. Round the back.'

'Right.'

In the lobby, under the on and the off, I hang up.

I open the door, Piggott awake, bringing a bucket of rain in with me.

'Where you been?'

'Phone.'

'Louise?'

'No,' and know I should have.

'Who did you call?'

'Jack Whitehead.'

'From the *Post*?'

'Yeah. You know him?'

'Of him.'

'And?'

'The jury's still out.'

'I need a friend, John.'

'Bob, Bob, you got me.'

'I need all the bloody ones I can get.'

'Well, watch him. That's all.'

'Thanks.'

'Just watch him.'

There's a knock.

Piggott tenses.

I go to the door, say: 'Yeah?'

'It's Jack Whitehead.'

I open the door and there he is, standing in the rain and the lorry lights, a dirty mac and a carrier bag.

'You going to let me in?'

I open the door wider.

Jack Whitehead steps into Room 27, clocking Piggott and then the walls:

'Fuck,' he whistles.

John Piggott sticks out his hand and says, 'John Piggott. I'm Bob's solicitor. You're Jack Whitehead, from the *Yorkshire Post*?'

'Right,' says Whitehead.

'Have a seat,' I say, pointing at the mattress.

'Thanks,' says Jack Whitehead and we all squat down like a gang of bloody Red Indians.

'I didn't do it,' I say, but Jack's having trouble keeping his eyes off the wall.

'Right,' he nods, then adds: 'Didn't think you did.'

'What have you heard?' asks Piggott.

Jack Whitehead nods my way, 'About him?'

'Yeah.'

'Not much.'

'Like?'

'First we heard was there'd been another murder, in Bradford, everyone over there saying it was a Ripper job, his lot saying nothing, next news they'd suspended three officers. That was it.'

'Then?'

'Then this?' says Whitehead, taking a folded newspaper out of his coat and spreading it over the floor.

I stare down at the headline:

RIPPER LETTER TO OLDMAN?

At the letter.

'We've seen it,' says Piggott.

'Bet you have,' smiles Whitehead.

'A surprise in Bradford,' I whisper.

'Kind of puts you in the clear.'

'You'd think so, yeah,' nods Piggott.

Whitehead says, 'You think it was the Ripper?'

'Who killed her?' asks Piggott.

Whitehead nods and they both look at me.

I can't think of anything, except she was pregnant and now she's dead.

Both of them.

Dead.

Eventually I say, 'I didn't do it.'

'Well, I've got something else. Another hat for the ring,' says Whitehead and tips a pile of magazines out of his plastic carrier bag.

'Fuck's all this?' says Piggott, picking up a porno mag.

'*Spunk*. You heard of it?' Whitehead asks me.

'Yeah,' I say.

'How?'

'Can't remember.'

'Well, you need to,' he says and hands me a magazine open at a bleached blonde with her legs spread, mouth open, eyes closed, and fat fingers up her cunt and arse.

I look up.

'Look familiar?'

I nod.

'Who is it?' asks Piggott, straining at the upside-down magazine.

I say, 'Clare Strachan.'

'Also known as Morrison,' adds Jack Whitehead.

Me: 'Murdered Preston, 1975.'

'What about her? You know her?' he asks and hands me another woman, Oriental, black hair with her legs spread, mouth open, eyes closed, and thin fingers up her cunt and arse.

'No,' I say.

'Sue Penn, Ka Su Peng?'

Me: 'Assaulted Bradford, October 1976.'

'Give the boy a prize,' says Whitehead quietly and hands me another magazine.

I open it.

'Page 7,' he says.

I turn to page 7, to the dark-haired girl with her legs spread, her mouth open, her eyes closed, a dick in her face and come on her lips.

'Who is it?' Piggott's asking.

'I'm sorry,' says Jack Whitehead.

Piggott still asking: 'Who is it?'

But the rain outside, it's loud, deafening, like the lorry doors as they slam shut, one after another, in the car park, endlessly.

No food, no sleep, just circles:

Her cunt.

Her mouth.

Her eyes.

Her belly.

No food, no sleep, just secrets:

In her cunt.

In her mouth.

In her eyes.

In her belly.

Circles and secrets, secrets and circles.

I ask: 'MJM Publishing? You checked it out?'

'I was over there yesterday,' says Whitehead.

'And?'

'Your run-of-the-mill porn publisher. Slipped a disgruntled employee twenty quid for the names and addresses.'

John Piggott asks, 'How did you find out about it?'

'*Spunk*?'

'Yeah.'

'An anonymous tip.'

'How anonymous?'

'Young lad. Skinhead. Said he'd known Clare Strachan when she was calling herself Morrison and living over here.'

I say, 'You got a name?'

'For him?'

'Yeah.'

'Barry James Anderson, and I'd seen him before. Local. He'll be in the files.'

I swallow; *BJ*.

'What files?' asks Piggott, playing catch-up, years behind.

'Can't you have a word with Maurice Jobson,' presses Whitehead, ignoring Piggott. 'The Owl's taken you under his wing, hasn't he?'

I shake my head. 'Doubt it now.'

'You told him anything about any of this?'

'After that last time we spoke, I went to him to get the files.'

'And?'

'Gone.'

'Fuck.'

'A Detective Inspector John Rudkin, my bloody boss, he checked them out in April 1975.'

'April '75? Strachan wasn't even dead then.'

'Yeah.'

'And he never brought them back?'

'No.'

'Not even after she did die?'

'Never even fucking mentioned them.'

'And you told Maurice Jobson all this?'

'He worked it out for himself when he tried to pull the files.'

'Which files?' asks Piggott again.

Whitehead, foot down, ignoring him again: 'What did Maurice do?'

'Told me he'd deal with it. Next time I saw Rudkin it was when they came and picked me up.'

'He say anything?'

'Rudkin? No, just took a fucking swing.'

'And he's suspended?'

'Yes,' says Piggott, a question he can answer.

'You spoken to him?'

'He can't,' says Piggott. 'It was one of the stipulations of his release. No contact with DI Rudkin or DC Ellis.'

'What about Maurice?'

'That's OK.'

'You should show him these,' says Whitehead, pointing at the carpet of pornography before us.

'I can't,' I say.

'Why not?'

'Louise,' I say.

'Your wife?'

'Yeah.'

'The Badger's daughter,' smiles Whitehead.

Piggott: 'You going to tell me which fucking files you're talking about. I think I should know . . .'

Mechanically I say, 'Clare Strachan was arrested in Wakefield under the name Morrison in 1974 for soliciting, and was a witness in a murder inquiry.'

'Which murder inquiry?'

Jack Whitehead looks up at the walls of Room 27, at the pictures of the dead, at the pictures of the dead little girls and says: 'Paula Garland.'

'Fucking hell.'

'Yeah,' we both say.

Jack Whitehead comes back with three teas.

'I'm going to go see Rudkin,' he says.

'There's someone else,' I say.

'Who?'

'Eric Hall.'

'Bradford Vice?'

I nod, 'You know him?'

'Heard of him. Suspended, isn't he?'

'Yeah.'

'What about him?'

'Turns out he was pimping Janice.'

'And that's why he's suspended?'

'No. Peter Hunter's mob.'

'And you think I should pay him a visit?'

'He must know something about these,' I say, pointing at the magazines again.

'You got home addresses for them?'

'Rudkin and Hall?'

He nods and I write them out on a piece of paper.

'You should talk to Chief Superintendent Jobson,' Piggott is telling me.

'No,' I say.

'But why? You said you need all the friends you can get.'

'Let me talk to Louise first.'

'Yeah,' says Jack Whitehead suddenly. 'You should be with your wife. Your family.'

'You married?' I ask him.

'Was,' he says. 'A long time ago.'

I stand in the lobby, under the on/off strip lighting, and I die:

'Louise?'

'Sorry, it's Tina. Is that Bob?'

'Yeah.'

'She's at the hospital, love. He's almost gone.'

In the lobby, under the on/off lighting, I wait, everything gone.

'Bob? Bob?'

In the lobby, under the on and the off, I hang.

Caller: They got the right idea in France for once.

John Shark: What's that?

Caller: Bloke raped and murdered some eight-year-old little lass and they guillotined bugger.

John Shark: You'd like to see us import some of that French justice over here, would you?

Caller: French justice? It was a Yorkshireman invented guillotine, John. Everyone knows that.

> *The John Shark Show*
> Radio Leeds
> Wednesday 15th June 1977

Chapter 19

I sat in the Redbeck car park between two Bird's Eye lorries, my head spinning from that room, those memories, and these options:

See Rudkin and Hall, or tail Fraser.

Heads or tails:

Heads.

I took out the scribble Fraser had given me:

Rudkin lived nearer, Eric Hall further.

Rudkin dirty, Hall dirtier.

Hall dirty, Rudkin dirtier.

Heads or tails.

Staring across the car park at that room.

That room, those memories.

The writings on those wailing walls.

Eddie, Eddie, Eddie, always back to Eddie.

In the rearview mirror, Carol waited on the back seat; white flesh and bruised tones, red hair and broken bones, the pictures from the wall, the pictures from my Nursery Walls, the pictures from down the Memory Lane.

I sat there in a car full of dead women, a car full of Rippers, and tossed the two-pence coin again.

Heads or tails:

Heads.

Durkar, another Ossett, another Sandal:

Another piece of White Yorkshire –

Long drives and high walls.

I drove past Rudkin's, saw two cars in the drive and pulled up on Durkar Lane and waited.

It was 9.30 on the morning of Wednesday 15 June 1977.

I wondered what I'd say if I walked up that drive, rang that bell:

'Excuse me, Mr Rudkin. I think you might be Yorkshire Ripper and I was wondering if you had any comment to make?'

And just as I was thinking that, another car pulled into his drive.

Five minutes later and Rudkin pulled out of his drive in his bronze Datsun 260, another man in the passenger seat, and headed down Durkar Lane.

I followed them down into Wakefield, stalling at the lights on the way in, out along the Dewsbury Road, over Shawcross, past the tip, down through Hanging Heaton and into Batley, through the centre until they pulled up outside RD News on the Bradford Road, on the outskirts of Batley.

Batley, another Bradford, another Delhi:

Another piece of Black Yorkshire –

Low walls and high minarets.

I drove past RD News and pulled up just beyond a Chinese take-away and waited.

Rudkin and the other man stayed inside the car.

It was 10.30 and the sun had come out.

Five minutes later and a maroon BMW 2002 pulled up just past Rudkin's Datsun and two men got out, one black, one white.

I span round in my seat and made sure:

Robert Craven.

Detective Inspector Robert Craven –

'They are outstanding police officers who have our heartfelt thanks.'

Craven and his black buddy went over to Rudkin's car and Rudkin and a fat man got out.

Mike Ellis, I was guessing.

Then the four of them went inside RD News.

I closed my eyes and saw again rivers of blood in a woman's time, umbrellas up, bloody showers, puddles all blood, raining cats and blood.

I opened my eyes, the sky blue, clouds moving fast up the hills behind the shops.

I got out of my car and crossed the road to a telephone box.

I dialled her flat.

She answered: 'Hello?'

'It's me.'

'What?'

'I want to know. About the pictures, I need to know.'

'It was a long time ago.'

'It's important.'

'What?'

'Everything. Who took them? Who arranged it? Everything.'

'Not on the phone.'

'Why not?'

'Jack, if I tell you on the phone, I'll never see you again.'

'That's not true.'

'Isn't it?'

I stood in the red telephone box, in the middle of the red river of blood, below the blue sky, and I looked up at the window above the newsagent's.

John Rudkin was looking out of the window, one hand on the frame, the other square, palms open, smiling from ear to ear.

'Jack?'

'I'll come over then.'

'When?'

'Soon.'

And I hung up, staring at John Rudkin.

I went back to the car and waited.

Thirty minutes later, Rudkin came out of the shop, shirtsleeves, jacket over his shoulder, followed by the fat man and Craven.

The black man didn't come out.

Rudkin, Craven, and the fat man shook hands, and Rudkin and the fat man got into the Datsun.

Craven waved them off.

I sat there, waiting.

Craven went back inside the newsagent's.

I sat there, waiting.

Ten minutes later, Craven came back out.

The black man didn't.

Craven got into his car and drove off.

I sat there.

Five minutes later, I got out and went into the newsagent's.

Inside it was bigger than it looked, selling Calor gas and toys as well as papers and fags.

There was a young Pakistani behind the counter.

I said to him, 'Who owns this place?'

'Pardon?'

'Who's the boss? Is it you?'

'No, why?'

'I wondered if the flat above was for rent?'

'No, it's not.'

'I'd like to put me name down if it ever comes up. Who would I see about that?'

'Don't know,' he said, thinking about it, thinking about me.

I picked up a *Telegraph & Argus* and handed him the money.

'Best speak to Mr Douglas,' he said.

'Bob Douglas?' I nodded.

'Yes, Bob Douglas.'

'Thank you very much,' I said and left, thinking:

'They are outstanding police officers who have our heartfelt thanks.'

Thinking, fuck off.

The Pride, Bradford, just down from the *Telegraph & Argus*. Tom was already there, coughing into his beer at the bar.

I put my hand on his shoulder and said, 'Sorry, springing this on you.'

'Yeah,' he smiled. 'Awful having to drink with the enemy.'

'Sit down?' I said, nodding at the table by the door.

'Not getting a drink?'

'Don't be daft,' I said and ordered one and another for him.

We sat down.

'Not very nice,' I said. 'That piece about the letter.'

'Nothing to do with me,' he said, palms up, genuine.

I took a sip and said, 'They're hoaxes anyway.'

'Fuck off.'

'They're not from the bloody Ripper, tell you that.'

'We had them tested.'

'We? Thought it was nowt to do with you.'

'There was evidence and all.'

'Fuck it. It wasn't why I phoned.'

'Go on,' he said, relaxing, relieved.

'I want to know about one of yours, Eric Hall?'

'What about him?'

'Been suspended, yeah?'

'Him and rest of them.'

'Right. What you got on him?'

'Not much.'

'You know him?'

'Say hello, that way.'

'You know this last one, this Janice Ryan?'

'Yeah?'

'Well, I got me a bloke saying she was Eric's bird, that Detective Inspector Hall pimped her a bit and all.'

'Fuck.'

'Yep.'

'Doesn't surprise me like but, these days, not much bloody would.'

'So you don't know anything else? Anything extra on him?'

'They're a law unto themselves, Bradford Vice. But it's same with your lot, I bet.'

I nodded.

'To be honest,' he continued. 'I always thought he was a bit on thick side. You know, at press conferences, after work.'

'Thick enough to murder the prostitute he was pimping and try and make it look like a Ripper job?'

'Be beyond him, mate. Out of his bloody league, he'd be. Never pull it off.'

'Maybe he hasn't.'

Tom was shaking his head, sniffing up.

I said, 'How well do you know lasses over here?'

'What you asking, Jack?'

'Come on. Do you know them?'

'Some.'

'You know a Chinese lass, Ka Su Peng?'

'The one that got away,' he smiled.

'That's the one.'

'Yeah. Why?'

'What do you know about her?'

'Popular. But you know what they say about a Chinky?'

'What?'

'An hour later and you could murder another.'

I knocked once.

She opened the door, said nothing, and walked back down the bare passage.

I followed her and stood there, there in her room, with its sticks of shit and stink of sex, and I watched her rubbing hand-cream into her fingers and into her palms, up her wrists and into her arms, down into her knees.

There were the spits of an afternoon rain on the window, the bright orange curtains hopeless in the gloom, her rubbing her childish knees, me staring up her skirt.

'Is this the last fuck?' she asked later, lying in the back bedroom with the curtains drawn against the rain, against the afternoon, against the Yorkshire life.

And I lay there beside her, looking up at the stains on the ceiling, the plastic light fittings that needed a wipe, listening to her broken words, the beat of her battered heart, alone and depressed with my come on her thighs, her toes touching mine.

'Jack?'

'No,' I lied.

But she was crying anyway, the magazine open on the floor beside the bed, her top lip swelling.

I parked outside a nice house with its back to the Denholme Golf Course.

There was a blue Granada 2000 sat in the drive.

I walked up to the door and rang the bell.

A gaunt middle-aged woman answered the door, fiddling with the pearls around her neck.

'Is Eric in?'

'Who are you?'

'Jack Whitehead.'

'What do you want?'

'I'm from the *Yorkshire Post*.'

Eric Hall came out of the living room, his face black and blue, nose bandaged.

'Mr Hall?'

'It's all right Libby, love . . .'

The woman gave her pearls another tug and went the way he'd come.

'What is it?' hissed Hall.

'About Janice Ryan?'

'Who?'

'Fuck off, Eric,' I said, leaning into the doorway. 'Don't be a silly cunt.'

He blinked, swallowed, and said, 'You know who I am, who you're talking to?'

'A dirty copper named Eric Hall, yeah.'

He stood there, in the doorway to his nice house with its back to the Denholme Golf Course, his eyes full of tears.

'Let's go for a drive, Eric,' I suggested.

We pulled up in the empty car park of the George.

I turned off the engine.

We sat in silence and stared at the hedge and the fields beyond.

After a while I said, 'Have a look in that bag at your feet.'

He opened his fat little legs and bent down into the bag.

He pulled out a magazine.

'Page 7,' I said.

He stared down at the dark-haired girl with her legs spread, her mouth open, her eyes closed, a prick to her gob and spunk on her face.

'That yours?' I asked him.

But he just sat there, shaking his head from side to side, until he said, 'How much?'

'Five.'

'Hundred?'

'What do you think?'

'Five fucking thousand? I haven't got it.'

'You'll get it,' I said and started the car.

The office was dead.

I knocked on Hadden's door and went in.

He was sat behind his desk, his back to Leeds and the night.

I sat down.

'Well?' he said.

'They've let Fraser go.'

'You seen him?'

'Yep,' I smiled.

Hadden smiled back, an eyebrow arched. 'And?'

'He's been suspended. Reckons Rudkin and some bloke from Bradford Vice are up to their ears in it.'

'What do you think?'

'Well, I went out to have a look and Rudkin's up to his ears in something, but I'm fucked if I know what.'

Bill Hadden didn't look very impressed.

'Saw Tom,' I said.

Hadden smiled. 'He apologise, did he?'

'Sheep-faced, he was.'

'And rightly-bloody-so.'

'Said they still reckon the letter's genuine.'

Hadden said nothing.

'But,' I went on. 'He didn't have anything on this Bradford copper.'

'What's his name?'

'Hall. Eric Hall?'

Hadden shook his head.

I asked, 'You got anything new?'

'No,' he said, still shaking his head.

I stood up. 'I'll see you tomorrow, then.'

'Right,' he said.

At the door, I turned back. 'There was one other thing.'

'Yeah?' he said, not looking up.

'You know the one in Preston?'

He looked up. 'What?'

'The prostitute they say was a Ripper job?'

Hadden was nodding.

'Fraser said she was a witness in the Paula Garland murder.'

'What?'

And I left him with his mouth open, eyes wide.

He was sitting in the dim lobby in a high-backed chair, his eyes on his hat, his hat upon his knee.

'Jack,' he said, not looking up.

'I dream of rivers of blood, women's blood. When I fuck, I see blood. When I come, death.'

Martin Laws leant forward.

He parted his thin grey hair between his fingers and the hole leapt from the shadows.

'There has to be another way,' I said, tears in the dark.

He looked up and said: 'Jack, if the Bible teaches us nothing else, it teaches us that this is the way things are, the way things have always been, and will always be until the end.'

'The end?'

'Noah was insane until the rain.'

'And there's no other way?'

'Must it be it must.'

John Shark: *See another Yard man resigned?*

Caller: *There's going to be none of them bloody left at this rate.*

John Shark: *Arrested Arthur Scargill and all?*

Caller: *And Ripper's walking around scot bloody free.*

John Shark: *Makes you laugh, does it Bob?*

Caller: *Not much, John. No.*

The John Shark Show
Radio Leeds
Wednesday 15th June 1977

Chapter 20

And Piggott drops me outside St James and is saying how if there's anything I need or there's anything more he can do, I should just give him a call, but I'm out of the car, door open, and up the stairs, out of breath, pulling myself up on the banisters, skidding across their polished floors, into the ward and shouting at that one and the other one, the nurses coming running, me pulling back the curtains on an empty bed, one saying how she's so sorry and it was quite sudden in the end, quite sudden after all that time and how it's always so difficult to predict but at least my wife was with him and in the end he'd closed his eyes like he just stopped and how upset she'd been but, in cases like this, it's for the best and the pain's gone and it wasn't that drawn out in the end, and I'm just standing there at the bottom of his empty bed, staring at the empty bedside table, doors open, wondering where all the barley water's gone and then I see one of Bobby's cars, the little Matchbox police car Rudkin got him, and I pick it up and stand there just staring at the little car in the empty corner of the ward, the other nurse telling me how peaceful he looked and how much better off he is being dead and not alive and in pain and I look up at her face, at the red folds in her neck, the white damaged hair, the big blue eyes, and I wonder what on earth would possess someone to do this job, and then I think the same about my own job before I remember how I'm suspended and I probably won't be doing my own job anyway, no matter what they say, and I look at my watch and realise how much I've lost track of the time, much I've lost track of the minutes, I've lost track of the hours, lost track of the days, track of the weeks, of the months, the years, decades, and I walk away down the polished corridor, the nurses still talking, another one coming out from the booth, the three of them watching me go until I stop and turn around and walk back up the corridor to thank them and thank them and thank them and then I turn around and I walk away again, down the polished corridor, the little police car in my hand, down the stairs and out the door into the morning, or what I think is a morning but the leaves on the trees are all tinged red and the sky is turning white, the grass blue, the people alien greys, the cars silent, the voices gone, and I sit on the steps, rubbing my eyes until they sting like bees and I stop and I stand up and walk down the long drive towards the road and wonder how the fuck I get home from here and so I stick out my thumb and stand there for a long time until I fall over and lie there beside the entrance to the hospital in the blue grass, staring up at the white sky, at the red leaves, and if I sleep, then I wake, and when I wake I get up and dust the blue grass off me and walk down the road to a bright red phone box and inside I find a white card for a taxi and I dial and ask a foreign voice in a foreign place for a cab and then I stand outside the box and watch the silent cars with all their Rippers at their wheels, watch them speeding up and down the road, watch them laughing and pointing at me, dead women in their boots, at their back windows, dead women waving and asking for help, white hands dangling from their boots, white hands pressed to their back windows, until at long, long, bloody last the taxi pulls up and I get in and tell him where I want to go and he looks at me like he doesn't know where the fuck I mean but off we set, me sat up front, the radio on, him trying to talk to me but I can't understand what on earth he's saying or why on earth he would want to say anything to me until I ask him where the fuck he's from and he doesn't say anything after that, just concentrates on the road ahead until we pull up some two days fucking later outside my house and I tell him I'm sorry but I haven't got any money so he'll just have to wait there while I go inside and find some, which upsets him no end but what can he do, so I go up to the house and put my key in the lock but it doesn't work any more so I ring the bell for the rest of the day until I go round the back and try another key in another lock but that doesn't work either, so I spend the night knocking until I put the brick that stops the garage doors banging, I put that brick through the little window next to the back door and stick my hand in there but that doesn't help at all so I set about the door with my fists and my feet until finally I get inside and go into the front room and take the milk money out of the top drawer and go back out down the drive to the taxi driver but if he hasn't fucked off after all that, not that I can blame him, so I wave to the neighbours across the road and go back inside to find Louise and Bobby, going from room to room, but they're not there, not in the drawers, not in the cupboards, and not under the beds, so I go back downstairs and pop round to Tina's to see if they've nipped round there or if she knows where the bloody hell they've got to, so I wave to all the neighbours again and go up Tina's drive and knock on her back door but she doesn't open the door so I keep knocking into the middle of next week, Kirsty the dog yapping away on the other side, and I keep knocking until at long fucking last the door opens and it's Janice, just fucking stood there, as large as life, and you could knock me down with a feather I'm that surprised, and I tell her straight, I thought you were dead I say, thought Eric Hall or John Rudkin raped you and hit you on the head and then jumped up and down on your chest, and she's crying and saying no, saying she's all right, and I ask if the baby's all right and she says it is and so I ask if I can come in because I feel like a right prick stood out there for all the world and his wife to see, but she says no and shuts the door and I try and open the door again and she's shouting and telling me how she's going to call the police and I remind her how I am the police, but it's obvious she's not going to let me in and then I know she can't really be Janice, because Janice would let me in, and I sit on Tina's back step and wish in my heart I was more like Jesus, until I get up and go back round to mine and when I get to the drive I see the garage doors are wide open and banging in the rain and so I decide to go for a drive to try and find Louise and Bobby, fucked as I am if I know where they could be or where to start, but I get in her car and set off anyroad because it's hardly like I've got a lot of bloody pressing engagements, is it?

Part 5
The damned

John Shark: *You see this [reads]: The hijacker who killed two people and wounded two others on a bus yesterday at Kennedy Airport said he had been inspired by a dream, the police say. Luis Robinson, a 26-year-old ordinary seaman, said he 'felt the country was going into chaos and somebody had to stop it.'*

Caller: *Thinks it's bad over there, it's good job he didn't come from round here, isn't it?*

John Shark: *Not been having them dreams again, have you Bob?*

Caller: *It's not the dreams, John. It's when you get up and pull back them bloody curtains. That's when it hits you.*

The John Shark Show
Radio Leeds
Thursday 16th June 1977

Chapter 21

I look at my watch, it's 7.07.

I'm on the Moors, walking across the Moors, and I come to a chair, a high-backed leather chair, and there's a woman in white kneeling before the chair, hands in angel prayer, hair across her face.

I lean down to scoop the hair away and it's Carol, then Ka Su Peng. She stands up and points to the middle of the long white dress and a word in bloody fingerprints there writ:

livE.

And there on the Moors, in the wind and in the rain, she pulls the white dress up over her head, her yellow belly swollen, and then puts the dress back on, inside out, the word in bloody fingerprints there writ:

Evil.

And a small boy in blue pyjamas comes out from behind the high-backed leather chair and leads her away down the corridor, the threadbare carpet, the dirty walls, the smell.

We come to a door and stop.

Room 77.

I woke with a start in my car, my chest tight, sweating and breathing fast.

I looked at the clock in the dashboard.

7.07.

Fuck.

I was on Durkar Lane, Durkar, at the bottom of Rudkin's drive.

I looked in the rearview mirror.

Nothing.

I sat there, waiting.

Twenty minutes later, a woman in her dressing-gown opened the front door and took in the two pints of milk from the doorstep.

I waited until she'd shut the door, then I started the car, put the radio on, and drove off.

Down into Wakefield, out along the Dewsbury Road, over Shaw-cross, down through Hanging Heaton and into Batley, radio on:

'Two masked men who broke into a sub-post office in Shadwell, beat up the sub-postmaster and his wife, and fled with £750, are being sought by the police. One of the men is said to be "very violent".

'Mr Eric Gowers, aged sixty-five, and his wife May, aged sixty-four, were taken to hospital but later allowed home.'

Through the centre until I pulled up on the outskirts of Batley, just beyond the Chinese take-away on the Bradford Road.

Just beyond RD News.

Just beyond a bronze Datsun 260.

I dialled her flat.

No answer.

I hung up.

I stood in the red telephone box again, looking up at the window above the newsagent.

'Is Eric there?'

'Who's calling?'

'A friend.'

John Rudkin was looking out of the window, one hand on the frame, the other square, palms open, not smiling.

'This is Eric Hall.'

'You got the money?'

'Yes.'

'Be in the George car park at noon.'

I hung up, staring at John Rudkin.

I went back to the car and waited.

Thirty minutes later, Rudkin came out of the shop carrying a child in his arms, followed by a woman in sunglasses.

The boy was wearing blue pyjamas, the woman black.

They got into the Datsun and drove off.

I sat there.

Five minutes later, I got out of the car and went round the back of the shops, down the alley, past the dustbins, the piled-up bin bags, the rotting cardboard boxes, counting the windows as I went.

I did my sums and looked up at two windows and two pairs of old curtains staring down from up above the back wall, the back wall with the broken bottles cemented in its lip.

I tried the red wooden door and opened it slowly.

All I needed now was the Paki from inside to pop his brown mug out.

I closed the door to the yard behind me and picked my way through the crates and the Calor gas canisters and got to the back door.

Wondering what the fuck I would say, I opened the door.

There was a passage out to the front of the shop, stacked high with boxes of Walkers crisps and old magazines. To my right were the stairs.

In for a penny, I took my chance and crept up them.

At the top was a white door with glass in it.

It was dark beyond the glass.

I stood there, listening.

Nothing.

In for a pound, I tried the door.

Locked.

Fuck.

I tried it again, knew it would give.

I took out my penknife and slid it in between the wall and the door.

Nothing ventured, I leant in.

Nothing.

Nothing gained, I tried it again.

The knife broke in the hinges, the frame of the door splintered, my hand cut and bleeding again, but I was in.

I stood there, listening.

Nothing.

Another dim passage.

I wrapped my handkerchief around my palm and walked

softly down the passage to the front of the flat, three closed doors off to the sides.

The flat stank, the ceilings as low and oppressive as the smell.

In the front room there was a settee, a chair, a table, a television, and a telephone on a box. Empty pop bottles and crisp packets littered the floor.

There was no carpet.

Only a big dark fucking stain in the floorboards.

I went back down the passage and tried the first door on the right.

It was a small kitchen, bare.

I tried the door on the left.

It was a bedroom, one with a pair of old curtains, thick, black and drawn.

I switched on the light.

There was a huge double bed, stripped, with another big dark fucking stain on the orange flowered mattress.

There were fitted wardrobes down one wall.

I opened them.

Lights, photographer's lights.

I closed the wardrobe doors and switched off the light.

Across the passage was the last door.

It was a bathroom and another pair of old curtains, drawn and black.

There were towels and there were mats, newspapers and paints, the bath spotless.

I ran cold water over my hand and wiped it dry.

I closed the door and went back down the passage.

I stood at the top of the stairs and pulled the splinters from the white door.

I tried to force the lock back in, but it wouldn't go.

I left the door as it was and went back down the stairs.

I stood on the bottom step, listening.

Nothing.

I went out the back way, into the yard, through the red wooden door, and out.

I walked down the alley past the dustbins, the piled-up bin

bags and the rotting cardboard boxes, a little yellow dog watching me go.

I went back round the front of the shops, past the Chinky, and got back into my car.

It was just gone eleven.

I dialled her flat.

No answer.

I hung up and dialled again.

No answer.

I hung up.

I drove past the George, Denholme, pulled up, reversed up a drive and turned back round.

I had a bad feeling, but I couldn't let it go, couldn't leave it like this.

I drove slowly back along the road and turned down the side of the pub, into the car park round the back.

It was almost noon.

There were four or five cars parked, three facing out towards the hedge and the fields, two with their noses against the back of the pub.

None of them were blue Granadas.

I parked in a corner, that bad feeling still feeling bad, looking out on the hedge and the fields.

I sat there, waiting, staring into the rearview mirror.

There were two men sitting in a grey Volvo, waiting, staring into their rearview mirror.

Fuck.

Two cars along, Eric Hall got out of a white Peugeot 304.

I watched him coming towards me, hands deep in his sheepskin.

He came round the back of the car and tapped on my window.

I wound it down.

He leant down and asked me: 'What you waiting for? Christmas?'

'You got the money?'

'Yeah,' he said and stood back up.

I was staring into my rearview, watching the two heads in the Volvo. 'Where is it?'

'In the car.'

'What happened to the Granada?'

'Had to fucking sell it, didn't I? Pay you.'

'Get in,' I said.

'But the money's in the car.'

'Just get in,' I said, starting the car.

He walked round the back and got in the other side.

I reversed out and down the side of the George.

'Where we going?'

'Just for a drive,' I said, turning into the traffic.

'What about the money?'

'Fuck it.'

'But . . .'

Eyes on the road, I was into the rearview every second glance. 'There were two blokes sat in a grey Volvo, back there. You saw them, yeah?'

'No.'

I hit the brakes and swerved into the side of the road, into the verge.

'Them,' I said, pointing at a grey Volvo flying past.

'Fuck.'

'Nothing to do with you?'

'No.'

'You wouldn't have been thinking of doing me in or shooting me or anything clever like that, would you?'

'No,' he said, sweating.

I reversed back down the verge and swung back round the way we'd come.

Foot down, I said, 'So who the fuck were they?'

'I don't know. Honest.'

'Eric, you're a dirty fucking copper. An old hack like me turns up on your doorstep and asks for five grand, you just going to roll right over? I don't fucking think so.'

Eric Hall said nothing.

We drove back past the George, the Volvo gone.

'Who you tell?' I asked him again.

'Look,' he sighed. 'Pull up, please.'

I went a little way on then parked near a church on the Halifax Road.

For a bit we just sat there, silent, no sun, no rain, nothing.

Eventually he said, 'I'm up to my bloody neck in it as it is.'

I said nothing, just nodded.

'I've not exactly played by the fucking rules, you know what I mean? I've turned a blind eye every now and again.'

'And not for free, eh?'

He sighed again and said, 'And who the bloody hell ever has or ever fucking would?'

I said nothing.

'I was going to pay you, straight up. Still will, if that's what it takes. Not five grand, I haven't got it. But I got two and half for the car and it's yours.'

'I don't want the fucking money, Eric. I just want to know what the fuck's going on?'

'Them blokes in the car park? I haven't a fucking clue, but I'm betting they're something to do with that cunt Peter Hunter and his investigation.'

'What did they suspend you for?'

'Backhanders.'

'That all?'

'It's enough.'

'Janice Ryan?'

'Shit I could do without right now.'

'When did you last see her?'

He sighed, wiping his palms on the tops of his thighs, and shook his head, 'Can't remember.'

'Eric,' I said. 'Fuck the money and tell me. By time Hunter's finished with you, you're going to need every fucking penny you can get your dirty little hands on. So start by telling me some fucking truth and save yourself two and half grand.'

He looked up out the top of the windscreen, up at the black

steeple in the sky, then he put his head back in the seat and said softly, 'I didn't fucking kill her.'

'Did I say you did?'

'Two weeks ago,' he said. 'She called me, said she needed money to get away, said she'd got some information to sell.'

'You meet her?'

'No.'

'You know what kind of information she had?'

'About some robberies.'

'Which robberies?'

'She didn't say.'

'Past or future?'

'She didn't say.'

I looked at the fat frightened face, saw it sweating in my passenger seat.

'You tell anyone this?'

He swallowed, nodded.

'Who?'

'A sergeant from Leeds. Name's Fraser, Bob Fraser.'

'When did you tell him?'

'Not long after.'

'Why'd you tell him?'

Eric Hall turned his face my way and pointing at his eyes said, 'Because he fucking beat it out of me.'

'Why'd he do that?'

'He was pimping her, wasn't he?'

'Thought that were you?'

'A long time ago.'

'That magazine, those pictures? What do you know about them?'

'Nothing. Straight up. She never mentioned them.'

I sat at the wheel, lost.

After a while, Eric Hall said, 'Anything else you want to know?'

'Yeah,' I said. 'Who the fuck killed her?'

Eric Hall sniffed up and said, 'I got my fucking theory.'

I turned to look at him, at that fat fucking slug of a man, a man happy to save himself two fucking grand though his soul was racked with lies, though hellfire and only hellfire awaited him.

'Do tell, Sherlock?'

He shrugged like it was no big deal, like it was on the front of every fucking newspaper, like the fat slug lived to fight another day, and smiled, 'Fraser.'

'Not Ripper?'

He laughed, 'The Ripper? Fuck's that?'

I stared up at the cross above us and said, 'One last thing.'

'Shoot,' he said, still smiling.

The cunt.

'Ka Su Peng?'

'Who?' he said, too quickly, not smiling.

'Chinese girl? Sue Penn?'

He shook his head.

'Eric, you're Bradford Vice right?'

'Was.'

'Sorry, was. But I'm sure you can still remember all your girls. Specially ones Ripper had a fucking pop at right in the middle of your bloody patch. No?'

He said nothing.

I said again, 'It was Ripper, yeah?'

'That's what they say.'

'What about you? What do you say?'

'I say let sleeping dogs lie.'

I started the car and turned back the way we'd come, driving in a fast silence.

I pulled up outside the George.

He opened the door and got out.

'Kill yourself,' I whispered.

'What?' he said, looking back into the car.

'Shut the door, Eric,' I said and put my foot down.

I dialled her flat.

No answer.

I hung up and dialled again.

No answer.
I hung up and dialled again.
No answer.
I hung up.

Back into Bradford, out of Bradford, back into Leeds, foot down all the way: Killinghall Road, Leeds Road, the Stanningley by-pass, Armley.

Under the dark arches, tempted by a last afternoon drink, succumbing in the Scarborough, a quick whisky into the top of a pint, down in one in the shadow of the Griffin.

Into the end of the afternoon, a breeze blowing through the centre, plastic bags and old papers round my shins, looking for a telephone that worked, just one.

'Samuel?'
   'Jack.'
   'Any news?'
   'They let Fraser go.'
   'I know.'
   'Well, don't let me keep you.'
   'Sorry.'
   'Don't suppose you know where he is?'
   'What?'
   'He was supposed to check in at Wood Street Nick this morning, but he never.'
   'He never?'
   'He never.'
   'Anything else?'
   'One dead darkie.'
   'Ripper?'
   'Not unless he's started on blokes and all.'
   'No, anything about Ripper?'
   'No.'
   'Bob Craven in?'
   'You sure?'
   'Put us through, Samuel.'

Two clicks and a ring.

'Vice.'

'Detective Inspector Craven please.'

'Who's calling?'

'Jack Whitehead.'

'Hang on.'

Two fingers over the mouthpiece and a shout across the room.

'Jack?'

'Been a while, Bob.'

'It has that. How are you?'

'Well, and yourself?'

'Keeping busy.'

'Got time for a pint?'

'Always got time for a pint, Jack. You know me.'

'When's best for you?'

'About eightish?'

'Yeah, fine. Where do you fancy?'

'Duck and Drake?'

'Eight o'clock it is.'

'Bye.'

Through the dirty afternoon streets, the breeze wind, the plastic bags birds, the newspapers snakes.

I turned into a cobbled alley out of the gale, searching for the walls, the words.

But the words were gone, the alley wrong, the only words lies.

I walked up Park Row and on to Cookridge Street, up to St Anne's.

Inside the Cathedral was deserted, the wind gone, and I walked down the side and knelt before the Pieta, and I prayed, a thousand eyes on me.

I looked up, my throat dry, my breathing slow.

An old woman was leading a child by the hand down the aisle towards me, and when they reached me, the child held out an open Bible and I took it from him and watched them walk away.

I looked down and I read the words I found:

During that time these men will seek death, but they will not find it;
They will long to die, but death will elude them.

And I walked through the Cathedral, through the double doors, through the afternoon, through the plastic bags and the snakes, I walked through it all.

Everything gone, everything wrong, only lies.

The office was dead.

I went down the hall and into records.

Into 1974.

I spun the microfilm through the reels, over the lights.

Into Friday 20 December 1974.

Front Page:

WE SALUTE YOU.

A photograph –

Three big smiles:

Chief Constable Angus congratulates Sergeant Bob Craven and PC Bob Douglas on a job well done.

'They are outstanding police officers who have our heartfelt thanks.'

I pressed print and watched those three big smiles, those outstanding police officers come out.

Watched that by-line:

BY JACK WHITEHEAD, CRIME REPORTER OF THE YEAR

I knocked on Hadden's door and went in.

Still sat behind the desk, his back still to Leeds.

I sat down.

'Jack,' he said.

'Bill,' I smiled.

'Well?'

'Fraser's done a runner.'

'You know where he is?'

'Maybe.'

'Maybe?'

'I have to check.'

He sniffed up and tidied up some pens on his desk.

I asked, 'You got anything new?'

'Jack,' he said, not looking up. 'You said something about Paula Garland, the last time you were in.'

'Yeah.'

He looked up, 'Well?'

'Well what?'

'You said something about a connection, a link?'

'Yeah?'

'Bloody hell, Jack. What have you found out?'

'Like I said, Clare Strachan . . .'

'The Preston Ripper job?'

'Yeah. She went by the name Morrison and under that name she'd made a statement as a witness in the Paula Garland murder.'

'And that's it?'

'Yeah. Fraser said Rudkin and maybe some other officers knew this, but it's never been officially recorded in the Preston inquiry. Or anywhere else.'

'And there's nothing else?'

'No.'

'Nothing you're not telling me?'

'No. Course not.'

'And you found this out from Sergeant Fraser?'

'Yeah. Why?'

'Just getting it straight in my mind, Jack. Just getting it straight.'

'You got it straight then?'

'Yeah,' he said, eyes on mine.

I stood up.

'Sit down a minute, Jack,' he said.

I sat down.

Hadden opened a drawer in his desk and pulled out a large manila envelope.

'This came this morning,' he said, tossing it across his desk. 'Take a look.'

I pulled out a magazine.

A nack mag, pornography.

Cheap pornography.

Amateurs:

Spunk.

The corner of one page folded down.

'Page 7,' said Bill Hadden.

I turned to the marked page and there she was:

Bleached white hair and flaccid pink flesh, wet red holes and dry blue eyes, legs spread, flicking her clit:

Clare Strachan.

I was hard again.

'This morning?' I asked, throat hoarse.

'Yeah, postmarked Preston.'

I turned the envelope over, nodding.

'Anything else?'

'No, just that.'

'Just the one issue?'

'Yeah, just that.'

I looked up, the mag in my hands.

Hadden said, 'You didn't know she was doing this kind of stuff?'

'No.'

'You any idea who might have sent it?'

'No.'

'You don't think your Sergeant Fraser's gone west do you?'

'No.'

'I see,' said Hadden, nodding to himself.

I said, 'What we going to do with it?'

'I want you to make some calls, find out what the fuck's going on out there.'

I stood up.

He was picking up a phone as he said, 'And Jack?'

'Yeah,' I said, one hand on the doorknob.

'Be careful, yeah?'

'I always am,' I said. 'I always am.'

*

I dialled her flat.
 No answer.
 I hung up and dialled again.
 No answer.
 I hung up and dialled again.
 No answer.
 I hung up and dialled again.
 No answer.
 I hung up.

I looked at my watch:
 Just gone six.
 Slight change of plan.
 Down the hall and back into records.
 Back into 1974.
 I spun the microfilm again, through the reels and over the lights.
 Into Tuesday 24 December 1974.
 Evening Post, Front Page:
 3 DEAD IN WAKEFIELD XMAS SHOOT-OUT
 Sub-headed:
 Hero Cops Foil Pub Robbery
 A photograph –
 The Strafford, the Bullring, Wakefield.
 A horrific shoot-out late last night in the centre of Wakefield left three people dead and three seriously injured in what police are describing as 'a robbery that went wrong'.

 According to a police spokesman, police were called after shots were reported at the Strafford Public House in the Bullring, Wakefield, at around midnight last night. The first officers on the scene were Sergeant Robert Craven and PC Bob Douglas, the two officers who last week were commended for their part in the arrest of the man suspected of the murder of Morley schoolgirl Clare Kemplay.

 When the two officers entered the Strafford they discovered a robbery in progress and were shot and beaten by unidentified gunmen, who then escaped.

 Members of the West Yorkshire Metropolitan Police's Special Patrol

Group arrived minutes later to find the two hero cops and another man suffering from gunshot wounds and three people dead.

Roadblocks were immediately set up on the M1 and M62 in all directions and checks ordered at all ports and airports but, as yet, no arrests have been made.

Sergeant Craven and PC Douglas were described as being in 'a serious but stable condition' in Wakefield's Pinderfield Hospital.

Police are refusing to release the names of the dead until the next-of-kin have been contacted.

An Incident Room has been set up at Wood Street Police Station, Wakefield, and Detective Superintendent Maurice Jobson appealed for any member of the public with information to contact him in confidence as a matter of urgency. The number is Wakefield 3838.

I pressed print and watched those big lies, those outstanding lies come out.

Watched that by-line:

BY JACK WHITEHEAD, CRIME REPORTER OF THE YEAR

The Duck and Drake, in the gutters of the Kirkgate Market.

A gypsy pub, in the shadows of the Millgarth Nick.

Eight o'clock.

I took my pint and my whisky to the table by the door and waited, a plastic bag on the other seat.

I tipped the whisky into the pint and drank it down.

It had been a long time, maybe too long, maybe not long enough.

'Same again?'

I looked up and there was Bob Craven.

Detective Inspector Bob Craven.

'Bob,' I said, standing up, shaking hands. 'What happened to your face?'

'Bloody Zulus got a bit restless up Chapeltown couple of weeks ago.'

'You all right?'

'Will be when I get a pint,' he grinned and went off to the bar.

I moved the plastic bag on to my lap and watched him at the bar.

He brought two pints over and then went back for the whiskies.

'Been a while,' he said, sitting down.

'Three years?'

'Only that long?'

'Aye. Seems like a lifetime,' I said.

'A lot of water under the bridge. A bloody lot.'

'Last time must've been before Strafford then?'

'Must have been. Straight after that'd have been *Exorcist* business you had, yeah?'

I nodded.

He sighed: 'Fucking hell, eh? Things we've seen.'

'How's the other Bob?' I asked.

'Dougie?'

'Yeah.'

'Well out of it, isn't he?'

'You weren't tempted then?'

'Pack it in?'

I nodded.

'What the fuck else would I do? And you?'

I nodded again. 'But what about Bob, what's he do?'

'He's all right. Put his comp into a paper shop. Does all right. See him and I'm not saying there aren't times when I wish it had been me who took the bullet. You know what I mean?'

I nodded and picked up my pint.

'Little shop, little wife. You know?'

'No,' I shrugged. 'But tell him I was asking after him, won't you?'

'Oh, aye. He's still got your piece up on wall. *We Salute You*, that one.'

I sighed, 'Only three years, eh?'

'Another time, eh?' he said and then picked up his pint. 'Here's to them; other times.'

We touched glasses and drained them.

'My shout,' I said and went back to the bar.

At the bar, I turned and watched him, watched him sitting there, watched him rubbing his beard and flicking at the dust on his trousers, picking up the empty pint glass and putting it down again, watched him.

I brought the drinks over and sat back down.

'Anyway,' he said. 'Enough Memory bloody Lane. What they got you on these days?'

'Ripper,' I said.

He paused, then said, 'Yeah, course.'

We sat there, silent, listening to the noise of the pub: the glasses, the chairs, the music, the chat, the till.

Then I said, 'That's why I called you actually.'

'Yeah?'

'Ripper, yeah.'

'What about the cunt?'

I handed him the plastic bag. 'Bill Hadden got this in morning post.'

He took the bag and peeked inside.

I said nothing.

He looked up.

I looked at him.

'Let's go for a walk,' he said.

I followed him into the black Market, into the shadows of the stalls, the evening wind blowing the rubbish and the stink in with us.

Deep in the dark heart, Craven stopped by a stall and took out the magazine.

'Page is marked,' I said.

He turned the pages.

I waited –

Heart cracking, ribs breaking.

'Who knows about this?' he asked, his back to me.

'Just me and Bill Hadden.'

'You know who this is, don't you?'

I nodded.

He turned round, the page open and dangling from his hand, his face black and lost in the shadows and the beard.

'It's Clare Strachan,' I said.

'You know who sent it?'

'No.'

'There was no note?'

'No. Just what you got there.'

'They'd marked the page though?'

'Yeah.'

'You still got the envelope?'

'Hadden has.'

'You remember when and where it was posted?'

I swallowed and said, 'Two days ago in Preston.'

'Preston?'

I nodded and said, 'It's him, isn't it?'

His eyes flew across my face: 'Who?'

'Ripper.'

There was a smile deep in there, just for a moment, deep behind that beard.

Then he said quietly, 'Why you call me, Jack? Why not straight to George?'

'You're Vice, yeah? Your neck of the woods.'

He stepped forward, out of the shadow of the stall, and he put a hand on my shoulder. 'You did the right thing, Jack. Bringing this to me.'

'I thought so.'

'You going to print anything?'

'Not if you don't want me to.'

'I don't want you to.'

'Well then, I won't.'

'Not yet.'

'OK.'

'Thanks, Jack.'

I moved out of his grip and said, 'What now?'

'Another pint?'

I looked at my watch and said, 'Better not.'

'Another time, then.'

'Another time,' I said.

At the edge of the Market, out of the heart, the shit and the stink still strong, Detective Inspector Bob Craven said, 'Give us a call, Jack.'

I nodded.

'I owe you,' he said.

And I nodded again – unending, this whole fucking hell unending.

The footnotes and the margins, the tangents and the detours, the dirty tabula, the broken record.

Jack Whitehead, Yorkshire, 1977.

The bodies and the corpses, the alleys and the wasteland, the dirty men, the broken women.

Jack the Ripper, Yorkshire, 1977.

The lies and the half-truths, the truths and the half-lies, the dirty hands, the broken backs.

Two Jacks, one Yorkshire, 1977.

Down the hall and back into records.

Into 1975.

I spun the microfilm one last time, through the reels and over the lies.

Into Monday 27 January 1975.

Evening Post, Front Page:

MAN KILLS WIFE IN EXORCISM

Sub-headed:

Local Priest arrested

But I couldn't read, couldn't read another –

I dialled her flat.

No answer.

I hung up and dialled again.

No answer.

I hung up and dialled again.

No answer.

I hung up and dialled again.

No answer.

I hung up and dialled again.

No answer.

I hung up.

I pulled into the Redbeck car park and parked between the dark lorries, the empty cars, and switched off the radio with the engine.

I sat in the night, waiting, wondering, worrying.

I got out and walked across the car park, through the potholes and the craters, a black moon rising.

Outside Room 27, I paused, listened, knocked.

Nothing.

I knocked, listened, waited.

Nothing.

I opened the door.

Sergeant Fraser was lying on the floor in a ball, the chair and table splintered, the walls bare, lying on the floor in a ball under all the shit that had been up on the walls, lying on the floor in a ball of splintered wood, in a ball of splintered hell.

I stood in the doorway, the black moon over my shoulder, the night across us both.

He opened his eyes.

'It's me,' I said. 'Jack.'

He raised his head to the door.

'Can I come in?'

He opened his mouth slowly and then closed it again.

I walked across the room to him and bent down.

He was clutching a photograph –

A woman and child.

The woman in sunglasses, the boy in blue pyjamas.

His eyes were open and looking up at me.

'Sit up,' I said.

He gripped my forearm.

'Come on,' I said.

'I can't find them,' he whispered.

'It's OK,' I nodded.

'But I can't find them anywhere.'

'They're OK.'

He tightened his grip, pulling himself up on my arm. 'You're lying,' he said. 'They're dead, I know they are.'

'No, they're not.'

'Dead, like everyone else.'

'No, they're fine.'

'You're lying.'

'I've seen them.'

'Where?'

'With John Rudkin.'

'Rudkin?'

'Yeah, I think they're with him.'

He stood up, looking down at me.

'I'm sorry,' I said.

'They're dead,' he said.

'No.'

'All dead,' he said and picked up a table leg.

I tried to stand upright, but I wasn't quick enough.

I was too slow.

Caller: *And now all sodding coppers are refusing to do overtime. Bloody criminals must be laughing up their sleeves.*

John Shark: *You don't think the boys in blue deserve a pay-rise then, Bob?*

Caller: *Pay-rise? Don't make me bloody laugh, John. I wouldn't pay them bastards a fucking penny until they bloody caught someone. And someone who'd bloody done something and all.*

John Shark: *Arrested Arthur Scargill again.*

Caller: *And that's all they're bloody good for, isn't it? Nicking Arthur and grassing each other up.*

The John Shark Show
Radio Leeds
Friday 17th June 1977

Chapter 22

Kill them all.

Driving.

Radio on:

'The charred remains of an unidentified black man were discovered yesterday on Hunslet Carr.

'A post-mortem revealed that the man had died from stab wounds, before being doused in petrol and set alight.

'A police spokesman said that a definite attempt had been made to disguise the identity of the victim, leading police to believe the man may have had a police record.

'The man is described as being in his late twenties, about six foot tall, with a big build.

'Police appealed for members of the public with any information as to the identity of either the victim or his killers to contact their nearest police station as a matter of urgency. Police stressed that all information will be treated in the strictest confidence.'

Radio off.

Driving, scrrrrrrrrrrrrrrrrrrrrrrrrrrrreaming:

Kill them all.

It's dawn.

I stop at the bottom of Durkar Lane.

There's a car in his drive, milk on his doorstep, my family inside.

And I sit there at the bottom of his drive, wishing I had a gun, crying.

I stop.

Dawn, 1977.

I press the doorbell and wait.

Nothing.

I press it again and don't stop.

I see a pink shape behind the glass, hear voices inside, the door opens and there's his wife, and she's saying, 'Bob? It's Bob. Just a minute.'

But I can hear Bobby and I push past her, up the stairs, kicking open doors until I find them in the back bedroom, her sat up in bed holding my son, Rudkin pulling on his jacket, coming towards me.

'Come on,' I say. 'We're going.'

'No-one's going anywhere, Bob,' says Rudkin, putting a hand on me, starting the fight, me bringing the chair leg up into the side of his head, him holding his ear, swinging out, missing, me grabbing his hair and pulling his fucking face down into my knee, again and again, until I can hear shouting and screaming and crying, Rudkin's wife pulling me off him, scratching my cheeks, Rudkin still swinging out until he finally connects and I fall back through the door, turning and slapping his wife away, Rudkin punching me hard in the side of my face, my teeth into my tongue, blood everywhere, though fuck knows whose, her shielding Bobby, almost standing on the far end of the double bed, arms tight about him.

And then there's a pause, a lull, just the sobbing and the crying, the throbbing and the aching.

'Stop it, Bob,' she's crying. 'Stop it, will you!'

And all I can say is, 'We're going.'

Then Rudkin brings his fist down into my face and it all starts up again, me bringing my head straight into his, stars fucking everywhere, him reeling back, me following through, chasing exploding stars and meteorites across the room with my fists, across John bloody Rudkin's face, kicking and punching him into a big black fucking hole, reaching the bed and grabbing Bobby and trying to pull him free until Rudkin takes me round the neck and starts choking the living fuck out of me.

'Stop it,' she's crying. 'Stop it, will you!'

But he doesn't.

'Stop it, John,' she's crying. 'You'll kill him.'

Rudkin drops me to my knees and I fall forward into the bed, my face in the mattress.

He steps back and there's another pause, another lull, still the sobbing and the crying, the throbbing and the aching, and the longer it goes on, the pause, the lull, the longer I lie here, the sooner they'll relax.

So I lie there, eating bed, waiting until Louise, Rudkin, his wife, until one of them lets me get a look in, lets me get what's mine:

Bobby.

And I lie there, limp, still waiting until Rudkin says:

'Come on, Bob. Let's all go downstairs.'

And I can feel him weaken as he bends down to pull me back up, feel him weaken as I reach down for the chair leg, as I bring it up and round and into the side of his face, as he falls howling into the bedroom window, cracking the glass, her watching him go, so I can reach up and take Bobby from her and I'm on my feet and out the door and through the wife who's tumbling back down the stairs as fast as I'm following her, Louise on my heels, shouting and screaming and crying, until I trip on Rudkin's wife at the foot of the stairs and Louise topples over me, Rudkin stumbling into the pile-up, blood running down his face, into his eyes, blinding the cunt, me shouting, bellowing, howling:

'He's my fucking son and all!'

Her shouting, screaming, crying:

'No, no, no!'

Bobby pale with shock and shaking in my arms on top of Rudkin's wife, under the other two, me trying to pull us out from under them until Rudkin gets a punch, a kick, a fuck-knows-what into my ear and I fall back, Bobby gone, her pulling them free, Rudkin pinning me down, me doing the shouting, the screaming, the crying:

'You can't do this. He's my fucking son.'

And she's backing into their living room, her hand on his head, his head in her hair, until she says:

'No he's not.'

Silence.

Just this silence, *that* silence, just that long, long, fucking silence, until she says again:

'He's not.'

I try to stand, to push Rudkin's foot off me, like if I stand I'll be able to understand the shit she's saying, and at the same time Rudkin's wife is repeating over and over:

'What? What do you mean?'

And there's him, head to toe in blood, palms up, saying:

'Leave it. For christssakes, leave it.'

'But he needs to fucking know.'

'Not now he fucking doesn't.'

'But he was fucking a whore, a dead fucking whore, a dead fucking pregnant whore.'

'Louise . . .'

'Just because she's dead doesn't make it any fucking different. It was still his kid she was carrying.'

I get to my knees, arms out towards them, towards Bobby, my Bobby.

'Get away!'

Rudkin screaming, 'Louise . . .'

And then his wife walks over and slaps him across the face and stands there just looking at him, just looking at him before she spits in his face and walks out the front door.

'Anthea,' he shouts. 'You can't go outside like that.'

I stand but he's still got me, shouting at his wife:

'Anthea!'

And my hands are out to Bobby, the back of his head, my Bobby.

'Get away,' she says. 'John, get him away from us!'

But he's torn is John Rudkin, torn between letting his wife go and letting me loose, and it's making him weak and making me strong, me seeing Bobby just a couple of feet across the room and then I'm away and over there, a punch into the side of her lying fucking head and another until she lets me take what's mine, let's me have him, let's me have my Bobby, Rudkin walking straight into my fucking elbow, me with one hand on Bobby, the other holding on to Rudkin's hair, spinning him into his marble mantelpiece and on into Louise, him sending her flying so me and Bobby are out the room, into the hall, out through the door, and down the drive, Bobby crying and calling for his Mummy, me telling him it's all right, everything's going to be all right, telling him to stop crying, Mummy and Daddy are just joking, and all the time I can hear them behind me, hear their feet, hear her saying:

'John, no! The baby! Mind Bobby!'

And suddenly I feel my back go, like I don't have one anymore, and I'm down on my knees in his drive and I don't want to drop Bobby and I don't want to drop Bobby and I don't want to drop Bobby and I don't want to drop Bobby and I don't want to drop Bobby.

'No! You'll kill him!'

And then I'm lying face down in his drive and Bobby's gone, lying face down in his drive with them walking over me, running for the car, him clattering the cricket bat down on to the ground by my head, her saying:

'We're even, Bob. Even.'

And then they're gone, everything white, then grey, and finally black.

Caller: *You look through the paper and what do you see?*

John Shark: *I don't know, Bob. You tell me.*

Caller: *[Reads]: Baby battering claims six lives a week, injures thousands. Next page, every child in North waves at Queen. Then, seventy-four coppers quit every month and unemployment's up one hundred thousand. Rapes, murders, Ripper . . .*

John Shark: *What's your point, Bob?*

Caller: *Callaghan bloody said it himself, didn't he? Govern or go.*

The John Shark Show
Radio Leeds
Friday 17th June 1977

Chapter 23

I look at my watch, it's 7.07.

I'm riding in an old elevator, watching the floors pass, going up.

I step out of the elevator and on to the landing.

A young boy in blue pyjamas is standing there, waiting.

He takes my hand and leads me down the corridor, down the threadbare carpet, the dirty walls, the smell.

We come to a door and stop.

I put my fingers on the handle and turn.

It's open.

Room 77.

I woke on the floor, a terrible black and heavy pain across my skull.

I put my hand to the side of my head, felt the dried, caked blood.

I lifted my head, the room bathed in bright light.

Morning light, a morning light from out on the Common, from out on the Common where the steam rose from the backs of the ponies and the backs of the horses.

I sat up in that morning light, sat up on the sea of ripped-up paper, the smashed-up furniture, putting the photographs and the notes back together.

Eddie, Eddie, Eddie – every fucking where.

But all the Queen's horses, all the Queen's men, we couldn't put Eddie together again.

Couldn't keep Jackie together again either.

I tried to stand, felt sick in my mouth, and pulled myself over to the sink and spat.

I stood and ran the tap, cupping the cold grey water over my face.

In the mirror, I saw him, me.

Limbs of straw and will of wicker, trampled under hooves, horses' hooves, Chinese horses.

I looked at my watch.

It was gone seven.

7.07

I sat in my car in the Redbeck car park, squeezing the bridge of my nose, coughing.

I started the engine, turned the radio off, and pulled away.

I drove into Wakefield, past the ponies and the horses on Heath Common, black stacks where the beacons had been, and up through Ossett and down through Dewsbury, black slags where the fields had been, past RD News and out of Batley, into Bradford.

I pulled up on her street, parking next to a tall oak decked out in her best summer leaves.

Green.

I knocked again.

It was cold on the stairs, out of the sun, the leaves tapping on the windows.

I put my fingers on the handle and turned.

I went inside.

The flat was quiet and dark, nobody home.

I stood in her hallway, listening, thinking of the place above RD News, these places where we hid.

I went into the living room, the room where we'd met, the orange curtains drawn, and I sat down in the chair in which I always sat and I decided to wait for her.

The cream blouse and matching trousers, that first time. The bare bruised and dirty knees, the last time.

Ten minutes later I got up and went into the kitchen and stuck the kettle on.

I waited for the water to boil, poured it into a cup and went back into the living room.

And then I sat there in the dark, waiting for Ka Su Peng, wondering how I got here, listing them all:

Mary Ann Nichols, murdered Buck's Row, August 1888.

Annie Chapman, murdered Hanbury Street, September 1888.

Elizabeth Stride, murdered Berner's Street, September 1888.
Catherine Eddowes, murdered Mitre Square, September 1888.
Mary Jane Kelly, murdered Miller's Court, November 1888.
Five women.
Five murders.
I felt the tide coming in, the Bloody Tide, lapping at my shoes and socks, crawling up my legs:
'What happened to our Jubilee?'
The tide coming in, the Bloody Tide, lapping at my shoes and socks, crawling up my legs:
Carol Williams, murdered Ossett, January 1975.
One woman.
One murder.
Felt the waters rising, the Bloody Waters of Babylon, those rivers of blood in a woman's time, umbrellas up, bloody showers, puddles all blood, raining red, white, and bloody blue:
Joyce Jobson, assaulted Halifax, July 1974.
Anita Bird, assaulted Cleckheaton, August 1974.
Theresa Campbell, murdered Leeds, June 1975.
Clare Strachan, murdered Preston, November 1975.
Joan Richards, murdered Leeds, February 1976.
Ka Su Peng, assaulted Bradford, October 1976.
Marie Watts, murdered Leeds, May 1977.
Linda Clark, assaulted Bradford, June 1977.
Rachel Johnson, murdered Leeds, June 1977.
Janice Ryan, murdered Bradford, June 1977.
Ten women.
Six murders.
Four assaults.
Halifax, Cleckheaton, Leeds, Preston, Bradford.
The Bloody Tide, a Bloody Flood.
I closed my eyes, the tea cold in my hands, the room more so. She leant forward, parting her hair, and I listened again to her song, our song:
'To remission and forgiveness, an end to penance?'
I needed a piss.
Oh Carol.

*

I opened the door and switched on the light and there she was:

Lying in the bath, water red, flesh white, hair blue; her right arm dangling down the side, blood across the floor, deep snakes bitten into her wrists.

On my knees:

I pulled her from the bath, I pulled her from the waters, wrapped her body in a towel and tried to squeeze her into life.

On my knees:

I rocked her back and forth, her body cold, her lips both blue, the black holes in her hands, the black holes in her feet, the black holes in her head.

On my knees:

I called her name, I begged her please, I told her the truth, no more lies, just to open her eyes, to hear her name, to hear the truth:

I love you, love you, love you . . .

And she said:

'*I do, Jack. I have to.*'

Caller: *I read my Bible.*

John Shark: *I know you do.*

Caller: *[Reads]: And the rest of the men which were not killed by these plagues yet repented not of the works of their hands, that they should not worship devils and idols of gold, and silver, and brass, and stone, and of wood: which neither can see, nor hear, nor walk:*

John Shark: *What's your point?*

Caller: *Neither repented they of their murders, nor of their sorceries, nor of their fornication, nor of their thefts.*

> *The John Shark Show*
> **Radio Leeds**
> **Friday 17th June 1977**

Chapter 24

I park up on the Moors, in the place they call the Grave, the pain fading, the day too:

Friday 17 June 1977.

I take out my pen and go through the glove compartment.

I find a map book with some blank back pages and I rip them out.

I write page after page, before I stop and screw them up.

I get out and go to the boot, take out the tape and the hose and do what I have to do.

And then I just sit there until finally, finally I pick up the pen and start again:

Dear Bobby,
I don't want a life without you.
They'll tell you lies about me,
like the lies they told me.
But I love you and I'll be there,
watching over you, always.
Love Daddy.

I switch on the engine and put the note on the dashboard and stare out across the Moors where all I can see out there, beyond the windscreen, all I can see is his face, his hair, his smile, his little tummy sticking out of those blue pyjamas, making a telescope out of his hands, and then I can't see him for the tears, I can't see him for –

John Shark: Hello?

Caller:

John Shark: Hello?

Caller:

John Shark: Is anybody there? Hell . . .

The John Shark Show
Radio Leeds
Saturday 18th June 1977

Chapter 25

'Thanks,' I said and walked across the lobby.

I pressed seven and rode the Griffin's old elevator, watching the floors pass, going up.

I stepped out of the elevator and on to the landing.

I walked down the corridor, down the threadbare carpet, the dirty walls, the smell.

I came to the door and stopped.

I put my fingers on the handle and turned.

It was open.

Room 77.

The Reverend Laws was sitting in a wicker chair in the window, Leeds City Station grey amongst the chimneys and the roofs, the pigeons and their shit.

Everything was laid out on a white towel on the bed.

'Sit down, Jack,' he said, his back to me.

I sat down on the bed beside his tools.

'What time is it?'

I looked at my watch:

'Almost seven.'

'Good,' he said, standing.

He drew the curtains and brought the wicker chair into the centre of the room.

'Take off your shirt and sit here.'

I did as he said.

He picked up the scissors from the bed.

I swallowed.

He stood behind me and began to snip.

'Something for the weekend?'

'Just a little off the top,' I smiled.

When he'd finished, he blew across the top of my head and then brushed the loose grey hairs away.

He walked back over to the bed and put down the scissors.

Then he picked up the Philips screwdriver and the ball-pein hammer and stood behind me, whispering:

'Thy way is the sea, and thy path in the great waters, and thy footsteps are unknown.'

I closed my eyes.

He put the point of the screwdriver on the crown of my skull.

And I saw – *the two sevens clash and it happening again, and again, and again, coats over faces, boots placed on thighs, a pair of panties left on one leg, bras pushed up, stomachs and breasts hollowed out, skulls caved in, heavy duty manners, Dark Ages and Witch Trials, ancient English cities, ten thousand swords flashing in the sunlight, thrice ten thousand dancing girls strewing flowers, white elephants caparisoned in red, white, and blue with the prices we pay, the debts we incur, the temptations of Jack under cheap raincoats, another rollneck sweater and pink bra pushed up over flat white tits, snakes pouring from stomach wounds, white panties off one leg, sandals placed on the flabs of thighs, good-time girls with blood, thick, black, sticky blood, matting their hair with pieces of bone and lumps of grey brain, slowly dripping into the grass of Soldier's Field, the fires behind my eyes, a white Marks & Spencer nightie, soaked black with blood from the holes he'd left, so full of holes, these people so full of holes, all these heads so full of holes, Daniel before the ancient wall in the ancient days, playing with matches behind my eyes, there written* tophet: *white Ford Capris, dark red Corsairs, Landrovers, the many ways a man can serve his time,* HATE, *no subject, no object, just* HATE: *Yorkshire Gangsters and Yorkshire Coppers, the Black Panther and the Yorkshire Ripper, Jeanette Garland and Susan Ridyard, Clare Kemplay and Michael Myshkin, Mandy Wymer and Paula Garland, the Strafford Shootings and the* Exorcist *Killing: Michael Williams and Carol Williams, holding her there in the street in my arms, blood on my hands, blood on her face, blood on my lips, blood in her mouth, blood in my eyes, blood in her hair, blood in my tears, blood in hers, Blood and Fire, and I'm crying because I know it's over, and above the fireplace opposite the door hangs a print entitled* The Fisherman's Widow, *a man's pilot coat doubles as a curtain over the window, Philips screwdrivers, heavy Wellington boots, ball-pein hammers, the*

Minstrel by a neck, the ginger beer, the stale bread, the ashes in the grate, just a room and a girl in white turning black right down to her nails and the holes in her head, just a girl, hearing footsteps on the cobbles outside, the heart absent, the door locked from the inside, keeping on running but knowing you won't get far: shotguns in Hanging Heaton, shotguns in Skipton, shotguns in Doncaster, shotguns in Selby, Jubela, Jubelo, Jubelum, him stroking his beard, him shaking his head, winking once and gone, where you seek one there's two, two three, three four; where you seek four three, three two, two one, the ones that get away and the ones that never can, the man I love, up in the gallery in the last days, the time at hand, when your sons and daughters shall prophesy, your young men shall see visions and your old men shall dream dreams, no wonders for the dead, just dreams smiling through the gloom, meat between his teeth, patting his paunch, burping, primping his hair, stroking his moustache, grinning, arching an eyebrow, frowning and shaking his head, winking once and gone again after the horror: tomorrow and the day after, getting away again, wretched and close to death from my youth up, I suffer your terrors: I am desperate, my companions in darkness, and there's got to be another way, The Fisherman's Widow in wet red paint, sherry bottles, bottles of spirits, beer bottles, bottles of chemicals, all empty, just a room in hell, Twenty-five Years of Jubilee Hits, hell around every corner, every dawn, dead elm trees, thousands of them in dark panting streets, leering terrace backs, surrounded by silent stones, buried by the black bricks, through courtyards and alleyways, foot upon brick, brick upon head, the houses that Jack built, and he's coming, ring-a-ring of roses, a pocket full of posies, he's coming, fuck you – then you sleep/kiss you – then you wake, and he's here and there is no hell but this one, Lucky Cow, up to five now they say four but remember Preston '75, come my load up that one, Dirty Cow, God saves the People of Leeds and the cuts that won't stop bleeding, the bruises that won't heal, and I feel it coming on again so wear something pretty because this is why people die, this is why people, this is why, up to number five now you say, but there's a surprise in Bradford, get about you know, Eddie, Eddie, Eddie; outstanding police officers who have our heartfelt thanks, men seeking death but not finding it, longing to die but death eluding them, like remission and forgiveness, an end to penance, burning niggers on Hunslet Carr, gollums on the train, Nigerians face down in the Calder, the red and the white and the blue, the Valleys of Death, the Moors of Hell, lonely hells, endlessly: the set-ups and the frames, the fit-ups and the blame, the whispering grasses, the weeping, bleeding statues, neighbour against neighbour, brother against brother, families bound and slaughtered aboard Black Ships, mothers tied and watching daughters raped aboard Bride Ships, the White Ship sunk off Albion, me trapped on a train in a snowstorm on top of the Moors, in the rooms of the dead, in the houses of the dead, on the streets of the dead, in the cities of the dead, the country of the dead, world of the dead, us driving together along a road, after the rain, after the Jubilee, the fireworks spent, the red and the white and the blue gone, drowning in the bloody belly of the whale in the last few days, men eating shotguns, sucking gas, nigger gangs slitting the throats of fat white coppers as they sit in their houses watching Songs of Praise *with their backs to the door, their sons swearing revenge, their children crying for the rest of their lives, endlessly: lost in rooms, chimneys taller than steeples, minarets taller than chimneys, cursed Islam in every town, Backyard Crusades, crusades for the dead, crusades without end, mornings that are night, sat in sudden silences, making calls from red boxes, policemen tall and blond, covered from head to toe in blood, evil connecting with evil, green trees shining silver with the stuff, sleep-starved dreams stretching the bones, racking them, the long faces from hell, singing their songs of the damned and the doomed: odes to the dead, prayers for the living, lies for the lot, screaming coaches flying past empty, doors open, chunks of cancerous phlegm sliding down the sink-hole, standing in the shadows in the wings of the truth, bruised by sleep, help me, in the shadows of her thighs, the blacks of her eyes, fuck you – then you sleep/kiss you – then you wake, in rooms above shops, the real flesh, the stones in my shoes, sat together on bloody sofas, the night Michael Williams drove a 12″ nail into his Carol's head,* INTO MY CAROL'S HEAD, *to save her soul alive, my Carol, thinking I've forgotten something, Chinese horses flying past, backs empty, eyes open, talking nothing but surrender, futures written as pasts, people left behind in private, sovereign angsts, right royal hells, telling lies and telling truths full of holes, so full of holes, these people so full of holes, all these heads so full of holes, the time at hand, outside the dogs and sorcerers, the whoremongers and murderers crouched in Southern cemeteries raining down blows to the heads of Scottish slags with blunt household instruments, in 1977 suffering your terrors, in 1977 I am desperate, in 1977 my companions are in darkness, in 1977 when young men see visions and the old men dream dreams, dreams of remission and forgiveness, an end to penance, in 1977 when the two sevens clash and the cuts won't stop bleeding, the bruises not healing, the two witnesses – their testimony finished, their bodies lying naked in the streets of the city, the sea blood, the waters wormwood, women drunken with the blood and the patience and faith of the saints, and I stand at the door and knock, the keys to death and hell and the mystery of the woman, knowing this is why people die, this is why people, in 1977 this is why I see –*

He brought the hammer down.

– No future.

Nineteen Eighty

David Peace

Leeds 1980.

Women don't go out at night.

Ripper's out there. Yorkshire Ripper.

People are frightened. People are angry. Yorkshire police haven't laid a glove on him. Someone's got to take the blame. And someone's got to police the police.

Step forward Peter Hunter. The honest copper. Hunter digs deep into West Yorkshire police, Hunter finds corruption, murder and cover-up. Hunter digs too deep. West Yorkshire Police look after their own.

Hunter. Hunted. Haunted.

The third part of David Peace's acclaimed Red Riding Quartet sees Yorkshire terrorised by the Ripper while the corrupt police, familiar from *Nineteen Seventy Four* and *Nineteen Seventy Seven*, continue to prosper. Weaving his own extraordinary fiction around the terrible history of the time, David Peace has once more produced a thriller that goes above and beyond the limits of the genre to provide an unforgettably stark, strangely poetic portrait of a time and a place, and a world gone wrong.